Praise for
Katee Robert and the O'Malley Series

"Unspeakably hot."

—Entertainment Weekly

"Brilliantly imaginative and blisteringly hot."

—Booklist

"A tension-filled plot full of deceit, betrayal, and sizzling love scenes will make it impossible for readers to set the book down."

—Publishers Weekly

"Katee Robert never misses."

—Hannah Whitten, *New York Times*
bestselling author

"Buckle up and hold on, because *Forbidden Promises* is breathtaking romance with heart-stopping action and un-expected twists and turns."

—USA Today

beautiful
vengeance

Also by Katee Robert

The O'Malleys

Dark Succession
(previously published as *The Marriage Contract*)
Heated Rivals
(previously published as *The Wedding Pact*)
Twisted Secrets
(previously published as *An Indecent Proposal*)
Beautiful Vengeance
(previously published as *Forbidden Promises*)
Lovely Corruption
(previously published as *Undercover Attraction*)
Ruthless Redemption
(previously published as *The Bastard's Bargain*)

The Kings

The Last King
The Fearless King

beautiful vengeance

KATEE ROBERT

FOREVER

NEW YORK   BOSTON

Cover design by Emily Osborne. Cover images © Shutterstock. Cover copyright © 2024 by Hachette Book Group, Inc.

Forever
Hachette Book Group
1290 Avenue of the Americas, New York, NY 10104
read-forever.com

Originally published in mass market and ebook as *Forbidden Promises* by Grand Central Publishing in May 2017

First trade paperback edition: March 2024

Forever is an imprint of Grand Central Publishing. The Forever name and logo are trademarks of Hachette Book Group, Inc.

The publisher is not responsible for websites (or their content) that are not owned by the publisher.

The Hachette Speakers Bureau provides a wide range of authors for speaking events. To find out more, go to hachettespeakersbureau.com or email HachetteSpeakers@hbgusa.com.

Forever books may be purchased in bulk for business, educational, or promotional use. For information, please contact your local bookseller or the Hachette Book Group Special Markets Department at special.markets@hbgusa.com.

Library of Congress Control Number: 2023952432

ISBNs: 978-1-5387-5736-9 (trade paperback), 978-1-4555-9705-5 (ebook)

Printed in the United States of America

LSC-C

Printing 1, 2024

To Brock O'Hurn. Your man-bun selfies are pretty much directly responsible for Jude. So thanks for the inspiration!

beautiful vengeance

CHAPTER ONE

Y ou have...no job experience. In anything."

Sloan O'Malley did her best not to wring her hands when faced with the incredulous expression of the woman sitting across from her. Her potential future boss. Around them, the little diner bustled with early morning customers, either coming in before their day got started or ending their night shift. It felt like every single one of them was staring at her.

She realized she hadn't answered the question that wasn't a question and cleared her throat. "I'm a hard worker, and I learn fast." Sloan hoped it was true. She'd never had to put herself to the test, and it was slightly horrifying to realize just how sheltered she'd been when it came to actual life skills. "Please. I need this job."

The money her brother Teague had sent would last a few more weeks, but she didn't want to lose that precious cushion. Besides, she was so incredibly *tired* of sitting around while life passed her by. That was why she'd escaped her family to begin with, slipping out like a thief in the night and traveling from Boston across the country without a word to anyone. They would look for her—she'd be a fool to believe otherwise. And if Teague had to send her more resources, it would be too easy for her father to find her. Seamus O'Malley was a cold-hearted bastard who had millions in the bank and all kinds of unsavory connections. One daughter had already slipped his control, and Sloan wasn't sure his pride could take another hit.

She had to stand on her own two feet for the first time in twenty-four years.

She just hoped she wasn't about to fall flat on her face.

Taking a deep breath, she tried to produce a convincing smile. The owner of the diner, Marge, did not look convinced. What could Sloan possibly say that would make the woman hire her? "Marge—"

"Here's the deal." Marge sat back. She was an older woman with a no-nonsense face creased with laugh lines that spoke of a life well lived. Her graying hair was pulled back into a bun, and she wore serviceable clothes and a nondescript apron. She seemed like someone who could take anything life threw at her. "You look like trouble, and the last thing either I or this town needs is trouble."

Sloan tried not to wilt at that, but Marge wasn't through. She sighed. "But I have a thing for strays and you're nothing if not that. I'll give you a shot. You screw up, you're done. You're late, you're done. You bring any unnecessary drama to my door, you're done. Got it?"

She could hardly believe what she was hearing. "You're hiring me?"

"Isn't that what I just said?" Marge shook her head and

pushed to her feet. She had to be nearly six feet tall and she was built like a linebacker. "Show up tomorrow morning at seven. Dress comfortably, because I'm not going to be sending you home if your shoes pinch your feet. You complain—"

"I'm done."

A small smile graced Marge's lips, then disappeared as soon as it'd come. "Yep. Now get lost. You're distracting the menfolk and these fools have places to be." She turned and walked across the diner to the counter and snapped her fingers at the cook through the gap in the wall where the food was delivered. "Hurry up, Luke. You know damn well that the judge has places to be and he'll be wanting his breakfast as soon as he walks through the door."

Sloan got up and hurried out the door. *I got the job!* Her first impulse was to call Teague and tell him, but she had to remind herself she was only supposed to call in case of an emergency.

She missed her family, missed knowing that they were just a phone call away if she needed them. She hadn't counted on that.

She headed for the beach, needing to burn off her pent-up energy. With the way the interview had gone, she'd been sure Marge was going to tell her to get lost. She'd even prepared herself for it. To have the woman do exactly the opposite made Sloan's head spin. *She's taking a chance on me and she doesn't even know me.* Sloan could hardly believe it. In her world, people didn't take chances on strangers like that.

Except that wasn't her world anymore.

This was.

The sea air cleared some of the static in her head. She'd

spent her entire life in Boston, but the ocean felt different on this coast. Wild. Free. Vast beyond comprehension. She slipped off her shoes and dug her toes into the sand.

Callaway Rock was about three miles from one side of the town limits to the other, all of it stretched out along the beach. The little house where she was living was on the southern outskirts, and the diner was smack dab in the middle. It might have been smarter to drive over, but she liked the walk. There might come a time when she didn't crave the sand beneath her feet and the ocean breeze in her face, but that day wasn't today.

Two weeks ago, she'd been in the middle of humid eighty-degree weather in Boston, but here it could have been fall instead of early August. The air had a crispness that never seemed to go away, no matter the time of day. Even though it was warm enough that she wished for a tank top, the breeze coming off the water made it downright pleasant.

Everything about Callaway Rock was downright pleasant.

Her shoes dangling from her fingertips, she started walking, letting her mind wander. The last week had been the first time she had truly lived alone, and the learning curve was…strange. There were so many little things she'd taken for granted, things she'd never bothered with because the O'Malleys had a full-time staff to do everything from cooking to cleaning.

It turned out Sloan wasn't much of a cook.

I'll figure it out. All I have is time.

All she'd ever wanted to do was get away from life as the daughter of an Irish crime lord, to remove herself from the playing field where she'd never have control. And she had, with Teague's help.

Unfortunately, she couldn't turn off her brain, and she kept wondering how Keira was doing, and if Aiden was holding up under the increasing pressure as heir to one-third of Boston's underworld: O'Malleys, Sheridans, Hallorans. And Cillian. Last she'd heard, he'd been off in Connecticut with that woman. Had things turned out? They must have, because if something had happened to Cillian, Teague would have called her.

She hoped.

She trailed off to a stop, staring blindly at the tide coming in. Then there was Carrigan. Her big sister. The one she couldn't quite forgive, no matter how much time or distance was between them. It wasn't fair and it wasn't right, but Sloan couldn't let her betrayal go.

Maybe someday...

She inhaled deeply and started walking again. Thinking about her five remaining siblings, wondering what they were up to, wasn't going to do her a single bit of good. And thinking about Devlin, rotting away six feet beneath the ground...That way lay madness.

Up ahead, the bright green door of her house came into view. Well, technically it wasn't *her* house. Teague's wife, Callie, had gotten her aunt to agree to let Sloan live there. Sloan had woken every morning for the last seven days thinking that would be the day when Sorcha showed up, but the woman hadn't shown up. It was more than a little strange that she'd agreed to give Sloan a place to stay and then not been there upon her arrival. The only contact she'd had from the woman was a text from a random number saying to make herself at home. When she'd texted back, there had been no reply.

Frankly, a part of Sloan was relieved Sorcha hadn't made

an appearance. She didn't know much about the woman except that she owned this house and seemed willing to do her niece a favor by housing Sloan indefinitely.

Against her better judgment, her gaze drifted to the house directly north of hers. She'd mistakenly gone there her first night in town, and her encounter with the surly man who lived there still made her shiver. *Jude.* He'd been like a junkyard dog guarding his territory, more interested in getting her off his property than hearing her out about an honest mistake.

If she never ran into him again, it would be too soon.

Still...She couldn't help being a little curious. Nearly every other local she'd come across had been friendly and welcoming. When they learned she was in the old O'Connor house, they always perked up and prodded her for more information, but wasn't that what small towns were known for? Everyone took care of everyone else, and if there was a bit of gossip involved, that was to be expected.

It just made Jude's horrible attitude stand out even more. He didn't care where she came from, didn't care what she was doing in town, didn't care about anything but getting her away from his house.

If she were a more curious woman, she'd wonder if he was hiding something behind those closed curtains and barred shutters. *Who owns a beach house and keeps all the windows blocked?*

"None of my business." She had enough trouble without borrowing more. If that...that...*jerk* wanted her to stay away from him, that was exactly what she'd do. End of story.

As she passed, the door in question opened and Jude

emerged, a coffee mug in his hand. Sloan jerked to a stop, unable to tear her gaze away. His long dark hair was in a bun at the back of his head, which should have made him look delicate, but there wasn't a single delicate thing about the man staring at her. His jaw might as well have been chiseled from stone, and though she couldn't see his brown eyes across the distance, she knew they were like bitter dark chocolate and intense.

But what he was wearing...

Or, rather, *not* wearing.

Cargo shorts hung low on his hips, and he'd misplaced his shirt somewhere. Every muscle was defined, his body too perfect to be real. She blinked, but he didn't vanish like she'd half-expected. Instead, he lifted the mug to his lips, drawing her attention to his impossibly broad shoulders, which tapered to a narrow waist and, good gracious, what were those muscles called that created a V leading directly into his shorts?

Her face felt impossibly warm despite the mild August morning and she was suddenly sure that she was blushing furiously. *Keep walking. Just put one foot forward and keep walking.* She couldn't move. She couldn't do anything other than stand there and stare at him until he nodded briefly at her, turned around, and walked back into his house.

What in God's name just happened?

* * *

Jude MacNamara left his place as soon as night fell. He didn't like moving around Callaway Rock during the day. Fuck, he didn't like small towns in general. Everyone had too much time on their hands and felt like it was their

God-given right to stick their noses into their neighbors' business. He'd had to run off over a dozen attempts to welcome him into town since he moved here three months ago, and that hadn't done a damn thing to dissuade anyone. If anything, it made the locals *more* determined to figure out everything there was to know about him.

They were wasting their time. He was here for a job. He sure as fuck wasn't staying.

He stalked onto the beach, pausing only to make sure no teenagers had thought it was a brilliant idea to have a beach fire tonight. *Clear.* Unlike the towns farther north, Callaway Rock didn't get much in the way of tourists. Maybe if they had, he wouldn't have had to actually buy a house here while he waited for his target to reappear.

Jude lifted a pair of binoculars. In his dark clothes and with the ocean at his back, he was damn near invisible on a night like this, especially with clouds covering the moon. He gave the beach to the north and south of him a cursory look to reconfirm that there was no one but him out tonight and then he turned to his real target.

The O'Connor house.

It had been unoccupied since he'd gotten to town, but a little over a week ago, a woman had moved in. She was about fifty years too young to be Sorcha O'Connor, and the coloring was all wrong regardless. This woman—Sloan—had both dark hair and eyes, not the blond hair and blue eyes that ran through Sorcha's family.

He paused his binoculars at each window, taking in the little changes that had come with the new resident. After he'd moved to Callaway Rock, he'd broken in and gone through the entire house, looking for clues to where Sorcha might have gone and familiarizing himself with the layout in the event that he'd need to return. There was nothing of the former, and the latter was laughably easy. With the massive windows and fact that the curtains and shutters were never closed, he hadn't had to set foot in the place to figure out everything he needed to know. But it paid to be thorough.

What he couldn't figure out was who the hell this Sloan was and how she was connected to Sorcha O'Connor.

For a second, right when he found her peering into his windows that first night, he'd half convinced himself that she was actually Callista Sheridan, come to visit her long-lost aunt. A coup like that...It made his adrenaline spike just thinking about it. What better way to make Colm Sheridan suffer than removing his beloved daughter from the equation? She was the only child he had left, after all—though recently she'd been too protected for Jude to even consider. He'd have to wait until things died down to circle back to Boston.

But as soon as the woman stepped into the light, he'd realized his mistake. Even if her coloring could be faked, this wasn't Callista. He'd seen her a time or two over the years, and she carried herself as a woman used to having her orders followed without question, even before she took over the Sheridan empire.

Sloan? She seemed to have her shoulders perpetually hunched, as if expecting a blow. He couldn't tell if it was an abusive ex or something else, but she was fleeing something. *It's none of my fucking business if she is. She's not my target. Colm's sister Sorcha is.*

He'd bide his time and see how this played out. His vengeance had waited this long—it could wait a little bit more.

Every light was lit inside the house, and he watched Sloan walk through it, pausing to touch the marble kitchen counter, the thick mantel over the fireplace, the back cushion on the couch facing the massive windows. Then she disappeared, reappearing in the guest room, her hands going to the buttons at the front of her dress.

Jude's body sprang to attention when he realized what was happening. *Put the damn binoculars down. Sorcha isn't there, and this girl isn't your mark.* But he didn't put them down. Instead, he watched as she shrugged out of the dress, leaving her in only a pair of silk white panties and an equally white bra. She looked innocent, untouchable, and he could barely wrap his mind around it.

It took considerable willpower to lower the binoculars as she reached behind her to unhook her bra, but he wasn't a goddamn peeping tom. Jude laughed softly. *Sure, stand on your high moral horse. You fucking kill people for a living and you're going to be honorable about watching some woman who you've met once undress.*

There have to be lines. Even if they don't always make sense.

Mystery past or not, that woman *was* an innocent. It was...odd. These days, most of the people he associated with were people who made their living on the underbelly of society. They'd all seen things, same as him. They didn't blink at the choices he'd made or the path that had brought him to them.

Jude didn't spend much time around innocents.

He'd seen the way she looked at him this morning, though. Even across the distance between them, the hunger in her eyes had been readily recognizable. It made him hot just thinking about it. What would she do if he walked up to her front door right now and knocked? Would she answer in a robe? Would she submit if he closed the distance between them and kissed her?

Jude cursed long and hard, his cock so hard it was a wonder it didn't burst out of his jeans. He had no business thinking shit like that, not while he was on the hunt he'd spent his entire life preparing for and sure as fuck not about a woman who had some kind of connection with his target.

An innocent.

He was half-surprised he could even recognize that trait in another person. He'd never been one. He hadn't had a chance to be. That opportunity had been taken away the moment Colm Sheridan declared the death sentence on Jude's father and brothers—the same death sentence he would have delivered to Jude's mother if he'd known she was pregnant.

No, there was no room for innocence in his life.

There was only revenge.

CHAPTER TWO

Sloan's shoulders ached, and she was reasonably sure that her feet had signed off over an hour ago. Her most comfortable shoes couldn't hold up to an eight-hour shift at the diner. She'd thought she'd been prepared, ready to face anything Marge and her customers could throw at her. She'd been wrong.

The very thought made her want to cry.

She stared at herself in the mirror of the tiny employee bathroom. *One hour left. One hour and you can limp home and curl up with a blanket and cry yourself to sleep.* Millions of people held down jobs like this one—*harder* than this one. She *should* have been able to manage this without bringing herself to the brink. Reality was nowhere near as positive. In reality, everything hurt and she was constantly terrified that she'd make a mistake that would have Marge showing her the door.

Splashing a little water on her face didn't do a single

thing to center her. But there was no hope for it. She had an hour left in her shift, and for a diner in a tiny town, this place saw an overwhelming amount of business. Apparently hiring the new girl in town was part of Marge's business strategy because the entire population must have stopped by at one time or another. Most of them openly gawked at her, making her feel like a freak show.

Not too far from the truth.

She made an effort to keep her spine straight as she walked out of the bathroom and headed for the kitchen. A couple of fisherman had ordered fish and chips, and their meals should be ready by now.

Luke smiled when he saw her coming. It took her half the day to realize he was Marge's husband and that they owned this place together. He was as tall as his wife, but built leaner, more like a blade than a blunt object. He was kinder, too, always offering an easy smile or an uplifting word. God help her, but Sloan couldn't help waiting for the other shoe to drop.

Kindness for the sake of kindness wasn't something in her realm of experience.

Luke plated the fish and chips and scooted the food toward her. "You're doing great for your first day."

"Thank you." She caught herself hunching her shoulders and stopped. "I'll just get these out."

"Sloan."

She froze in the middle of picking up the two plates, and turned to face Marge. Excuses bubbled up—*I'm doing the best I can!*—but she didn't let them past her lips. She cleared her throat. "Yes?"

Marge surveyed her, the big woman's hands on her hips. "Take the rest of your shift off. I can handle it from here."

No. Oh God, don't fire me. She kept her death grip on the plates. *Show no fear.* "Ma'am, I haven't complained, haven't dropped anything, and I haven't messed up a single order."

Marge raised her eyebrows. "I'm not blind, girl. I know. You did good today—you even helped me haul in those massive bags of flour without whining. But if you stand for another minute longer, you're going to keel over and then you're no good to anyone. Take the rest of the day off and be back at seven tomorrow."

She blinked, hardly daring to believe it. "I did... good?"

"Don't make me say it again. Git." Marge took the plates out of her hands and strode through the doorway into the main dining area.

Luke chuckled. "That's my girl—as subtle as a two-by-four to the side of the head. Don't let her scare you. She's got a soft spot a mile wide."

"Forgive me if I don't take your word for it." Sloan rubbed a hand over her face, exhaustion weighing her down. "I guess I'll see you tomorrow, Luke."

"Hey." He waited for her to look at him before continuing. "Soak your feet and do some walking or something or your muscles will tighten up and you'll be a mess tomorrow. There's a yoga class one of the local girls, Jessica, runs out on the beach every morning at sunrise." There was no mistaking the concern in his eyes. "Might be something you could use."

Apparently for all her training at hiding what she was feeling, she'd done a poor job of it in this new setting. Sloan opened her mouth to beg off, but reconsidered. She couldn't spend the rest of her life hiding in a borrowed beach house in between shifts and wandering the coast alone. At some point she'd have to actually meet the people she served food to.

And I could use some of the peace yoga is supposed to bring.

She managed a smile. "I'll try it out."

"Good." He held up a container with another smile. "Now do as Marge says and git."

Judging from the heavenly smells wafting from the container, it was some of the very same fish and chips she'd just been about to deliver. Sloan took it, the feeling of being at a loss only getting worse. "Is food a perk of the job Marge neglected to mention?"

Luke gave her a strange look. "I'm not sure where you came from, but we take care of our own in Callaway Rock. You worked hard and don't think I missed the fact you haven't eaten since you started your shift. You need to keep up your energy." He started to pat her on the shoulder, but stopped the motion when she flinched. "Get some rest. We'll see you in the morning."

Sloan walked out of the diner feeling more confused than ever. She'd known this little town in Oregon wasn't anything like back home, but right now it didn't seem like it was on the same planet.

She kicked off her shoes as soon as she hit the stairs leading down to the beach, and couldn't stop a tiny moan of relief. She walked over the sand toward her house, which was fast becoming a home, and slowed to watch the people around her. The beach wasn't crowded by any means, but there was a group of teenagers lounging in the meager Oregon sunlight, the girls in bikinis and the boys throwing a Frisbee. They all looked so carefree, it actually made her heart ache. She'd never been like that as a teenager.

No, ever since she could remember, she was aware of the fate awaiting her because of the family she'd been born into. The O'Malley sons might grow up to take their place within the family business, both legal and illicit, but there was only one role Seamus O'Malley had for his daughters—marriage to the man most likely to accumulate power for the family.

Her sister Carrigan had bucked that rule and been exiled as a result. Sloan shook her head and resumed walking. *Exiled.* Here in Callaway Rock, it seemed impossible that such a thing even existed anymore, let alone in the US.

If we'd been born a fisherman's family instead of a mob boss's, Devlin would still be alive.

The pain in her chest that never quite went away grew at the thought, made worse by a young family playing in the surf. The mother sat with a baby beneath an umbrella, and the father chased his toddler through the shallow water. Sloan could hear the little girl's giggles from where she stood, but the sound only made her melancholy worse.

Stop it. You left it all behind by choice. Any children you decide to have won't grow up to be pawns in a game they want no part of.

Children.

The very idea was ludicrous. She could barely take care of herself right now, let alone herself and a tiny human who depended solely on her for survival. Frankly, she didn't like the theoretical child's chances.

When she'd left the diner, all she'd wanted was to go home and close a door between her and the rest of the world, but as soon as she'd showered and picked at the meal Luke packed for her, a restlessness had her pacing through the small house. She looked at the fireplace, considered building a fire, but then realized she had no idea how to go about doing that other than throwing some wood and paper in the fireplace and lighting it. *Maybe that's all it takes?*

Frustrated with yet another thing she didn't know without resorting to Google, she walked out the back door and onto the porch. Sloan tilted her head back and inhaled deeply, muscles she hadn't even been aware were tense relaxing one by one from the combination of briny air and the soft crash of the waves.

"This. This is why I came here."

Freedom.

If it came with costs, well, what thing worth having didn't?

A throat cleared near her and she opened her eyes to find Jude on his porch as well, a beer dangling from his big hand. Everything about the man was massive. He had to be at least six and a half feet tall, and even with several yards between them, he dwarfed her. Today, his long hair was down in careless waves that her fingers were itching to dig into.

Sloan clenched her hands. What was wrong with her? Not only had she just met this man, he'd been nothing short of hostile in the single interaction they'd had. She should *not* be eyeing the slice of his chest revealed through his unbuttoned shirt—did the man *ever* dress himself properly?—and yet...

And yet.

You said you were going to start living. He could be another step in the right direction.

She'd never had a fling. Sloan wasn't the type of girl who was interested in that sort of thing, and the knowledge of what her father planned for her had kept her from allowing anyone too close for fear that it would end in heartbreak.

That and the single time a boy had asked her out, all four of her brothers had cornered him and scared the ever-loving daylights out of him. Word had gotten around after that, and there had been no second offers. Neither of her sisters seemed to let that stand in their way, but Sloan was different. She was the one who kept her head down. The dutiful daughter, the quiet sister, the one who never stepped a foot outside of what was good and proper.

Until now.

She bolstered what little courage she had and made her way off her porch to the stairs leading up to Jude's. "Good evening."

He raised a single eyebrow. "You're pretty damn proper for a waitress."

Of course he knew she was a waitress. Gossip seemed to be the only thing Callaway Rock and Boston had in common. It wasn't something she was ashamed of. She had a job, which was more than many people could say. She glanced at his beer, but it wasn't a brand she recognized. "I don't suppose you have another one?"

Jude threw back his head and laughed, the sound deep and cruel. "Go home, honey. You couldn't handle me on your best day."

She took a step back, about to argue that she wasn't trying to handle anything, but her courage failed her. *Why did I think this was a good idea?* She pressed her lips together, hating that her eyes burned at his rejection. *Keira wouldn't cry over some man who probably isn't worth her time.*

Carrigan wouldn't have been rejected in the first place.

She spun on her heel and hurried back to her home, vowing that her explorations into this new life were strictly to exclude flirting from here on out. She'd gone this long without sex or a relationship. She could just keep on going for another twenty-four years.

* * *

Jude felt like a piece of shit as he watched Sloan scurry back to the O'Connor place. He took a swig of his beer, hating the guilt that rose when he pictured the hurt and humiliation on her face. He'd been doing her a fucking favor, not that she needed to know that. She might be a part of this because of her connection to Sorcha, but that didn't mean she had to be caught in the crossfire.

Must have taken some pep talk to get her ass over here to begin with.

And he'd shot her down in two seconds flat.

He drained the rest of his beer. What the hell was he supposed to do? Apologize? He might like her tight little body and soulful eyes, but that just meant he'd be down to rock her world for a few hours. Call him crazy, but Sloan didn't strike him as a woman who was down for a dark and dirty fuck. She was too *sweet* for that sort of thing.

Jude didn't do sweet.

But...

He set his bottle down and turned to consider the O'Connor place. If he went over and shared a beer with her, it didn't have to mean a damn thing. If she was living there, it was possible she knew where Sorcha was, or at least when the old woman would be back. He could be charming when it suited him.

Maybe.

Reconnaissance. That's all it was.

You're a goddamn liar.

Wouldn't be the first time I've been called it.

He ducked back into his place and grabbed two beers from the fridge. Ten minutes, thirty tops. He'd be in, get the information he needed, and get out. Then he could go back to researching and planning out his next step.

She answered the back door, her big dark eyes surprisingly shiny, which only served to make him feel more like an asshole. Jude held up the two beers. "I was out of line. Sorry."

She blinked. "I don't know if I want the beer now."

Well, hell, he didn't exactly blame her. But since he'd made the effort to come over here, he wasn't about to leave without accomplishing what he'd set out to do. Jude tried for a smile. "It's better than the shit they sell at the general store down here."

Her eyebrows slanted down, making him think of a disapproving kindergarten teacher. "That's rude. From my experience, beer isn't all that wonderful, regardless of its brand. You don't have to be a snob about it."

It never failed. Even when he was doing his damnedest to be charming and meld into the world around him, he invariably said something to set himself apart. He doubted Sloan had that problem. She fit right in with the people of Callaway Rock, sliding into the rhythm of life in this place without missing a step. He didn't really understand what that was like. He could fake it for a time, but the truth always outed.

And the truth was that Jude didn't fit in anywhere.

He held up the beer. "Do you want it or not?"

Her shoulders slumped, but she made a visible effort to pull herself together. "Yes."

He could do better than this. He had to. Jude sank onto

the wicker chair on the porch across from where she stood and popped the cap off his beer. She really was a petite little thing. He had the strangest urge to sit her down in front of a pile of food and make sure she ate. Jude shook his head and waited for her to take the other chair. They were delicate to the extreme, and he felt like an idiot perching there, half-sure it would break under his weight and send him sprawling on his ass.

But he was trying to be less threatening, so he didn't surge to his feet like he wanted to.

Sloan took a tiny sip of her beer and made a face. "This is ... good."

"Not much of a beer drinker then, even with all your *experience*?"

"Not much of a drinker at all." She took another sip, and he almost laughed. "If this is what the so-called good stuff is like, I don't think I'm going to start."

How old was this girl? He put aside his weird impulses, which seemed to pop up whenever he was around her, and surveyed her with a critical eye. Too thin, too much history, but she had a world-weary look in her brown eyes that only came with some years in the rearview. She'd seen things.

Still, he wasn't a man to leave things to chance. "Are you even old enough to drink?"

She glared, giving the first indication that there might be a backbone in there. "I'm twenty-four."

A baby.

Not that he was ancient. But thirty-five was a whole hell of a lot of living—and hard living—in comparison. He took a drink of his beer. "So you didn't have much of a twenty-one run."

"My older sister tried." She took a hasty sip of beer and set the bottle down. "It doesn't matter. Thank you for the beer."

He leaned back, carefully stretching his legs out and crossing his ankles. Going home was the right thing to do. He'd repaired whatever blow he'd delivered to her ego. Staying around was just asking for trouble.

Jude opened his mouth to say good-bye, but that wasn't what came out. "You have any vodka in this place?"

"What?"

"Vodka. The more expensive the better. I have some in my house, but you're a smart girl and that means taking drinks from strange men is something you don't do."

She blinked. "I would think inviting strange men into my house is also something smart girls don't do."

Not unless they're looking for trouble. He kept the words restrained, but only barely. Fuck, what was it about this woman that tried his control so thoroughly? He didn't know, and that made her dangerous in a way he wasn't used to. He couldn't afford distractions right now.

I could ask her about Sorcha.

But if he did, he'd spook her, and she might tip off Sorcha before the woman finally flitted back into town. So he affected a neutral expression. "What do you say?"

She seemed torn, but finally nodded more to herself than to him and stood. "I saw some liquor, but I didn't investigate to see what kind of bottles they were."

He had when he'd been snooping around, so Jude knew there were three bottles of Belvedere stashed in one of the cupboards. He noted the tense set of her shoulders as he followed her into the house, and fell back another step so he didn't loom over her. It didn't seem to help.

Sloan pulled out one of the bottles and held it up. "Vodka."

"Good." He decided waiting for her to take the lead just wasn't going to happen, so Jude nudged her to the side and went through the cupboards like it was his first time here, coming up with two tumblers, a carton of cranberry juice, and one of those little lime-juice things. He caught her staring and shrugged. "Just sit down and I'll make you a drink that you don't have to choke down."

"I don't..." She looked away and then back. "Why?"

"Why what?" He dropped a handful of ice into each glass and poured healthy dashes of vodka. He didn't necessarily want her sloppy drunk, but the tight set of her shoulders could do with some loosening up.

Right. Because you're such a fucking white knight.

He wasn't. The longer he spent in her presence, the clearer it became he didn't have any intention of leaving her alone. It had been a while since he'd had sex—too long if he was really considering taking *this* woman to bed.

But ever since the thought occurred to him last night, he hadn't been able to get it out of his head. He wanted her, and it was only some long-dead honor demanding he stay the hell away from her.

His honor had died with the rest of his family.

Any chance he'd had of resurrecting it had died with his first mark when he was twenty-one.

Jude finished the drinks off with the cranberry juice and a squirt of lime and then found a spoon to stir them. He slid one over. "Try it."

She took a sip and gave him a cautious smile. "That is a bit better."

He downed half of his drink in one swallow, not sure if

he was searching for the drive to leave or to make a move on her. At this point, it could go either way.

Sloan took another drink, longer this time. Little circles of pink appeared high on her cheeks, giving her some much-needed color. She licked her lips, and he damn near groaned. "You never answered my question. Why are you doing this?"

Jude finished his drink. "I was a dick before for no reason. You caught me off guard. So I'm sorry."

"You don't like me." She smoothed back her dark hair. "You haven't since we met."

"I thought you were breaking into my house. I got a little territorial."

"A little?" Sloan shook her head and drank more. "I don't think there's a realm on earth where manhandling me on your front porch in the dark could be qualified as a little."

He couldn't very well tell her that he thought she might be one of his targets, wandered into his lair. *Lair? Dramatic to the very end.* Jude poured more vodka over his ice, not bothering with the juice this time.

She watched him drink it, her gaze lingering on his mouth. It wouldn't take much. He could touch her in some innocent way, lower his voice so she'd lean close, cup the back of her neck and...

Fuck. Jude finished his drink and set it on the counter. "Thanks for the drink. We should do it again sometime." And then he walked out before he could talk himself out of it.

Or into a whole different set of mistakes.

CHAPTER THREE

Sloan finished her drink, the alcohol buoying her and making her feel ten feet tall. As tall as Jude. She wandered over to lock the back door, but hesitated. She might not be good at the flirting game, but she wasn't stupid. He wanted her. He might be holding back for unknown reasons, but he was interested.

The question remained... Was she?

She laughed softly. The man was so overwhelming, she wouldn't know what to do with him even if she was interested—and she was. He was just so *big*, and that hair should have been ridiculous, but it gave him the air of a wild thing that could never be tamed. In truth, they couldn't be more opposite.

Not to mention she didn't know a single thing about him.

He'd charged in here, taken control of the situation, made her a delicious drink, and charged back out into the night. She rested her forehead against the cool wood of the door. If she were braver, she'd follow him home. She'd flirt. She'd issue an invitation that couldn't be misinterpreted...

And he'd say no just like he did to the initial offer for drinks.

Sloan opened her eyes and straightened. "The only reason he came over was because he pitied me." Call her naive, but she didn't want her first time with a man to be because he felt sorry for her.

So she turned the deadbolt, and then did her normal circuit of the house to ensure everything was closed and locked. Satisfied and feeling a little silly—what were the odds that someone would choose *this* house to break into?—Sloan shook her head. She knew better. She might have left the past and the dangers of Boston behind, but that didn't mean she should be careless.

Someone would be coming for her. It was only a matter of time. She just hoped that Teague had hidden her well enough, and that she could keep under the radar on her end as well.

She needed to stay out of trouble, and Jude had trouble written all over him.

Stripping, she allowed herself to imagine, just for a moment, what it would have been like if he'd stayed. He'd take control in the bedroom the same way he had over drinks. There was no doubt about that. Sloan closed her eyes and ran her hands down her body, imagining it was his touch. Her fingers stopped just north of the band of her panties.

I shouldn't.

But she wanted to.

She slipped beneath the covers and took off her underwear. She never slept naked, and it felt downright decadent to have the silky sheets rubbing against her nipples with every breath. Would he kiss her there? Or even between her legs?

She closed her eyes again, refusing to feel self-conscious as she ran her hand down her stomach to stroke herself between her thighs. She might be thinking of him, but no one had to know. It was her private little fantasy, something that would never happen in the real world.

Her body was already primed, and she spread her wetness up and over her clit, nearly gasping with the shock of pleasure the move brought. She'd masturbated before, but there was something just naughty about doing it while visualizing the man who lived next door. If she concentrated, she could almost feel his whiskers against her inner thigh, his tongue following the path her finger traced. Her body tightened, the pleasure so acute, it almost hurt. Sloan arched her back, a moan slipping free despite herself. Her orgasm stole her breath, but she managed to whisper Jude's name as she came.

What in God's name was I thinking?

She opened her eyes, feeling so incredibly foolish. "It doesn't matter, because it's just pretend. It won't ever happen." Something like disappointment banged inside her, but she ignored it. She had a life here, a life that she'd chosen for herself. She had nothing to be ashamed of. She smiled to herself and rolled over, pulling the covers up to her neck. Tomorrow would come soon enough. She'd get up with the sun and attend yoga, and then she'd go to her shift at the diner. After? Well, maybe she'd give cooking another shot.

Things were finally looking up.

* * *

Jude's grip on the railing was so tight, he'd have slivers for sure. It didn't fucking matter. He couldn't tear his gaze away from the window into the spare bedroom. The bedroom where Sloan had just coaxed herself into orgasm and moaned *his* name upon release. He tightened his grip, the pain reminding him that he could *not* go into her room, pull the tease of sheets off her body, and show her what a real orgasm looked like.

It took every ounce of control he had to let go of the railing and walk down the stairs to the beach. And just keep walking.

She hadn't invited him into her bed. Maybe she would have if he'd stuck around, but the girl was a lightweight if he'd ever seen one, and Jude wasn't a fan of the idea of taking advantage of her being more than a little tipsy. Another line he refused to cross, even after he'd left so many in the rearview. He didn't take contracts for kids, or for anyone without a track record to rival his.

And he didn't take advantage of innocents.

He snorted and picked up his pace until he was jogging. The wet sand clung to his boots, but he relished the effort each step took. Anything to distract him from imagining what Sloan might taste like. She gave the impression of someone with little experience, and a primal part of him raged to the forefront at the thought of being the one to show her how much pleasure she'd been missing.

Hold on, asshole. You're acting like it's a sure thing. You're the one who put on the brakes.

Yeah, he had.

But as far as he was concerned, she'd issued an open invitation when she'd touched herself while fantasizing about him. It didn't matter if she didn't realize what she'd done. It was like waving a red flag in front of a bull.

He wouldn't force her. He wouldn't have to.

She just needed permission to take what she wanted...to allow him to take what *he* wanted.

He circled back to their houses, heading for his. As tempting as it was to appear at her bedside like some sort of incubus, he doubted she'd respond well to it. So he went back to the drawing board—his go-to time consumer.

Jude pulled out the gun he'd taped beneath the cupboard just inside the back door—one of many secreted throughout the house—and checked to make sure it was loaded and hadn't been tampered with. Satisfied everything was as it should be, he cleared the house, one room after another. It was unlikely that anyone had broken in, but he couldn't afford to be careless.

Not when he was so close to his goal.

Sorcha was the only Sheridan who'd left Boston, and it had made tracking her down a hellish job. But just because she was out of Boston didn't mean she was completely out of the family business. Jude's sources had come back with info that he couldn't ignore—about Sorcha and her nephew, Ronan. It didn't strain Jude's skills too much to make it look like Ronan had an unfortunate accident. But finding Sorcha had proven much tougher.

He moved to the room at the back of the house. It had originally been a guest room, but he'd converted it into a place to lay out his research. He unlocked both the door and the deadbolt and let himself in. Just like in the rest of the house, nothing here was tampered with.

The map spread across most of one wall, little blue pegs marking the various homes Sorcha owned across the world, courtesy of her late second husband. She never stayed too long in one place, never moved about with any pattern that could be tracked.

If he was going to be perfectly honest with himself, he'd hesitated at first. After all, Sorcha and Ronan had almost done him a favor. Once he'd finished with Sorcha, he fully intended to send Colm the information he'd compiled—information confirming how the man's beloved son and sister had fully intended a coup that would leave half the Sheridan force dead. That old saying about the apple not falling too far from the tree applied to Ronan Sheridan—with interest.

It took a sick son of a bitch to kill his own father in a quest for power.

And what better way to hurt Colm than to first take his scheming son away, and then to pour salt on the wound by using the truth as a weapon?

But first—Sorcha.

The *only* reason he had some assurance that she would come to Callaway Rock was that a contact of his had heard that Callista Sheridan had recently spoken with Sorcha for the first time in her adult life. No one knew why—though it sure as fuck wasn't because Callie had found out that her aunt fully intended to murder her just one year before—but the contact had heard Callaway Rock mentioned.

That was it.

It wasn't much as leads went, but it was more than he'd had.

And now Sloan was occupying the O'Connor house.

He'd have to be an idiot to ignore the possible connection. There were too many facts adding up to a mystery he had no answers to. Sloan, with her delicate personality, who flinched like she'd been someone's punching bag. Callista, contacting her aunt for the first time in her life. Sorcha, coming to a predetermined location despite all evidence pointing to her never once doing that. It all boiled down to one fact.

Sloan was the reason Callista had called Sorcha.

While that might seem like something profound, it didn't mean a damn thing when push came to shove. Sloan wasn't a Sheridan. He knew every single one of them inside and out. And she wasn't on the list.

A part of him was profoundly grateful for that fact.

He could seduce her, could pump her for information, but he wouldn't have to put an end to her. She'd been in town a grand total of a week and he'd actually seen her finding her feet as day after day went by. He'd hate himself a little if he had to put an end to that—to *her*. He'd compromised damn near every line he'd ever had in the pursuit of vengeance. He refused to kill an innocent, no matter her apparent connection to his enemies.

But she wasn't a Sheridan, so it wasn't an issue.

Jude stopped in front of the photograph that had started all this. The one his mother had kept with her always, right up until sorrow finally won and she took that last step into permanent sleep. She'd managed to stay alive until he was grown, which was astounding when held against the truth that a vital part of her had died with her husband and other sons. If she hadn't been pregnant with Jude—her late-in-life miracle baby—she would have finished what Colm Sheridan started the same day that she buried her boys.

He touched the photograph, the faces familiar because of how often she'd pointed to them, telling him stories about how Neal had been a little hell-raiser, even from infancy, and how Carey had been quiet and solemn and watched everything around him with wide green eyes. About how they'd grown up big and strong and become a threat Colm couldn't ignore.

About how he'd butchered them in one fell swoop, he

and his men attacking in the wee hours of the morning and killing every single man the MacNamaras had to call their own, whether family or hired help.

It had been a slaughter.

He turned the photograph facedown, unable to stand the happy faces staring back at him. It was for his mother he'd gotten into the killing business, honing his already considerable skills. She'd prepared him as best she could and when she couldn't do any more, she'd slipped away to be with her lost loved ones. Her death had been the final push he needed to move forward and take that first contract.

He couldn't blame her. What did one son compare to the two who were lost? To the beloved husband who she'd never stopped mourning?

It didn't make him miss her less, though.

Almost there. I'm so close to bringing justice to the Sheridans once and for all. The rest of Boston can rot for all I care.

What would he do after he'd avenged his family?

Jude turned, facing the direction of the O'Connor house despite the fact he couldn't see it from his position. There was no future for him—not the kind that included a woman or a family of his own or any sort of stability. He'd seen too many things, had *done* too many things. There was no coming back from that, even if he wanted to. He'd never even stayed in one place for more than a few months, and he didn't imagine he was going to start now.

But that didn't mean he wouldn't use his time waiting for Sorcha O'Connor in Callaway Rock well.

CHAPTER FOUR

Sloan delivered a plate of eggs Benedict to the judge—who didn't seem to have a name other than his title—with a smile. "Let me know if I can get you anything else."

"I know that accent." He studied her from beneath his bushy gray eyebrows. They gave him the look of a quizzical owl. "East Coast...New York?"

She froze, then mentally berated herself into relaxing. "Philadelphia." It wasn't the truth, but Philly natives' accent was close enough to Boston's for someone to mistake the faint trace of accent she had if they weren't familiar with it.

His frown cleared. "Ah, yes, that's it. You'll have to tell me sometime how you came to end up here in our little town."

Sloan's smile slipped. "Of course. Another time, if that's all right?"

"Yes. Go, go. Don't let me keep you from your work." He focused on his breakfast, releasing her, but her panic didn't dissipate as she headed for the kitchen. She'd thought leaving her past in the past would be as easy as relocating and starting a new life. It had never occurred to her that everything from the way she carried herself to the way she spoke could give her away.

It doesn't matter. None of these locals care where you came from, other than wanting a good story.

Knowing that didn't change the fact that the walls felt too close. Sloan stopped just inside the door to the kitchen and concentrated on breathing in slowly through her nose like Jessica, the yoga instructor, had taught her this morning. Three breaths and she wasn't in danger of fleeing out the back door and never returning. Another five and she even managed to turn around and head back into the main dining area.

All her hard-won calm disappeared when she saw Jude lounging in the corner booth. Lounging wasn't the right word. He looked like a big cat who was as likely to tear out her throat as purr and rub against her.

Rub against…

She tried and failed to shut the thought down. From there, it was a slippery slope to thinking about what she'd done last night while picturing him.

It was almost enough to make her flee into the kitchen again. Or it would have been if not for the knowledge that Marge had given her a chance, and the woman wouldn't take kindly to her hiding in the back when there were customers to be served.

Sloan took a careful breath and approached Jude. "What can I get you?"

"I feel like I'm perpetually apologizing to you, but I left abruptly last night and I'm sorry." He didn't wait for her to respond. "Come out with me after your shift."

She blinked. *Did he just...* "I'm sorry, what?"

"I'm going to take you out. Tonight." His intense dark eyes never wavered, though she was wondering how she ever labeled them cold. Right now, they were so hot, they were liable to turn her into a pillar of flame.

The only question was if she'd perish in the fire or emerge as something altogether different.

That thought should have scared her, but she'd been afraid for so long. Maybe it was time to do more than think about taking the first step into the future. Maybe she needed to actually put herself into motion. Sloan licked her lips, aware of the way he tracked the move. Everything about Jude was intense. He'd toned it down for her last night, but he wasn't even trying right now. She shifted her stance, still torn. "I'm not exactly in a good place to date right now."

He considered her, and she suddenly got the impression that he was choosing his words with care so as not to spook her. "What is it, exactly, that you think I'm asking?"

"I, ah..." She clutched her little notebook to her chest, painfully aware that the handful of diners in the place were blatantly eavesdropping. "I don't know."

He lowered his voice to the point where she had to inch closer to hear him clearly. "Let me show you."

And, suddenly, she wanted to do exactly that. Sloan found herself nodding even though every instinct she had said that Jude was trouble in the worst way. But, whatever he was, he was vitally different from her brothers and father back home. He might seem brutal and dangerous and intense to a criminal degree, but this wasn't Boston. This was Callaway Rock. No matter how dangerous he seemed, odds were that he wasn't a man who had skeletons in his closet—literal or otherwise.

That made him safe in a way none of the men she'd ever known were.

Jude's gaze sharpened. "That's a yes."

"That's a yes." Her voice was too breathy, too irregular to pass for anything other than nerves, but she didn't care. If she fell flat on her face, at least she was *living*.

Get control of yourself.

She cleared her throat. "Can I get you something?"

"You." He drummed his fingers on the table, ignoring her jaw dropping. "In the meantime, some coffee to go would be great."

Did he... He didn't... He did.

Sloan walked back to the kitchen in a cloud of white noise. She'd never been talked to like that. She wasn't even sure it could be considered flirting, because he wasn't feeling her out in any manner—he was talking to her like their being together was already predetermined.

Like she was a sure thing.

She wasn't certain he was wrong.

* * *

Jude knew he'd crossed the line with Sloan, but there was something about the woman that drove him to it. He couldn't help pushing, poking, prodding her into a corner just to see how she'd react. The interest that had flared in her eyes at his blatant invitation had been reward enough.

Kind of like the dazed look on her face when he told her *exactly* what he wanted.

Well, not exactly. He could have gone into explicit detail about every single thing he planned on doing to her body, but she'd already been half a second from freezing up or bolting.

You're supposed to be pumping her for information. Not pumping...

He shut the thought down as she scurried back to him, a coffee mug and pot in her hands. Marge was an old battle-ax who used to have no problem sending people down to the beach with paper coffee cups, but the second those things started showing up in the sand and ocean, she drew the line. So she allowed ceramic mugs to travel outside the diner, and people sure as shit brought them back when the alternative was to be eighty-sixed out of the only decent place to eat without leaving Callaway Rock.

He waited for Sloan to pour the steaming hot liquid before he spoke again. "What time are you off?"

"Three."

"Good."

She started to say something, seemed to reconsider, and then hurried away, her head down and shoulders bowed. He'd take it personally, but she seemed to default to that body language when she wasn't paying attention. The few times he'd seen her straighten and stride forward with purpose, it had very obviously been something she'd made herself do. Once again, he caught himself wondering what the hell her story was.

And who had hurt her.

Jude made an effort to unclench his hands. That was the crux of it—someone had hurt her. People didn't walk around trying to squeeze themselves into as little space as possible without a damn good reason—without conditioning to do exactly that. He rubbed a hand over his chin, considering what he could find out about her. Sloan wasn't a very common name, and adding in her likely connection to the Sheridans would narrow the search further. He could tap a couple of his sources and see what shook out.

Or he could wait and talk to her and see if she told him anything.

He almost smiled. Giving people the benefit of the doubt wasn't what he did. If his family's history had taught him anything, it was that if left to their own devices, people would barely wait for a person to turn around before stabbing them in the back. It was smarter to go into any situation, whether it was a date or a confrontation, with all the cards and a plan for every contingency. Jude pushed to his feet and headed for the door.

He almost made it, too.

Jerry Steinback, town mayor and all-around pain in the ass, appeared as if out of thin air, a wide smile on his face showing off too-white teeth. Everything about him was trying a little too much. Skin too tanned to come from Oregon summers, hair too perfectly combed, clothes always impeccably pressed as if he'd just put them on. There was nothing overtly wrong about him, though, other than his making it his personal mission to find out Jude's story. He held out a hand. "Nice to see you in town."

Torn between the desire to walk right over this little man and the need not to make a damn scene, Jude gritted his teeth and took his hand. "Jerry."

The mayor gave him a significant look. "Our new waitress has perked everyone's curiosity. I knew you'd be in eventually." He extracted his hand from Jude's with a grimace, which was what made Jude realize he'd been gripping it too tightly. Jerry continued, undeterred. "So, you and the new girl, huh? One town stranger and another, traveling across untold distances to end up living right next door to each other. It sounds like something out of a novel, though not one of yours, of course."

That was the other thing about Jerry that pissed him the fuck off—the man had more imagination than was good for him. Jude took a drink of his scalding hot coffee and strove for patience. "If you'll excuse me..."

"Right, right. Those words won't write themselves." He stepped out of the way quickly, almost as if he was uncomfortable being in Jude's shadow. "It was nice seeing you in town for a change, though. We're a family here, for better or worse."

Jude wasn't staying. Even if by some freak accident he ended up stuck in this little town, he sure as fuck wasn't interested in a family. He'd lost the only family he'd had before he knew them and he wasn't looking for a replacement. Caring about people was like issuing handwritten invitations to his enemies telling them how best to hurt him. He couldn't afford to miss a step because he was worried about anything other than his mission. He wouldn't allow himself to.

But he couldn't say any of that to Jerry. The man was already too curious by half, and while Jude wasn't above taking out problematic individuals, he'd hate to have to kill a man because *he* couldn't keep his shit together.

So he faked a smile. "See you around, Jerry." Then he walked out the door and into the cool summer morning.

The interaction had served to remind him what he was here for. It wasn't Sloan. She might be a source of information, and she might be an enjoyable distraction in the meantime, but she wasn't his endgame.

Which meant he had no reason to play nice.

His questionable honor only went so far, after all.

Jude walked out onto the beach, putting some much-needed distance between him and the rest of the town. Only when there wasn't a single person in sight did he pull out his phone and dial. It only rang once, just like always.

"What?"

"I need some information and I don't have much to go on."

Stefan snorted. "When do you ever have much to go on? It's a good fucking thing I'm a goddamn miracle worker, isn't it?"

It was true that no one seemed as adept as ferreting out information as the hacker. Jude had only met him in person once—and only because he refused to work with someone he hadn't seen face-to-face—and Stefan reminded him of a mole or some other underground creature. He kept his apartment closed off from the outside, not even opening the curtains, and surrounded himself with more computer monitors than any man had a right to. From what Jude could tell, he lived on Cheetos and Mountain Dew and didn't leave his nest, but none of those things mattered, because he was the best at what he did.

Information.

"You're wasting my fucking time. Give me what you got and I'll get you what you need."

Jude glanced over his shoulder, but there was still no one in sight. Even if there had been, the sound of the tide coming in would have drowned out his low words. "A woman—dark hair, dark eyes, petite. Her name is likely Sloan, and she's just as likely got a connection with Boston and/or the Sheridan family."

Stefan barked out a laugh. "You really like making things interesting, don't you?"

"I'll pay double if you can get me the information in the next twenty-four hours."

"Forty-eight."

He clenched his jaw. It was never simple with Stefan. "It is of the utmost importance that I have this goddamn information as soon as humanly possible."

"That's fucking fine, but you've given me shit-all. This girl could be a cousin to a cousin of some rando who works for Sheridan. Or she could be not named Sloan at all. Or a hundred different options. I know my work, asshole. You want it that fast, you're paying triple."

Jude turned to stare out over the ocean. Arguing wasn't going to accomplish a damn thing. He wanted that information, and he'd pay dearly for it. Stefan knew it and he knew it, so there was no point in negotiating. "Fine. Hurry the fuck up." Jude hung up and headed for his house. He had several hours before Sloan would be finished with work, and he fully intended to put them to good use.

CHAPTER FIVE

Marge met Sloan as she was clocking out. The big woman looked down at her, her expression unreadable. "You weren't a total disgrace today."

"Thank you." Two days of working alongside the woman, and she knew enough to recognize the gruff sentence for the praise that it was. Warmth kindled inside her, the steady satisfaction of a job well done. It didn't matter that her feet hurt badly enough that she was fighting not to limp, or that she was sore in places she hadn't known she *could* be sore.

She'd done a good job.

Marge nodded like she'd said more than she had. "Take tomorrow off."

Sloan's gaze flew to her face. "But—"

"You work yourself too hard, you're going to fall apart. Take tomorrow off. Soak your feet. I know Luke sent you to Jessica for yoga, so keep that up—it'll stretch out your muscles gone tense from carrying plates. Do whatever you want, but take care of yourself." She paused, her brows furrowed into a frown. "Be here at seven on Thursday."

She's not firing me. She released a breath she hadn't realized she was holding. "Okay." She made it all of three steps before Marge's voice stopped her.

"And Sloan?"

She turned to look at the other woman. "Yes?"

"You be careful with that man, you hear? He hasn't done anything wrong since he moved into town, but he makes the small hairs on the back of my neck stand up." She shook her head. "Makes me think of my cousin. He was a SEAL. The man was never right after the war. He'd look at people and you could almost see him mentally listing all the ways he could kill them and hide the body."

Sloan pressed her lips together. It was sweet that Marge was worried about her, so she didn't laugh at the woman. Jude might be intense, but the thought that he could be murderous... "I'll be careful. I promise."

Marge's expression softened. "You're a good girl. Now git. We'll see you on Thursday."

She left the diner, half expecting to find Jude waiting for her. She still couldn't decide if she was intimidated or attracted, though it was realistically a bit of both. He said he was going to take her out, but what did *out* even mean?

She stopped short. *I've never even been on a date.* She didn't even know what to expect.

It was entirely possible that all the dates in the world wouldn't be enough to prepare her for Jude.

She made her way back to the house, moving slowly enough that she wasn't hurrying, but not dallying in the least. Every step that brought her closer spiked a strange combination of anticipation and something almost like fear. *Maybe he changed his mind. I'll get back to the house and he won't be anywhere to be found.*

If that was the case, she wasn't about to go searching for him. Sloan had never considered herself very prideful, but the thought of him changing his mind and her begging him to change it back didn't sit well. The whole point of this was that she was taking her life into her own hands, beholden to no one.

Except Teague, who had done all the heavy lifting to transport her out here.

And the still-absent Sorcha, whose house she was staying in rent free.

Temporary. I'll save up enough of my *money to find another place.*

Eventually.

She shut that train of thought down, because she could feel depression hovering at the edges of her mind, waiting for her to stop moving long enough to suck her under. Well, that was just too bad. She wasn't going to stop moving, or allow the sheer amount of things beyond her control to bring her down. She was finally, *finally*, in a place where she had a modicum of control over her life, and she wasn't going to drive herself to distraction thinking about all the things that could possibly go wrong.

Because the list is too long to number.

Stop it.

She was almost to her steps when Jude appeared on his porch. "Sloan." He didn't raise his voice, but she heard him clearly all the same.

And, suddenly, it was too much. She yanked her hair out of its ponytail. "I need a shower. You can wait." She marched into her house before he could respond, slamming the door behind her.

The shower didn't do a single thing to calm the turmoil inside her, and neither did dressing in her favorite white sundress and a comfortable pair of sandals. If anything, each move only spiked the sickening twist of emotions coiling themselves through her, demanding a release.

She nearly tripped over Jude when she opened the door, and that was the last straw. "What is your problem?"

He raised a single eyebrow, not looking perturbed in the least. "Sorry?"

"No, you're not. You're not sorry that you turned me down last night, or that you left in a hurry, or that you were an...an insufferable jackass this morning."

If anything, his eyebrow inched higher. "You're in a mood."

"Are you *kidding* me?" She pushed at his chest, but he didn't even pretend she had the strength to move him. "You weren't interested last night, so you don't get to waltz into the diner and *order* me to go out with you. I've taken orders my entire life, and I'll be damned before I take one from you." The outburst left her feeling deflated, but she clamped her mouth shut and refused to apologize. Maybe she was being the slightest bit dramatic, but that didn't mean she was wrong.

Jude took a step closer, towering over her, his shoulders so broad, they filled the doorway. "Are you done?"

Just like that, she had a whole lot more to say. "Actually—"

"That was a rhetorical question, sunshine." His big hand cupped the back of her neck, his thumb tracing over her jaw and up to drag against her bottom lip.

The touch shocked her into silence.

For a moment. "Jude—"

Apparently he wasn't finished. "I didn't say no last night because I wasn't interested. I wouldn't have apologized—twice—if I wasn't interested."

"But—"

"You want to know the truth? The truth is that I can't look at you without wanting to strip you down, to run my hands over that tight little body of yours, to spread those sweet thighs and fuck you with my tongue until you're screaming my name and begging for mercy."

She swayed, her anger, her ability to think or move or talk or do anything except stare helplessly at him, all gone. She licked her lips, forgetting that his thumb was there, and stroked him with her tongue instead. His chocolate eyes went even darker, and he suddenly seemed larger.

Say something.

"You shouldn't say things like that."

"It's the fucking truth, sunshine." He stroked her bottom lip with his thumb, his hand gentle yet holding her in place easily. "You're a good girl. I don't have to spend any time with you to know that. You deserve better than the likes of me, even for a fuck. But that's the difference between us. I'm not good. I might as well be the goddamn devil as far as you're concerned, but I've never been good at walking away when I have my mind set on something. And, sunshine, I have my mind set on *you*."

She couldn't speak, couldn't take a step, though she was at a loss if she'd move away from or toward him. It was like he held her captive with only a single hand, stalling out any and all reasoning ability.

Jude's grip tightened, ever so slightly. "I was going to

take you out. It's not my scene, but I was willing to give it a shot. I changed my mind." He stepped into her, his chest lightly pressed against her breasts, his thighs bracketing hers, his... *Oh my good Lord.* His hard length pressed against her stomach, and it felt perfectly in proportion with the rest of his massive body, not that she was an expert on these matters.

His other hand came to rest on her hip, fingers bunching the fabric of her dress as he kneaded her. "Tell me to stop, and it's done. I'll walk away, and I'll do my damnedest to leave you alone. Tell me to walk away, sunshine. Just say the words."

She knew he was right. He was no good for her, and this would only end in tears on her part. The man wasn't asking to date her. He didn't want to get to know her. He was telling her all the things he'd do to her body.

But she couldn't say the words to make him leave.

Sloan had never taken anything for herself in her entire life. She'd stayed in the background and gone with the flow and done everything in her power to play least in sight. Her brothers ran off any boy remotely interested in her, and she'd allowed it to happen. If her father had decided to move forward on his plans to marry her off, she would have walked down the aisle to a man of *his* choosing.

She'd never done a single selfish thing in her life until she asked Teague to help her escape.

Until she tentatively ran her hands up Jude's chest, sucking in her breath at the way his muscles tensed beneath her fingers. Until she looked up into his stormy dark eyes and said the word that would damn them both. "Stay."

* * *

Jude didn't give Sloan a chance to change her mind. He pulled her more firmly against him and kissed her. As much as he wanted to pin her to the doorframe and have her right then and there, a part of him that he didn't realize existed kept that desire reined in. She was sweet. She might have walked right into the lion's den and given him permission to ravage her in exactly the way he'd described, but nothing worth having had been attained by rushing headlong into a situation.

He teased her mouth open, guiding the kiss, nipping her bottom lip and then sliding his tongue in to stroke hers. Sloan made a surprised sound, and he froze. *No fucking way.* But he didn't stop, easing her into the kiss until her hands were fisting the front of his shirt and she was going onto her tiptoes to get closer to him.

Only then did he kiss down her jaw to her neck, allowing his whiskers to rasp against her sensitive skin, pitching his voice low. "Are you a virgin, sunshine?"

She went still and tense. "How did you—"

Damn it. He kept up his light stroking of her body, the small honorable part of him that he'd thought long dead reared up to demand he back the fuck away from this woman and back away from her *now.* "You were surprised when I slipped my tongue into your mouth."

"Not surprised, just..." Her voice was breathy, her body slowly relaxing against him again. "I didn't know it could be like that."

That hadn't even been a kiss. Not really. He'd been testing her, tasting her. *Thank Christ I started slow. The woman has never been properly kissed before.*

Back off. Back the fuck off now.

He already knew he wasn't going to. The thought of

being the one to show her pleasure—true pleasure—was too intoxicating. He was a bastard for feeling that way, but he'd been worse things than a bastard in his life. So he set his teeth to the lobe of her ear. "I'm going to take you to bed now." He lifted her, liking the way her legs instantly wrapped around his waist. She was a slight little thing, but fuck if they didn't fit perfectly.

He walked through the house, hesitating for her murmured directions even though he knew damn well where her bedroom was. Jude kissed her as he laid her on the bed, settling between her thighs.

The move made her sundress ride up to her hips, and he wasted no time stroking her thighs even as he deepened the kiss. Whoever said a woman's first time had to be painful was a piece of shit. Jude was going to make it good for her. Better than good.

"You change your mind at any time, you tell me to stop. That's it, sunshine. One word and it's over."

She dug her fingers into his hair. Her eyes might be shut, but every part of her body was responsive to a criminal degree. She shivered. "What you said before. I, ah, I want that."

It cost her to say it aloud. He could feel how tense she was and the words came out in a rush as if she needed to give them voice before she lost her nerve.

"You want my hands on your body." He coasted his hands up her sides, tugging up her dress as he did. She had to arch up to allow it past her breasts, and his mouth actually watered at the sight of her in her white panties and bra. Jude ran a single finger down the center of her chest, purposefully avoiding her breasts, and over her stomach to the band of her panties. "You want me to drive you out of your mind with my touch."

He eased back, spreading her thighs as he did. Without his body covering her, she shook, half fighting him as he spread her wider. He paused. "Do you want me to stop?"

"No, I just..." Her breath shuddered out. "I feel exposed."

"That's because you are." He traced the edge of her underwear with each thumb, down the dip where thigh met hip, to where it covered her pussy. "Before the night's through, sunshine, I'm going to see every single part of you." He stroked over her clit, earning a gasp that shot straight to his cock. Jude did it again, torturing them both. "I'm going to take off these damn panties, and I'm going to spread your folds and explore parts of you that no one else has. And then I'm going to kiss you there. In fact, I'm tired of waiting."

He slid down to settle between her thighs and pressed an openmouthed kiss against her panties. Sloan's shocked moan was music to his ears, spurring him on. He kissed and licked and played with her until the fabric was soaked and her hips moved restlessly against his mouth. "I'm taking these off now."

Her breath sobbed out. "You don't have to narrate every move you make."

"Maybe not." He pulled the white fabric down her legs and tossed it to the side. "But you love every single filthy word that comes out of my mouth." He nipped her thigh, causing her to spread her legs wider. "You get off on knowing that I've thought about this—that after we're done, I'll be thinking about this, reliving your every move, every sound, every single fucking taste."

He sucked her clit into his mouth, letting go almost immediately when she made a keening sound. She was so fucking close, she practically vibrated with the need to get off. He'd bring her to orgasm, but not yet.

First he had to do what he promised.

Jude gripped her hips, keeping her legs spread and fucking her slowly, thoroughly, with his tongue. She cried out, her hands immediately going to his hair, but she didn't try to push him away or pull him closer, seeming content to ride out the pleasure he dealt her. It was sexy as fuck.

"You taste so goddamn good." He licked up and over her clit and back down again, savoring every single detail. "I could lick you until you come so many times, you forget your fucking name."

"Jude."

The desperation in the way she said his name steadied his frenzy a little—enough that he remembered his purpose. Her pleasure. Not his. Not now. Not until she was ready for him. When she was ready, he'd fuck her as hard and long as he craved.

It just wouldn't be tonight.

Tonight was about *her*.

CHAPTER SIX

Sloan couldn't think, couldn't breathe, couldn't do anything but take the pleasure Jude gave her. It rose, spiking through her, until she couldn't stop small, helpless sounds from escaping her mouth. They evolved into his name, a curse and a plea. "*Jude.*"

"We're getting there." He shifted, letting go of one of her hips, and that was the only warning she got before his finger pushed into her.

Her eyes flew wide and she arched half off the bed. "Oh my *God.*"

"Fuck, sunshine, you're tight." He stroked her, stretching her. "It's going to feel so goddamn good when you come around my cock. But first . . ." He licked her, flicking her clit with the tip of his tongue.

Combined with the intrusion of his finger, it was too much. She cried out as her pleasure crested, stronger than she'd ever felt before. He barely waited for the aftershocks to move up her body, slipping her out of her bra. She stared at him, dazed, her nerves still sparking with pleasure. "Jude."

He cupped the back of her neck the same way he had when they'd stood in the doorway. "I'm going to fuck you now."

When he didn't immediately move, she realized he was waiting for some kind of response. She opened her mouth. *We haven't even had sex and he already made me feel like this. Maybe there is something to this whole thing.* Sloan swallowed hard. "Yes."

She half expected him to get down to business, but he kissed her again, taking her mouth with more purpose than he had previously. She tasted herself on his lips, and it wasn't unpleasant. In fact, it was erotic to a terrifying degree.

Finally, Jude lifted his head. "Do not move."

She held herself perfectly still, feeling a bit silly, as he pushed to his feet. The feeling faded as he pulled his shirt over his head, revealing the body she'd fought not to ogle before. He was in better shape than most gods, his muscles clearly defined, his skin bronzed from the sun. With his dark brown hair falling about his shoulders, he truly did look more god than man.

Then his hands went to the button of his jeans, and she forgot everything. His pants hit the floor, revealing that Jude didn't bother with underwear.

I was right. He really is *as big there as he is everywhere else.* For the first time since she'd told him to stay, a fissure of fear went through her. *Too big.*

He correctly interpreted the direction of her thoughts. "I won't hurt you, Sloan. I promise."

There was no logical reason for her to trust him, but he'd been careful with her up to this point. Perhaps he'd be careful with her with what came next. She nodded mutely, watching as he rolled on a condom that he'd retrieved from his pocket. Her body hummed in anticipation and trepidation, but she didn't let it show as he moved back to join her on the bed.

Jude palmed her between her legs, his big fingers exploring her. It didn't seem possible that he could spark pleasure with a few specific touches, but it didn't take much to have her relaxing, letting him once again take the lead. He kissed her neck. "Feels good, huh?"

"Well, I—*oh*." Her eyes went wide when he pushed a second finger into her. It stretched her, the feeling not entirely pleasant at first, but he merely waited, pulsing the slightest bit, until pleasure took hold once more. She clutched his shoulders. "Kiss me again. Please."

"You don't have to ask twice." He took her mouth like he owned it—like he owned every part of her. Jude slid between her legs, his body rubbing deliciously against hers. His hard length slid through her wetness, creating a friction that sparked a tide of desire deep inside her. *Again? I couldn't possibly...*

He nipped her bottom lip and then soothed the slight ache with his tongue. "Ready?"

There was no mistaking his meaning. She nodded. Despite the earlier orgasm and how good it felt to have him moving against her, she was so incredibly *empty*. Instinct had her hooking a leg around his hips and arching up to meet him, needing more, so much more.

Jude reached between them, and then he was at her entrance. He kissed her, tongue twining with hers as he pushed into her, just a single inch. It was too much and not enough and she couldn't help but thrash, pinned in place by his big body, overwhelmed by her helplessness and what he was doing to her. "Jude, I—"

"Shh. I've got you." He rolled, taking her with him. One second she was on her back, finding it hard to breathe, and the next she was straddling him where he sat with his back against the headboard.

Sloan looked down, daunted by the sheer size of him. "I don't know if this is going to work. You're too big."

He laughed, deep and full-throated, the sound rolling through her like the tide. "You can take every inch of me, sunshine. I promise you that." He gripped her hip with one hand and spread his other across her lower stomach, his thumb finding her clit. "Does this hurt?" He asked the question like he already knew the answer.

She spread her legs a little more, her wiggling taking him deeper inside her. Sloan sucked in a harsh breath. "It's too much."

"Do you want to stop?" His thumb brushed her clit, the gentlest of circles. Combined with him inside her, even partially, it made her whole body go hot like she'd been thrown into a fire.

She opened her mouth to say...She wasn't sure what she wanted to say. All she knew was that she'd never felt anything this intense in her life, and she'd be damned if she walked away before it was finished. "Don't stop. Just...slow."

"You're on top. You set the pace." His eyes were intense on hers, his thumb never stopping that intoxicating movement.

She didn't know what she was doing. But she wasn't

about to let that stop her—not this time. She gripped his shoulders and sank onto him. This time it wasn't the least bit unpleasant. The ache inside her only got worse, as if her body knew she was depriving it of all of him. She eased down another inch.

"Just like that." His grip on her hip pulled her off him a little, and she cried out. "I can feel how wet you are for me, even through the fucking condom." He guided her lower, reclaiming the lost ground and then some, sealing them together. Jude closed his eyes, his mouth tight, his grip unrelenting. The only part of him not tense was his thumb, coaxing her pleasure higher and higher. "Fuck, you feel so goddamn good."

She rocked a little, experimenting. "You feel good, too." Sloan rolled her hips, her orgasm looming closer. But just out of reach. She sobbed out a breath. "Jude, please."

"A man could lose himself with the sound of his name on your lips." He let go of her hip and claimed the nape of her neck, forcing her to meet his eyes. "I know what you need, sunshine." Using his grip, he led her up until his length was almost completely free of her. She fought him, needing that delicious fullness, not wanting to let him go.

He released her, and she slammed down on him. He hit some spot deep inside her, and that was it. Sloan cried out, her pleasure cresting. He flipped them again, hitching one of her legs up and out, rolling his body so that his pelvis ground against her clit, making the orgasm go on and on. She couldn't get enough, clinging to him even as her body took on the tempo as if it had been made for this.

Made for him.

* * *

Jude tried to maintain control, but Sloan reared up and sucked on his neck, her teeth setting against his skin, and it was too much combined with the way her pussy gripped him like a fucking vise. He came with a curse, trying to keep from driving into her, but it was no use. She took everything he gave, her legs wrapped around his waist, her hands tangled in his hair until he was spent.

He rolled partly to the side to avoid crushing her. The sound of their harsh breathing filled the room, and she maintained her grip on his hair as if unable to control her body enough to let go. Jude kissed her lips once, twice, a third time, keeping it light. With her looking up at him with her dark eyes gone hazy with pleasure *he* provided, he wanted nothing more than to just keep fucking her. It wouldn't take much. He palmed her breast, her pebbled nipple dragging against his palm.

Already, he was getting hard again.

She's a fucking virgin.

She was. She's not anymore.

But the reminder was enough to have him sliding reluctantly out of her. She made a sound that was half protest, half pain, and he felt like an ass all over again for considering taking his pleasure over hers. As it was, she'd be sore as fuck tomorrow. "Stay here."

He got up and headed into the attached bathroom. It was quick work to dispose of the condom and get a hot bath running. He didn't make a habit of sticking around after sex, but this was different for multiple reasons. He needed information she had—and he'd be damned before he scared her off sex for life.

"What are you doing?"

He turned to find Sloan standing in the doorway, looking

well and thoroughly fucked. Her dark hair tumbled around her shoulders, her mouth swollen from his kisses, and whisker burn on her neck and thighs. He wanted to leave his marks all over her goddamn body. He motioned her closer, and then pulled her against him when she obeyed. "You're going to be sore."

"I already am." She made a face. "Is it always like this?"

Something like guilt rose up inside him. In some ways, she seemed younger than twenty-four. It made him feel like a fucking cradle robber. But she ran her hands up his chest, much like she had earlier when she told him to stay, and he let the guilt go. She was a grown-ass woman. She'd known exactly what she was getting into when she invited him into her bed.

Or as much as any virgin could know about such things.

He prodded her a little with a hand on her back. "Some of it is unavoidable, but the bath will help."

She raised her eyebrows, looking amused. "Do you seduce many virgins?"

"Just you."

The amusement disappeared like it'd never been, replaced by a heat he couldn't do a damn thing about. Not tonight. Not if he didn't want to actually hurt her. So Jude guided her into the bath and sat back, forcibly reminding himself why he couldn't join her. It wasn't just the size of the tub holding him back.

Still…

He reached over and cupped her chin, dragging his thumb over her bottom lip. Her breathing picked up, and hell if that didn't make him harder than a rock. "Tonight, you're going to recover. I just used your body in ways it's not accustomed to, and you're going to be feeling it tomorrow."

"Mmm." She leaned her head against the back of the tub, her eyes closing and her tongue flicking out to taste his thumb.

Fuck.

He couldn't let that stand, the little flirt. He stroked down her chest, cupping her breast where her nipple peeked through the surface of the water. "You liked riding my cock."

She opened her eyes. "I liked what we just did, yes."

"That's good, sunshine, because I plan on having that tight little pussy of yours whenever I damn well feel like it." He pinched her nipple lightly. "I'm going to fuck you in every way imaginable, until you can't move without feeling the echoes of what I've done to your body." He dipped his hand beneath the water to cup her gently, well aware that she'd be sore. "I'm going to tongue your pussy right there in your living room with the lights on, so every single fucking person walking on the beach can see how you come so sweetly for me."

She licked her lips, her gaze on his mouth. "You're more dangerous than any drug I've heard of."

She was right, though not in the way she meant. He brushed her clit, just enough to tease. "Think so?"

"There is no rational reason I should let you talk to me like that—that I should want exactly what you're describing." She covered his hand with her own, keeping him in place. "Even though I ache, I want you again. How is that even possible?"

Get up, you piece of shit. Get up and walk away from this woman right now.

She deserves better than you.

But she turned those dark eyes on him, and he found

himself rooted in place. "Stay, Jude. You're probably right that more sex would be a poor idea, but…just stay."

It took more strength than he could have dreamed to slide his hand from beneath hers and stand. "That's not what this is. We don't sleep together. You come for me. I come. We fuck until we're tired of each other. Then we move on. End of story." He should have just left it there, but the wounded look on her face spurred him to his knees. He hooked the back of her neck and pulled her up into a kiss, splashing water everywhere. Her hands came to his chest, not pushing him away, but not drawing him closer.

He shifted and licked the shell of her ear. "This might not be forever, sunshine, but you're mine for the duration. And I take care of what's mine."

CHAPTER SEVEN

Aiden O'Malley stared at the papers on his desk, wanting nothing more than to throw them into the fire. His brother Cillian had brought in the report with the mail earlier today, but he'd only gotten around to opening it now. A small miracle, since for once he was alone in his father's massive office. No one needed to see what he'd just read, the undeniable proof in photos and phone taps, showcasing one seriously fucked-up truth.

They had a rat.

One who was high enough up in the ranks as to pose a very true threat. One he couldn't touch without inciting the war they'd all worked so hard to hold off. All of that was bad, but it wasn't the worst part of the whole situation. He sat back and ran his hands over his face, feeling a hundred years old.

His motherfucking *brother*.

Cursing under his breath, he picked up the envelope

62   KATEE ROBERT

and flipped it over. There was no return address, but that fact was less important than the contents of the file. There were pictures of his brother meeting with the FBI, wiretaps detailing the information he'd shared, even a report detailing how the FBI had saved Teague's life when shit had gone down with the Hallorans, transporting him and Callie to the hospital before they went forward with their sting. There were only a handful of people capable of this level of surveillance—and who had reason to put this much effort into following his brother around.

Aiden flipped through the photos again, part of him wishing he'd see something different this time, while the practical side of him knew better. "God*damn* it, Teague. What the fuck were you thinking?"

More importantly, what had he let slip? Their entire business—their entire *life*—depended on flying below the radar of law enforcement, and his goddamn brother had been willingly handing that information over in return for...Fuck, he didn't know. There weren't payoffs, though that sort of thing would be hard to track. The only one messing with O'Malley business appeared to be Dmitri Romanov, and Aiden highly doubted *that* man was in bed with the feds. The only thing that stood out as too coincidental was the raid on the Hallorans. Teague had definitely had something to do with that.

Even then, only a few of their men were arrested. Those fuckers had their eyes on the prize—Victor Halloran. That old bastard was currently living out what remained of his days in federal prison. Good riddance.

Doesn't mean they won't come for us eventually, armed with whatever information my brother gave them.

The *only* silver lining to the whole shit show was that

Teague had never been privy to certain information because he was neither the heir nor the one running the books.

But he still knew plenty to damn them and the Sheridans, both. God, what would Callie say?

Aiden eyed the phone. He could call Teague right now, arrange a meet up, and... *What? Try to force him to confess everything? Threaten him?*

It's what their father would have done.

But, as everyone was so fond of reminding him, he wasn't their father. He might be close these days, but he couldn't make himself go through with it. They'd already lost a brother to circumstances that might have been avoidable. To lose another over shit like this? Maybe he was weak, but Aiden couldn't pull the trigger, proverbially or otherwise.

Not to mention, he was pretty fucking sure Teague was behind Sloan's convenient disappearance two weeks ago. Of them all, Teague was the only one not going mad with worry. New papers weren't hard to get ahold of if someone knew where to look.

Especially when that someone had the goddamn FBI in his pocket.

His gaze shifted to the other man in the photos, one John Finch. Aiden drummed his fingers on the desk, considering. He might not be willing to take irreversible steps with Teague, but this agent had no such protections in place.

He picked up his phone and dialed without taking his gaze from the photo. Liam answered almost immediately. "What can I do for you, boss?"

"I need you to find everything you can on an FBI agent named John Finch. And I mean everything—I want to know who he cares about most in the world, and if he has any vices that can be exploited, and every noteworthy case he's had in the last decade."

Liam hesitated. "There a reason you don't want Cillian on this? The kid's getting pretty damn good at hacking. Give him a half an hour, and he could get you everything you need to know."

If he did, Cillian would find out about Teague.

Aiden shook his head, even though the other man couldn't see. "I want you on this. Only you. And, Liam, it goes without saying that this stays between us."

Another hesitation, longer this time. "Is there something going on that I need to know about?"

They'd been friends for a long time. Aiden didn't like taking the boss man tone with him, and, truthfully, Liam didn't need threats to do his job. He sighed. "There's trouble, but until we have this information, there isn't a damn thing I can do about it." The cat was already out of the bag where Teague was concerned—he'd already talked to the feds. Now it was just a matter of figuring out *what* he'd told them.

And doing damage control.

"Got it. I'll see what I can do and pass along the information as soon as I have something."

"Thanks." Aiden hung up and sat back, releasing a pent-up breath. He'd fix this. It might not be the way his father would have gone about it, but he'd fix it all the same. Their family had taken too many blows in too short a time, and he'd be damned before he let one of their own bring them down for good. Depending on what Teague had told the feds, their father could be looking at jail time right alongside Victor Halloran.

Aiden could be looking at jail time.

He stared at the phone again, the tightness in his chest making it hard to breathe. Hurting Teague right now, even to get information, would do more harm than good, but he *had* to know what his brother had told John Finch—and he had to know it sooner, rather than later.

If he didn't...

If Seamus returned and found out what Teague had done...

Aiden cursed and scrubbed his hands over his face. Sloan's disappearance had broken something in their father. He'd gone out to the house in Connecticut with their mother and just...not come back. Aiden spoke with him daily, but he'd more or less handed over everything. Aiden kept thinking that one day Seamus would show up and take control again, but it hadn't happened yet.

Now he was starting to wonder if it would never happen.

He'd been trained to expect a knife in the back from everyone around him—from ally to enemy. In their world, everyone was out for themselves and willing to play dirty to get what they want.

He just hadn't expected the hand holding the knife to belong to his brother.

* * *

It took Sloan the better part of the day to put a name to the emotion sinking its barbs into her. *Fury.* She hadn't seen Jude since he walked out of the bathroom last night, though she hadn't really expected to. Her body ached with the memory of what he'd done to her, and even as angry as she was, she enjoyed the remnants a little too much. Last night was the first time she'd truly taken control.

And look how that ended up.

Wonderful sex with a less-than-perfect man. She stretched and stood. Though she'd had every intention of attending the yoga session at sunrise, she'd slept until ten. Between the diner and Jude, apparently she'd needed the sleep.

Restlessness drove her to clean, but it hadn't taken long, since the house was in immaculate condition. So she'd gone to the little market, but short of a few select items, she didn't know what to shop for. *I need a cooking class.* Maybe that way she could expand her diet to something other than diner food and salads.

At least I can't burn salads.

A knock on the door had her freezing. *It could be Jude.* Sloan shook off her initial impulse to rush to open it, and made her way slowly to the front of the house. If it was him, he could very well wait on her whim—especially after how last night had ended.

Except, when she opened the door, a curvy blond woman stood there. It took a second for Sloan to place her, but when she did, she smiled. "Jessica."

"Sloan, right?" Jessica held out a hand, her high ponytail bouncing with the motion. "You were there and gone at yesterday's class before I had a chance to formally introduce myself."

She hadn't been aware that chatting was part of yoga class. Some of the older folk had stuck around, but Sloan had felt a little like a kid hoping not to be picked last for a group project. It had been easier to walk away. "I had a shift at the diner."

"I know." Jessica grinned. She wore a pair of purple yoga pants and a loose gray wrap thing over a white tank top. The wrap defied comprehension, leaving gaps to show the tank beneath it. "Sorry, that was creepy and stalkerish.

The truth is that everyone pretty much knows everything about everyone else in Callaway Rock. So, I promise I'm not snooping around, but I had heard that you got a job from Marge." She spoke so fast, Sloan wasn't sure if she was supposed to interject a response or not, so she just stood there and waited. Jessica wasn't done. Her smile brightened. "I'm babbling on, and it's terribly rude. I'm sorry. The whole reason I came by, aside from introducing myself, was to tell you that I offer one-on-one sessions. I can tell you haven't done much yoga before, but you have a knack and you're bendy. And, forgive me for saying it, but you are tense enough to be brittle. Yoga will help with that."

Sloan started to beg off, and then stopped. The truth was, she'd enjoyed the class yesterday, but she *had* felt more than a little lost going from position to position. She opened the door a little wider. "I would love to do that. What is the cost of the classes, though? I haven't gotten my first paycheck and—"

"First session is on me." Jessica bounced on her toes. "After that, it's twenty-five for an hour, or one hundred fifty for a month's worth of a couple times a week. We can work it out if that's what you decide you want to do."

Purchasing a month's worth of anything seemed like a large commitment right now—a declaration that this was her final settling place. Sloan pulled at the hem of her shirt. *And getting a job doesn't?* She finally looked up. "When are you free?"

"Right now, in fact." Jessica's grin widened. "I'm being pushy. Sorry again for that. I'm just excited to meet some fresh blood in this place—which goes doubly because you're my age instead of twice that."

She had noticed that most of the residents skewed to

their forties and beyond. "I just need a few minutes to change."

"Go for it." Jessica danced back with a little twirl. "I'll meet you on the beach."

Sloan wasted no time. She dug out a pair of yoga capris and, after some consideration, pulled on a tank top over a sports bra. She didn't make a habit of showing much skin, but the less fabric to slide around and suffocate her the better. She'd learned that the hard way yesterday.

Had it only been yesterday? It seemed like a lifetime ago.

She couldn't stop herself from shooting a glance at Jude's house as she stepped onto her back porch, but the door was closed and the shutters drawn. If she thought too hard about it, she might half convince herself that last night never happened.

It happened. He took everything you offered and walked away.

It shouldn't matter. She was an adult. She wasn't young or foolish enough to think that sex meant anything other than a potential pair of mutually satisfying orgasms. Between Cillian and Carrigan, she'd learned that lesson through observation.

The pang in her chest hit again, sharper than it had a right to be. *Carrigan.* She missed a step and almost stumbled. It was easier not to think of her sister out here. Carrigan would hate this place, would feel confined by the lack of anything resembling city life, by the small population, by the thought of a life of settling down. She wouldn't understand.

Devlin would have.

It doesn't matter what Devlin would have understood. Devlin is dead.

"Over here."

Jessica's voice brought her out of her spiral, and not a moment too soon. She couldn't manage a smile as she approached where the other woman had dropped her water bottle onto the sand, but at least this was one potential relationship uncomplicated by a past that went back...Well, her entire life.

She pulled her hair back into a ponytail that wasn't nearly as bouncy as the other woman's, and eyed the ground. "We had mats yesterday."

"The older folk find it comforting." Jessica shrugged. "Honestly, it's better to have a connection to the earth. It grounds you, makes you feel like a small cog in a very large system."

Though the words sounded suspiciously like some sort of hippie dogma, she couldn't deny the attractiveness of the vision Jessica painted. So she nodded. "Where do we begin?"

The next hour passed in a blur. It started with the breathing technique she'd learned previously, which was relaxing in and of itself. Jessica turned out to be incredibly helpful once they began going through the poses. She demonstrated and then helped Sloan adjust to the correct form before moving on. Between the steady whisper of the waves coming in and the clear air and the slow burn of her muscles, her thoughts emptied out of her head one by one, until there was only blessed silence in their wake.

At the end of the session, they spent ten minutes lying flat on their backs and just being.

Jessica stretched and sat up. "You did amazing. How do you feel?"

"Good." And, for the first time in a very long time, it was

the truth. She could feel all her worries and anxieties waiting to crowd back in, but for the moment they felt curiously
distant. "Thank you. I didn't realize how much I needed that
until just now."

"It's addicting like whoa." Jessica tipped her head back
and closed her eyes. "Runners have their high, but yogis
have serenity like no others. It's worth its weight in gold in
today's world."

Sloan couldn't argue that. "I'll be at the class tomorrow."

"Great! I keep things pretty steady there, but you'll be
moving on to more advanced moves before you know it."
Her face lit up. "Just wait until we get to inversions. They're
a trip."

"I look forward to it."

Jessica's expression changed, sharpening with curiosity.
"Holy crap. Don't look now, but our resident brooding
writer is staring at you like he wants to eat you alive."

Naturally, she looked. She couldn't help it.

Sure enough, Jude stood on his porch, a beer dangling
from his fingers, and even across the distance, she could
read his hunger for her. Could feel her body already re-
sponding despite the fury she still felt over how he'd walked
out last night.

He wanted her? *Well, that's just too bad.*

She turned back to Jessica, gathered her newly found
courage around her. "Is there a place around here to get a
drink?" One night didn't make her much of a drinker, but it
seemed like a big deal to ask the other woman to a meal.

Jessica slanted her a look. "Are you sure? If he was looking at *me* like that, I'd already be in his bed."

"He can wait." She couldn't believe she'd said the
words, couldn't believe she was going to ignore the way

her body called to him, even after the single time together, but apparently she had some of that pride that seemed to run through the O'Malleys like bedrock. Jude had hurt her last night when he left, intentionally or no.

And his bold words didn't hold up to the light of day.

Or that was what she told herself as she ignored his silent command to come to him, and smiled at Jessica. "So what do you say?"

Jessica's green eyes twinkled. "I say that you're a woman I want to get to know better. Let's do it."

CHAPTER EIGHT

Jude watched Sloan walk away, blatantly ignoring his silent command, and couldn't stop a sliver of admiration. She was so damn quiet—more mouse than woman—but she seemed to be growing a spine by the second. Or discovering she had a spine beneath all the delicate layers. He shouldn't like it. She'd be more biddable and controllable if she was the mouse he'd originally planned on.

But he found himself smiling a little as he drained his beer and headed back inside, the late afternoon sunlight warm and heavy on his back. She'd come around. She wouldn't be able to stay away, no matter how pissed she was about his leaving—and she *was* pissed. No woman worth her salt would allow him to walk away like that without so much as a ripple of *something*.

She's a means to an end. That's it.

He locked the door behind him and stripped off his shirt, moving to the punching bag he had strung up in the corner of the room. His computer's screen saver taunted him, tempting him to go over his notes on the Sheridan family for the millionth time. He wouldn't find anything new. Fuck, he had all the information memorized.

Jude rolled his shoulders and paused to wrap his hands. He didn't always take that extra step when he wanted to use the bag, but he didn't need Sloan asking questions about why his knuckles were all messed up. Checking the wrap, he nodded to himself. It'd hold.

He delivered a devastating punch that sent the bag rocking. It felt good. Better than good.

Colm Sheridan had, for all accounts and purposes, calmed the fuck down after he massacred Jude's family. And now a Sheridan-O'Malley alliance dominated the majority of Boston.

The Sheridan-O'Malley alliance that had been created when Callista Sheridan married Teague O'Malley.

Jude hit the bag again and again, his adrenaline spiking. Taking out Callista Sheridan was the blow that would break Colm. More than his son's death. More than finding out that said son had been plotting his betrayal. More than anything else Jude could do to him.

His muscles warmed with each punch. Right hook. Left hook. Jab. Jab. Jab. It wasn't enough to escape that woman's face.

It shouldn't matter that Callista was a woman. She was no more innocent than he was. Even if he'd never found evidence that she knew what her traitorous brother and aunt were up to, she'd killed her goddamn fiancé just under two years ago, which should put her firmly in the same category that Jude was in.

Except, from all accounts, Brendan Halloran had been a monster.

And it was entirely possible she'd killed him in self-defense. *Fuck.*

He moved faster, ignoring the ache in his knuckles, and switched up the hits, using his elbows as well as fists. It wasn't pretty. There was no bouncing on his toes or shadowboxing. It was just punishing blow after punishing blow, designed to put his opponent on the ground and keep them there.

That was the problem, though. The only opponent in the room was the niggling guilt that appeared when he thought about killing Callista.

Jude snorted. A hit man with guilt issues. It wasn't a problem he'd had for the entire fourteen years he'd spent taking out targets. He had his code, and if the mark didn't fit the criteria, he passed. It didn't make him a saint by any means—and only a fool would call him a vigilante—but it allowed him to sleep at night. He didn't feel guilty for the lives he'd taken.

Guilt hadn't stopped Colm Sheridan from doing what he thought was necessary—murdering Jude's father, his brothers, his brothers' wives. So many innocent lives lost. And if Ronan Sheridan had been in charge back then, he would have done the same thing his father had.

Jude stopped punching and caught the bag as it swung back to him, letting his weight rest against it as he blinked sweat from his eyes. The violence hadn't helped. He couldn't escape the past any more than he could escape the future. It was already written in stone.

Maybe if his mom had been able to move on... Maybe if she hadn't been constantly teetering on the edge of a black pit that was only too willing to suck her in forever when she felt her duty was done... Maybe, maybe, maybe.

Maybe could drive a man to distraction if he let it.

Jude shook his head and straightened. *Enough.* He didn't have to make a decision about Callista Sheridan right now. He didn't even have to make a decision about Sorcha. The old woman had allowed him the gift of time, even if he'd just been chafing at the delay a few short minutes ago. He moved to the window and looked out, his gaze finding and holding the O'Connor place. There was still the intriguing puzzle that was Sloan. He'd told her the truth last night— this thing between them couldn't last forever.

But he sure as fuck wasn't going to let go until absolutely necessary.

* * *

"You didn't." Sloan took the shot in front of her, something fruity with an absurd name that she couldn't remember, and eyed the grinning blonde across the table from her. "You...did."

"Dudes dig yogi chicks." Jessica shrugged, not looking the least bit repentant. "So, yeah, I might have picked my tiniest shorts and itty-bittiest sports bra and done some really excellent balance poses when I knew he'd be jogging down the beach." She laughed and downed her shot, not grimacing in the least. "I'm a little amazed that he managed to drag me back to his place and not do me right there in the sand."

Jessica's sheer brazenness was daunting. She reminded Sloan of Carrigan. Sloan sat back, forcing the thought away. She hadn't come here to brood about the things best left behind. She was having fun, despite her initial reservations. Jessica was irresistible and had a laugh that made people around the bar turn and look whenever she unleashed it. Sloan pressed a hand to her face, feeling flushed, though she couldn't begin to say if it was because of the alcohol coursing through her system or the topic of conversation.

Jessica leaned forward, her eyes alight. "Okay, I've shared more than one slightly scandalous story. Your turn. Explain to me what's going on with the new guy."

"I, ah, oh." She pressed her lips together, but ultimately decided this was a safe enough topic of conversation. As safe as a rabid animal ready to attack.

But it was much safer than speaking about anything connected with her past.

She took a deep breath. "It's nothing, really. He's a bully, albeit a very attractive bully. Every time I turn around, he's *there*."

"Well, he does live next door."

She shot the other woman a look. "Yes, I am aware. Painfully aware. The man says things that aren't even remotely appropriate and I should slap him, but..." Her body flushed hot at the memory of his growling parting words.

"But they get you hot and bothered and make you stupid." Jessica nodded. "I know the type, though I bet our writer friend puts them all to shame."

"You keep saying that. He's not a writer. That's impossible." Sloan tried to picture him hunched behind a computer, putting words to paper for hours at a time, and failed miserably. There was something too...*alive*...about Jude. Restless and dangerous, and if he could sit still for more than a few minutes at a time, she'd be shocked. "I thought he was a fisherman." That seemed to be the prevailing job market in Callaway Rock.

But Jessica shook her head. "No way. I would know,

because I'm up by the time they take the boats out. I see him, but only at weird hours. Plus, that's what he told Marge when she asked last month."

She just couldn't see it. Sloan stood, weaving slightly on her feet. "That's absurd. I'm going to go tell him exactly how absurd that is. Marge is a nice lady and he shouldn't be lying to her."

Jessica laughed. "Right. I'm sure that's *exactly* why you're going over there."

She found herself laughing, too, and sobered. Or tried to. "I'm very angry with him. I think I'll tell him that, too." She looked at the old clock on the wall behind the bar. Between half the numbers being faded and the alcohol making the room swim, it took her a few seconds to translate. It was after ten. She hadn't realized she and Jessica had been here quite so long.

It's not that late. He'll be awake.

"Go get him, tiger." Jessica tossed two bills on the table and stood. "I'll see you bright and early tomorrow morning."

It took her mind a few seconds to catch up. *Right. Yoga.* "Looking forward to it." And she was. She understood how addicting the practice could get. Kind of like her growing addiction to Jude.

No. I'm angry with him. I'm going over there to give him a piece of my mind.

Of course you are.

She ignored the snide little voice inside her that sounded remarkably like her older sister and walked out into the night. Sloan paused to stretch, her muscles protesting faintly. It felt good, though, like she'd really pressed herself today. She started for the beach, but she only made it about a block before it dawned on her how dark it actually was on the streets of Callaway Rock.

In her time here, she hadn't made a habit of going out after sunset—especially since sunset was at nearly nine in the evening—so she hadn't noticed that there weren't many street lamps. With all the businesses shut down for the day, there was only the faintest of lights shining through the windows lining the street. It should have made the whole town look sleepy and comfortable, but some instinct she hadn't realized she had perked up and sounded the alarm.

Sloan turned a slow circle, studying her surroundings as well as she could through the shadows holding dominance. There was no one out, and though she'd only walked a block, the relative noise of the bar seemed worlds away. Anything could happen to her and no one would know about it until morning.

"Stop it," she told herself. Her voice sounded small and scared. "Stop it right now. This isn't Boston. You aren't in danger here." But she *felt* like she was, as if some sniper had her in his scope and was currently caressing the trigger.

She took a big step back, reaching behind her for the brick wall of the market, her heart beating too hard. *No one knows where I am…that I know of.* That thought wasn't nearly as comforting as it should have been. Someone could have found her. They could be waiting just around the corner to throw her in a car and take her home.

What if it isn't my family who's found me?

Fear wrapped itself around her throat, making it hard to breathe. She knew the O'Malleys had enemies. Her youngest brother, Devlin, had paid the price because of those enemies. They might not be actively at war at the moment, but that didn't mean that snatching her off the street wouldn't be a coup for whoever managed to do it.

Oh God, I am so incredibly stupid.

She started moving, because the only other option was to stand still and wait for morning. Her tennis shoes beat a quick rhythm on the pavement, and she could almost swear she heard a second set of footsteps echoing hers, just a breath off. Panic swelled, swallowing any ability to rationalize away her fear. She glanced over her shoulder, saw a shadow detach from the market building, and couldn't contain herself any longer.

Sloan full-out ran.

CHAPTER NINE

Jude bolted awake to the sound of someone pounding on his door. He surged to his feet, halfway to the door before he registered that he'd been asleep in the first place. *What time is it?* He checked the peep hole, frowned, and shoved his gun into the nearest drawer before opening the door. "Sloan? What are you doing here?" How long had he slept? The last thing he remembered was showering and sitting on the couch to figure out his next step.

Can't believe I fell asleep.

"Jude, thank God." She rushed inside and stopped short, as if realizing that it might be rude to charge in uninvited. She raised shaking hands to tuck her hair behind her ears, and only then did he notice how pale she was.

He glanced outside, noting that she'd come to the street-side entrance, rather than up from the beach, and shut the door. "You look..." *Fucking terrified.*

He went to her before he could think better of it, pulling

her into his arms. Shivers racked her body, and her breath came too fast, as if she'd just sprinted here. He hesitated and then smoothed back her hair. The move seemed to calm her a little, so he did it again. "What happened?"

"It's silly." She buried her head in his chest, which made it impossible to gauge her expression.

" 'Silly' isn't a word I'd use to describe you. Tell me."

She took a shuddering breath, held it for exactly three seconds, and exhaled. "I was walking back from the little pub in the middle of town. I didn't realize how dark the streets would be, and I spooked myself. That's all. It's nothing."

It didn't sound like nothing. Sloan might be edgy around him, but he'd observed her enough to know that she didn't jump at shadows. All he knew was that something had scared the living daylights out of her, and she'd just run some distance to come to *his* door. It would have taken her a grand total of five seconds to reach the O'Connor house and bar herself inside, but she hadn't done that.

She wants me to protect her.

The thought staggered him. He held her closer without meaning to. No one came to him for protection. They feared him, even if they weren't able to put a name to their fear until he stood before them, their death in his eyes. He stalked, hunted, killed, leaving destruction in his wake.

He didn't *protect*.

But he suddenly wanted to make an exception for this woman. She was so small in his arms, her strength gone in an instant, her body shaking even as she tried to calm herself. He wanted to stand between her and the world, to fight whatever demons plagued her.

Jude almost snorted. That wasn't who he was. That

wasn't what he *did*. He might forget that from time to time when he was around Sloan, but that didn't change his reality.

He still wasn't going to make her leave while she was terrified.

He guided her over to the couch and sat down, taking her with him. She curled her legs up, fitting in his lap with laughable ease. They sat like that for a long time. Jude didn't know what to say. He wanted to know what really set her off, but she obviously didn't want to talk about it. Fuck, he wanted to know a whole lot when it came to Sloan, but she wasn't the sharing type.

"I was so angry at you today." She spoke so softly, he thought he'd imagined it until she raised her head and looked at him. Sloan sighed. "It seems rather petty right now, though."

He'd known she was pissed. He'd done it on purpose. "I don't lie, not when it comes to sex." Only everything else. "If you go and get your heart broken, it won't be because I filled your head with false promises."

She blinked and then laughed, the sound harsh. "Oh my *God*, could you be any more arrogant? If you remember, *I* am the one who invited you in last night. Yes, I invited you to stay, but I'm prepared to chalk that up to temporary insanity. I like how you make my body feel—that's the sum of it. I'm not ready to date anyone right now, and even if I was, I certainly wouldn't date *you*."

That should reassure him. It was exactly what he wanted, after all.

Instead, it made him fucking furious.

He glared at her, half-surprised when she glared right back. Sloan shook her head. "Coming here was a mistake." She started to get up, but he hooked the band of her yoga pants and pulled her down. She ended up straddling him with a hiss of fury. "I dislike you intensely."

"No, you don't." He palmed her ass, sliding her forward so she rode the ridge of his cock. "You *dislike* feeling out of control. Guess what, sunshine. You don't get control when it comes to fucking me."

Her nipples pebbled, showing through her thin tank top. They teased him even as she put her hands on his chest, her fingers kneading him and making him think of a kitten who had just discovered her claws. "And if I want control?"

"You don't." He wrapped one arm around her waist and used his free hand to palm her over her pants. "I've barely touched you and you're so fucking wet, you're practically panting for me."

"You are *insufferable*." But she rolled her hips, rubbing herself against his hand. "I'm leaving."

"No, you're not. You're going to stay here and let me lick that pretty pussy of yours until you come." He lightly pinched her clit through the fabric, watching her face. She liked the slightest bit of pain, if the way her eyes went heavy lidded was anything to go by. "And then I'm going to bend you over this couch and take what's mine." *Until you forget why you were frightened in the first place tonight.*

He wanted to hear her say yes. For all his pushing her, if she actually wanted to leave, he wasn't about to stop her. She *wanted* him to push her, to corner her, to let her pretend she wasn't making this decision every step of the way. *Fuck that*. He gripped her hips, lifting her and standing her on her feet. She blinked, obviously confused. "I thought..."

Jude unbuttoned his jeans, drawing the zipper down, his gaze never leaving hers. "You thought I'd take what we both know you want to give me? Newsflash, sunshine—I might get off on the lady protesting too much, but that only goes so far. We both know you want to be here the same way you wanted me there last night, even if your pride is still pissed that I left instead of cuddling you like some soft-hearted asshole.

"You want to leave, leave. I'm not going to chase you down and club you over the head, no matter how much I want you."

She swayed a little. "That's not fair."

"What's not fair is how goddamn hard I am for you. I watched your little yoga show this afternoon—don't even pretend you didn't know because I saw you shooting looks this way. Seeing that pert little ass of yours in the air, like you were offering yourself to me, and not being able to take what I wanted?" He grabbed her hand and pressed it against his cock. "I've been like this for hours. Because of you."

"Because of me?" She didn't take her hand away even after he let her go.

"Don't play coy. It doesn't suit you. You know you were teasing me on purpose. I wanted to tell the blonde to get lost and play with you right there. How long do you think you could hold downward dog with my mouth on your pussy?"

Her whole body shivered, her hand clenching around his cock. Sloan's brows slanted down. "You're doing it again. That thing where I should slap you across your face for talking to me the way you do."

"Do it." Jude took her free hand and set it against his cheek. "But whatever you're going to do, if you're not leaving, then get those fucking pants off. I'm starving for you." He flashed her a grin, even though he didn't feel the least bit amused. "If it will make you feel better, you can pretend you don't have a choice in the matter, but we both know that's a fucking lie. You want me as much as I want you."

* * *

Sloan almost gave in. With his length in her hand and his whiskers scraping against her other palm, she already ached in a way she was coming to fear only he could assuage. The things Jude did to her made her weak in the knees, and with him challenging her with his dark chocolate eyes, she wanted nothing more than to climb into his lap and let him chase away the last of the fear clinging to her.

But she hadn't left her entire life behind to hand over what little freedom she had to another man.

She took one step back, and then another. "You're wrong. I don't want to give up control."

"If you say so." His tone told her exactly what *he* thought. That she was biddable. A sure thing. Meek. Everything that Sloan used to be.

She wasn't that woman anymore. She refused to be.

So she took another step back. The way he eyed the distance between them made her body spark, as if he'd cross it in a bound and take her to the floor. She wanted him to...but it wouldn't solve anything and, when they were done, she'd still be left with a different kind of ache. One he'd told her multiple times that he couldn't—wouldn't—be responsible for.

She reached the front door, hesitating. Even though the feeling of danger had passed, the thought of going back to her empty house left her cold. Or perhaps that was the fact that she'd put half a house between her and Jude and, without the warmth of his big hands on her, the entire world seemed a little bit colder. She clutched the doorknob, her heart beating too fast. *Lay the terms out. You don't want this to end, but he can't run the whole show. You can't let it happen like that.*

Sloan lifted her chin, faking a confidence she didn't feel in the least. "I want you, that much is true."

"I know."

She ignored him. "But even if this is temporary, I want it on *my* terms."

Jude went still, completely unbothered by the fact that he was exposed to her. "I'm listening."

The only way you can get what you want is to say it. She bit her lip and then charged on. "If you're sleeping with me, then you're *sleeping* with me. I don't care if you aren't a fan of cuddling. It's something I require to continue this thing."

He raised a single eyebrow. "You want me to whisper sweet nothings in your ear while you're at it?"

"I think we can both agree that's not how you operate." She didn't want the lie of sweet nothings, but she'd take the lie of his big body in bed next to hers.

Maybe it would make her feel a little less alone.

He buttoned his pants with careless efficiency. "I don't sleep."

Her earlier anger flared. "Then lie there and count sheep for all I care. If I'm yours for the time being, then you see to all needs of the physical nature—for me, that includes sleeping." She couldn't believe she was pushing this. It would be so much smarter to retreat back to the safety of her home. Lonely, yes. But at least no one could hurt her there. She was opening herself up for rejection and potentially worse when Jude shot her down.

But he didn't say anything, just continued watching her with a strange look on his face. "This will only end in tears for you. You want things I'm not capable of giving, even if I was staying in Callaway Rock."

Her heart gave a pang, but she ignored it the same way she'd been ignoring it for her entire life. "You seem to think I haven't shed more than my fair share of tears, Jude. What are a few more?" She took a careful breath. "Those are my terms. Take them or leave them."

And then he was towering over her, his hand sifting through her hair to tug her head back so she looked him directly in the eye. "I'm taking them, sunshine. More importantly, I'm taking *you*."

His thumb traced her jaw, unspeakably tender, but then his eyes went hard, making the bottom of her stomach drop in a way that wasn't altogether pleasant. *I have the tiger by the tail.*

Jude tugged on her hair again, a little harder this time. "Now get those fucking pants off. I'm not going to tell you again."

CHAPTER TEN

Jude watched Sloan sleep. It was the first time he'd seen her truly unrestrained, her arms stretched over her head, her legs tangled in the sheets. One finger kept brushing his biceps, and it drove him damn near to distraction.

I never should have agreed to this.

He hadn't been lying to her—he didn't sleep much. He wasn't dramatic enough—or conflicted enough—that the dead haunted him. The lives he'd taken weighed on him, sure, but he'd researched each mark before he agreed to the contract. They'd all been monsters, which someone like Sloan might take to mean he was some sort of romantic vigilante.

He wasn't.

Jude was just a bigger monster than any of his victims had been.

His phone buzzed, drawing him from his thoughts. *Stefan.* He slid out of Sloan's bed without making a sound and padded into the hall, closing the door softly behind him. He'd promised he wouldn't leave, but there was no missing this call.

"What have you got for me?"

"A proposition."

Jude froze, icy calm cascading over him at the unfamiliar voice on the line. Russian accent, a tone that spoke of old money, and the fact that the man had *this* number all added up to one person. *Dmitri Romanov.*

He knew the man by reputation alone. Dmitri Romanov, head of the Russian empire in New York City. They were worse than the Irish bastards in Boston. They were like some behemoth monster, gobbling up everything in front of them and still hungry for more. It was more than mere ambition—it was starvation when sitting down at the head of a feast. That kind of addiction knew no bounds, and they couldn't be trusted as a result.

Playing dumb might garner him more information—and lead to the Russian underestimating him—so he said, "I hope you haven't done anything to my man. I would take it poorly."

"Stefan is perfectly fine. We had a discussion, and he decided it was to his benefit to pass over your contact information."

Meaning Dmitri had offered Stefan more money than Jude did. *Stefan always was a mercenary little bastard.* Jude eyed the big windows with their open blinds, all too aware that a sniper could take him out easily, even without the lights on. *Damn it.* "You have me at a disadvantage."

"I hardly think I do. Like recognizes like, Jude Mac-Namara. You know who I am, so let's dispense with the games."

So much for playing the fool. He moved back down the hall to check on Sloan. Satisfied she was still asleep and this whole call wasn't some ploy, he closed the door and leaned against the wall. "What have I done to earn a personal phone call from the head of the Romanov family?"

"It's come to my attention that you're in contact with a woman I'm seeking. Petite, brunette, large doe eyes, couldn't begin to imagine hurting a fly."

The same woman sleeping in the bed not ten feet away? He narrowed his eyes. "Who's she to you?"

Dmitri sighed. "Her family and I have a complicated history. It would serve my purposes to have possession of the woman."

The pieces clicked into place with a snap that had Jude feeling like a fool. On its own, the Romanovs had more enemies than the beach outside this house had grains of sand. Add in the connection to the Sheridans...

Fuck. Fuck, fuck, fuck.

He should have goddamn well known it by her fucking name. "Sloan's an O'Malley."

"You didn't know?" The Russian laughed softly. "So you aren't perfect. I had started to wonder if the rumors could possibly be true."

He would have figured it out. It was just shitty that it was right in front of his face and he'd been more concerned with getting between her thighs than with using his goddamn brain. "Killing her will only ensure her family burns yours to the ground."

"They can try." Dmitri continued, his tone downright imperial. "However, it's a moot point. I have no intention of harming the girl."

Jude didn't believe that for a single second. There were

so many ways to break a person, many of them possible without ever laying a finger on the victim. Jude eyed the open windows again. This house wasn't fortified in the least. He could take it by himself, but he couldn't *defend* it by himself. Three or more men, and he might lose.

Dmitri wasn't fool enough to send fewer than three men.

He stalked into the kitchen and reached over the top of the upper cabinets to where he'd stashed a .45 behind a dusty pot with some sort of seaside flower arrangement in it. "I'm disinclined to give her up."

He'd told her this wasn't forever, but he would have to be without a soul to hand her over to Romanov. Especially when it was clear she'd fought so hard to get out of Boston and leave that life behind.

You didn't run far or fast enough, sunshine.

Dmitri snorted. "You and the waif? Forgive me if I find that incredibly amusing."

"Forgive me if I tell you to fuck right off."

All amusement disappeared from the Russian's voice. "Play with the girl for now. I don't care. But I will require her at some point, and I'll pay any price to ensure it happens. The amount is of no consequence."

No, it wouldn't be. The Romanovs were richer than God. "I'll think about it."

"You won't. You've already made up your mind." Dmitri laughed again. "Like I said, Jude MacNamara. I don't need her quite yet. And many things can change in the course of a few short weeks. Enjoy her—for now."

Jude readjusted his grip on the gun, not liking where his head was at. He knew better than to borrow trouble when the end was in sight. He pictured the light dying in Sloan's eyes when she realized he'd betrayed her. He couldn't do it.

He might be more monster than man, but he couldn't hurt her like that. "As delightful as this conversation has been, I'm hanging up."

"I have a business proposition for you."

Now we get down to it. Threatening Sloan was just foreplay to get a read on me. He leaned against the wall. "I'm listening."

"We seem to find ourselves with a common purpose."

"How do you figure?"

Dmitri tsked. "You're smarter than that, so do us both the favor of ceasing with this act. You want Colm Sheridan in the ground. That happens to align with my endgame, and I'm willing to pay handsomely to see it done."

The plot thickens... "I'll consider it."

"You're playing coy. I'll see half of your going rate deposited into your account, with the remaining half provided once you've eliminated our mutual acquaintance." He ended the call, leaving Jude fighting to keep his curses internal.

Jude considered his options. He might have conflicting feelings about removing Callista and Sorcha, but he had no qualms about killing the Sheridan patriarch. If anyone of that family was guilty, it was the man who pulled the trigger all those years ago. He'd been fully intending to do the job for free—for his mother—but if he could get something else for it in the process, he'd be a fool to say no. In addition to that, if Romanov didn't already know where they were—and that was doubtful—he would soon. He might have given a slight reprieve for his own purposes as long as Jude fell in line, but if he disagreed, Romanov would come eventually.

And he would come in force.

Jude set his phone gently on the kitchen counter. What

the fuck was he supposed to do? Whisk Sloan away and spend the rest of his life protecting her? It wouldn't work. There were too many men out there like Jude, men who had no qualms about taking offered money and tracking their target to the ends of the earth.

He could give her a month, a year, even a few years, but eventually the past would catch up with her.

I could kill them all.

No, he couldn't. He was good—one of the best—but he was still just one man. To take out the entirety of both the Boston underworld *and* the Romanovs... He shook his head. It was impossible.

"Jude?"

He forced his body to relax and turned to face her. Barefoot and wearing an oversized sleep shirt that made her legs look a mile long, she looked younger, if that was even possible. Innocent.

Fuckable.

"Come here." He didn't wait for her to obey, crossing the kitchen in two steps and pulling her against him.

Her eyes went wide, her body arching into his, but she frowned. "Is everything okay?"

No. It's turned goddamn complicated while I wasn't looking. Because sometime earlier tonight, when Sloan stood in his doorway, making demands he should have shot down immediately, he'd found himself wishing Sorcha O'Connor wouldn't come back. Not today, not tomorrow, not anytime in the foreseeable future. That he wouldn't reach the point of no return—the *true* point of no return.

That she wouldn't show up while he was so enjoying watching Sloan find her feet.

He captured her chin between his thumb and forefinger.

"The only thing that's wrong is your mouth isn't around my cock."

She licked her lips, and he nearly groaned. But apparently she wasn't done. "You're lying."

"And if I am?"

A line appeared between her brows. "You said you don't lie."

"No, sunshine. I said I don't lie about sex." He leaned down, his lips brushing hers with each word. "All the bullshit can wait for morning. I want you on your knees. Be a good girl and I'll fuck you right here on the kitchen floor."

"We're going to talk in the morning—really talk." Before he could deign to answer that, she was on her knees. He hadn't bothered to put on pants when his phone rang, so she had no barrier to bar her from his cock.

She wrapped her fingers around him, making a sound low in her throat that had his balls tightening almost painfully. He held still as she eased his cock into her mouth, letting her drive the encounter. For now. If she was a virgin in every other way, he doubted she'd ever given head before, and he'd be damned before he did something to spook her or fuck up her experience.

Sloan explored him with her tongue and lips, until it took everything he had to maintain his stillness. Jude allowed himself to run his fingers through her hair, pulling it back from her face so he could see everything she did to him. "You have no idea how sexy you look like this."

She pinned him in place with her dark gaze as her tongue darted out to lick the head of his cock. "Tell me more. I like to hear you talk."

"I thought you wanted to slap me for the things I shouldn't say to you."

A little mirth appeared on her face. "I do."

That startled a laugh out of Jude. Every time he thought he had her number down, she went and did something to surprise him. It made him think of a foal walking for the first time, all gangly limbs and jarring motions, but the second the animal found its stride, it was fluid and perfect and beautiful.

Just like Sloan.

Something in his chest tightened, but he did his damnedest to ignore it. "You might crave giving up control, but when you're like this, you have it all. You keep sucking my cock like that, and..." And what? He couldn't promise her a damn thing, even before the call from the Russian.

Jude had nothing to give.

This isn't forever.

She's so goddamn pure. You aren't worthy to touch her, let alone think of some kind of tomorrow.

He pulled away from her, desperate to drive the inner voice to silence. He went to his knees in front of her, kissing her before she could say something to shine the light on how goddamn fucked up he was.

Common sense, something he never could quite get away from, spoke up. *Condom.*

Jude stood, lifting her with him, and set her on the counter. "Don't move." He wasted no time striding into the bedroom and finding one of the many condoms he'd stashed in her nightstand. He rolled it on as he made his way back to her, finding her exactly where he left her. "Good girl."

She lifted her chin as he pulled her to the edge of the counter and pushed a finger into her. *Wet and wanting, just like I like her.*

Sloan gasped. "Do I have to tie you down in order to actually get to finish you like that?"

"It'll never happen." He wasn't the type of man who could be tied down. Not like that. Not in any way. Jude skimmed off her shirt, needing to see all that creamy skin laid out for his pleasure.

He notched his cock in her entrance and spread her thighs wide. "I'm not going to be gentle, sunshine." He didn't know if he had it in him with the tangled mess of emotions riding him.

She braced her hands on the edge of the counter, which arched her back and put her breasts almost within reach of his mouth. "I can take it."

"I know." He shoved into her and dropped his head to kiss where her shoulder met her neck, pursuing the peace he only seemed to be able to find between her thighs.

CHAPTER ELEVEN

Sloan gave up on clinging to the counter after the third stroke. Jude was too strong, too driven by something she had no name for. So she clung to him instead, riding out the storm she could feel growing inside him. It had started with the look in his dark eyes, one she'd recognized from seeing it in the mirror often enough in the last few years.

Desperation.

And he'd come to her, to what she could give him, to escape it.

He hitched her higher, sliding his hands under her bottom so she no longer had contact with the counter. Jude used his hold to slide her up and down his length, his mouth against her ear and his words filling her even as his body did. "I can't get enough of you. The little cries you make, the way your pussy tightens around my cock like you never want me to leave, your taste. I *crave* you." He turned, and her back hit the wall. "I could spend hours fucking you, switching between my cock, my fingers, my tongue."

"Do it." She wasn't sure she'd survive it, but only he seemed to be able to ease the emptiness she'd had inside her since Devlin's death. Sloan hadn't been actively living for a very long time, but when she was with Jude, she didn't feel like she was just existing.

She felt *alive*.

His grin was almost feral. "You think you can take it?"

"I can take anything you give me, Jude."

He cursed, shoving all the way into her, until he bumped against her cervix. She cried out, so close to coming, she felt more animal than woman. He knew. He always seemed to know. Jude kept her pinned there, pumping just slightly enough that he hit that spot over and over again. "I love how you say my name when my cock is buried inside you. I like it even better when you're coming."

He ground against her, and that friction was all it took. She orgasmed, her fingernails digging into his shoulders, her body becoming more and less at the same time. Distantly, she could have sworn she heard him say, "It makes me want to keep you."

But that couldn't possibly have been right.

Jude slammed into her, again and again, riding out her orgasm. He was close—she could tell by the tight expression on his face—but she also knew he wouldn't come yet if he had any say in the matter. A few days into this and she already knew that he liked to make her orgasm several times before he finished.

Not tonight.

She twisted a little, sliding her hand around her leg to cup his balls. His eyes went wide and then narrowed. "Sunshine—"

She squeezed, letting her nails prick him, just a little, and that was all it took. He cursed and drove into her harder, until it felt like the entire house shook with the force of his strokes. Sloan squeezed him once more for good measure, pushing him over the edge.

Jude buried his face in her neck, her name on his lips as he came, his strokes becoming inconsistent and almost spasming.

He lowered them to the ground, still inside her, and lifted his head. "That was a shady little trick."

"Mmm." She'd discovered that part of him was sensitive last night, completely by accident, though she'd half convinced herself it was a fluke. It wasn't, and she fully intended to torture him with the knowledge the same way he seemed to find pleasure torturing her by inexplicably knowing her body almost better than she did.

"I'm going to punish you for that." He kissed her lightly. "And you're going to love every single fucking second of it."

"I'm looking forward to it." She pushed on his shoulders. "Now get off me. I'm liable to suffocate before you get around to the punishment."

Jude laughed and thrust against her one last time before he pulled away. Her smile died at his harsh curse. Sloan sat up. "What's wrong?" But she saw what he held in his hand, and her body went cold, the last remaining pleasure disappearing as if it'd never been. "Please tell me that I'm not seeing what it appears I'm seeing."

"*Fuck.*" Jude pulled her to her feet and dragged her to the bathroom.

She watched in disbelief as he turned the knobs of the shower to get the water going. "What exactly do you think you're doing?"

"The goddamn condom broke, Sloan. I didn't pull out, and you were a fucking virgin until less than a week ago, so unless you've been hiding some sort of birth control, you need to get my motherfucking come out of you. Now."

Perversely, his near panic made her calmer. She stepped into the shower mostly to appease him, even though she knew her next words would negate that completely. "It's not going to be enough. I need..." She thought fast. "I need the day-after pill."

He stared at her. "Do you really think there's a pharmacy closer than Portland with one of those?"

She hadn't thought about it. She hadn't thought about *anything*—she'd been too busy enjoying her time with him. The thought of birth control had been a distant one because they were using protection, but now she felt incomparably stupid for not having gone and gotten a prescription for the pill after the first time they were together.

Except you need a doctor to get a prescription and I don't have one of those locally, and I can hardly call up Doc Jones and ask her.

She ducked her head under the spray and when the water ran from her eyes, she found him staring at her. "What?"

"This is beyond fucked."

She couldn't argue that, but his obvious distress wasn't exactly reassuring. "I'll call around and see if I can find it." She scrubbed down, feeling like he'd pointed a spotlight on her. "Actually, I have a shift in a few hours and nothing will be open before then. You'll have to do it."

"Call in."

She glared. "Absolutely not. Broken condom or no, I need this job and I can't start calling in after a grand total of two shifts spent working for Marge. She'll fire me on the spot."

"Everyone knows Marge has a soft spot a mile wide. Call in. This is more important than your fucking waitressing job."

That he so casually dismissed something she was proud of grated. She turned off the water and grabbed a towel. "You're free to feel that way. But you aren't my father or my…my boyfriend." She shook her head. "Pretend I never said that. The point is that you don't get a say, Jude. As you're so fond of pointing out, this is just sex. We set out the terms, and nowhere in those terms did it say you can tell me when I will and won't go into work."

"That was before this." He waved between them as if that really meant something. "And that was before—" Jude cut himself off.

Another time, she might press to know what he'd been about to say. Right now, Sloan just didn't care.

She strode past him and back into the bedroom. A quick glance at the clock told her that it was barely five. Sunrise yoga would be starting relatively soon, which was fine by her. She found the idea of staying in this house with an irrational Jude for a second longer than necessary stressful in the extreme.

Sloan pulled on a pair of yoga pants and was reaching for a sports bra when Jude grabbed her wrist. "What do you think you're doing?"

"Sitting here worrying about something that is unlikely to happen isn't going to do a single thing but stress us both out." She pulled, but he didn't release her. "For heaven's sake, Jude. People have unprotected sex all the time, and it doesn't result in…" *Pregnancy. A baby.* She couldn't quite say either.

She'd spent too much of her life sitting and worrying

about things beyond her control. It didn't change anything except to make her feel helpless and useless. She might as well be proactive about the things she *could* control instead. "Unless you're about to tell me that you have an STD and I need to go to a doctor immediately, let go of me."

"I'm clean."

She released a breath she hadn't realized she'd been holding. "Okay." She shouldn't trust him, but he had no reason to lie about it now. The horse was out of the barn, or whatever that saying was.

"It's the damnedest thing." He said it so softly, she wasn't sure if he was talking to her or himself. "Even knowing what could happen, I still want you. If it's possible, I want you *more* knowing that I could fuck you right now without a condom and it wouldn't make a damn bit of difference."

Her body flushed hot at the thought of being with him without a single thing between them. She wanted it. She wanted it so badly she almost said yes.

Almost.

"It would make a difference." She met his dark gaze and forced herself to be reasonable. "It would increase the chance of there being consequences."

"I know." But he still moved closer, and turned her around to face the dresser. She could see his expression in the mirror, see the familiar desperation there that called to her. He ran his hands down her sides and back up to cup her bare breasts. "I could have you just like this. It'd feel so fucking good, and seeing every inch of you in the mirror would be...Fuck, there are no words." He let go of one breast and slipped his hand into her yoga pants, stroking her. "You like that thought."

"Yes." She spread her legs a little, giving him better access. "But it's still a bad idea."

"Every single thing about this is a bad idea." He kissed her neck, his finger drawing her wetness up and around her clit before he pushed it back into her. "Say yes."

She wanted to. She could picture exactly what he described, could see him sliding her yoga pants off, spreading her legs farther yet, and pushing into her. The dresser was low enough that she'd be able to see him enter her, be able to see him watch her in the mirror as he took her.

I can't. It's too much of a risk. "No."

He hesitated, and for a second, she thought he might press the issue. Sloan bit her lip, almost hoping he would. She wanted it as much as he did, all common sense aside. But that was the problem—*common sense aside*. In reality, they had likely just dodged a bullet. Having unprotected sex *again* was beyond foolish. Jude would realize that the second he started thinking clearly.

She gripped his wrist, all too aware of how much bigger he was, and pulled. He let her slide his hand out of her pants. "No," Sloan repeated.

Jude exhaled harshly and gave himself a shake as if waking from a dream. "You're right."

"I know."

He shook his head again. "I'll find the fucking pill." He left the room, left her feeling more alone than she'd ever been.

* * *

"Stop the car here." Dmitri Romanov climbed out and paused to take in the building in front of him. It was a nondescript brick, with no windows and only a single service door. He'd seen many like it, though this one was being used for a distasteful purpose.

A rave.

Someone should tell the attendees that raves were something from the nineties and should be left in that godforsaken decade. Under normal circumstances, he would have sent one of his men if attending was required. That wasn't an option tonight.

He nodded at his driver and strode to the door. A few terse words and the password—*the password, God save him*—later and he was inside, every sense assaulted. He stood just to the left of the doorway, attempting to adjust to the sheer onslaught of sensation. Multicolored lights strobed, music shrieked loud enough to make every cell in his body vibrate, and the whole room smelled of sweat and sex.

The things I'm required to do.

He searched the crowd, looking for one person in particular. His man had followed her here, watching as she slipped her guard detail and made her way to this building. *Aiden, you haven't been taking care of your possessions.*

A flash of dark hair caught his attention, and he turned to find the very woman he was looking for staring at him, not ten feet away. Keira O'Malley had all the beauty of her oldest sister, but it was sharper, more likely to cut than seduce. She watched him with the jaded gaze of a woman who'd seen so much that nothing surprised her any longer. He took in the torn-up jeans that bordered on indecent and the shirt that hung from her thin frame, revealing a lacy black bra that was expensive enough to buy a night's worth of drinks for every person here.

Dmitri waited, part of him curious to see how she'd react. Would she run? Attempt a poorly thought-out attack? But Keira gave him a look that only an idiot would mistake as anything other than a challenge.

And then she slipped into the pulsing crowd and disappeared.

He followed, with his familiar harsh expression that made people retreat. A small path cleared, and it was enough for him to move freely after her.

Except when he reached the other side of the crowd, she had disappeared.

Dmitri turned a slow circle, irritated at himself for being drawn in. Of course she'd used the crowd to her advantage and slipped away. She was likely halfway back to the O'Malley house by now. *Fool.*

"You're looking for me." A voice in his ear had him turning to find the woman in question less than six inches from him. She went up on her tiptoes, giving him a good view of her dilated pupils, and spoke in his ear—or, rather, yelled, because anything less would be drowned out by the sad excuse for music. "What brings Dmitri Romanov to a rave in Boston?" She leaned back and pressed a hand to her chest. He didn't need to hear the words she mouthed to understand. *Little old me?*

He could take her. She was drugged nearly out of her mind and alone. It would be child's play to lead her to the back door where one of his men waited. They'd be in New York before the O'Malleys knew she was missing.

But, despite himself, he was intrigued by her.

Keira snagged his tie, studying the muted blue pattern as if it held the answer to the meaning of the universe. When she tugged on it, he allowed her to lead him to one of the little niches that had been built into the exterior walls. This one had a raggedy couch that had seen better days, but the music was slightly less than deafening, so it was an improvement regardless.

She pushed him, and he sat on the couch. Dmitri went still when Keira straddled him, her expression strangely contemplative despite the fact she was very blatantly blitzed. She ran her hands down his chest. "You're awfully pretty for an evil bastard."

"So I'm told."

Her eyes went wide. "And a sense of humor. God really gave with both hands when he made you, too, didn't he?" She palmed him. "Or should we make that three hands?"

Dmitri grabbed her wrist and removed her hand. "I don't enjoy being fondled by children."

She raised her eyebrows and mimicked his accent. "Do you not? Your hard cock says otherwise, Mr. Romanov." She leaned down, giving him a good view of where her breasts were in danger of spilling free of their confinement. "I think you came here looking for a little revenge." She rolled her body against him, and despite his control, his cock became even harder.

Keira's lips brushed his ear. "It's your lucky day. I'm a big fan of self-destructive tendencies and filled with self-loathing, so riding your cock would meet both needs nicely. What do you say?"

Yes.

He forced himself to take hold of her shoulders and move her back. "No."

"Pity." Keira shrugged like she couldn't care less. She rose to her feet in an eerily graceful motion. "See you around, evil bastard." Then she was gone, sliding back into the crowd. He suspected this time, if he followed her, he wouldn't be successful in cornering her.

Dmitri stood, and it was only then that he realized she'd relieved him of both his wallet and his watch. He blinked, turned to look out at the crowd, and shook his head in reluctant admiration. *She played me.*

He surprised himself by chuckling, amusement high as he walked out of the building and climbed into the back of his car. Then he let it fall away and spoke to his driver. "Next time Keira O'Malley slips her leash, I want to be informed immediately." He would keep his lead on Sloan because it paid to maintain several balls in the air, but his interest in the youngest O'Malley daughter was piqued.

More the pity for her.

CHAPTER TWELVE

It took Jude all fucking day to find the goddamn Plan B pill. As expected, he'd had to drive into Portland to retrieve it, every hour he was away from Sloan increasing the chance that she was pregnant.

And you almost took her again.

He pulled up in front of his house and turned the car off. There was no excuse for the idiocy that the woman brought out in him. He got around her and he couldn't think, couldn't reason, couldn't take a step back and claim the icy rationale that had gotten him to this point.

If he was smart, he'd call Dmitri Romanov and hand her over as fast as humanly possible.

Except she might be pregnant with my child.

A fucking kid. He hadn't been able to hold down a single relationship in his thirty-five years—hadn't wanted to—and now he was looking at potentially bringing a helpless kid into the world. What the fuck did he know about raising a child? His old man was dead before he was born, and his mother had spent his entire life checked out and clinging to a past that no longer existed.

Jude wouldn't know healthy if it kicked him in the face.

There was no way he wouldn't fuck this kid up.

He grabbed the small bag with the two pills in it and climbed out of the car. Sloan's shift would be done about now, so he grabbed a shower and decided to check in with Stefan before he met her at her place. When he called, the phone rang and rang, Jude's irritation turning to concern.

"You have the worst fucking timing."

The concern vanished, irritation taking hold. He leaned against the kitchen counter. "And you have the morals of a back-alley whore. You sold me out."

Stefan cursed. "What was I supposed to do? Romanov showed up *here*. Or where here used to be. I've moved shop, which is why it took me so long to answer—I couldn't find my phone."

Jude shoved his wet hair back into a ponytail and took the phone off speaker. "How did he find you?"

"It's that fucking girl of yours. One of his men had tagged searches for anything concerning her. By the time I realized I'd sent vibrations up the spider web, he was at my front door."

He still wasn't sure that Romanov was preferred to one of Sloan's brothers finding her, but at least the Russian had offered him a reprieve—mostly because he wanted the same thing Jude did: Colm Sheridan dead. It didn't matter. The end result was that it gave him time to plan—or at least figure out what the fuck he was going to do. He sighed. "What have you got?"

"Sloan O'Malley, sister-in-law to Callista Sheridan. She's

the fly on the wall in a family of strong personalities, always in the background. Her sisters were—and are—wild party girls, one of whom defied their bastard of a father to marry her heart's true love." His sarcastic tone said exactly what he thought of that.

Jude was inclined to agree, but this was old news. "I'm aware of who Carrigan O'Malley is fucking. Focus."

"That's it, man. Her brothers are looking for Sloan, but Teague appears to be stalling them, probably because he's the one who got her out. I can't track how she got out of Boston, and if I can't do it, no one can. She disappeared on a Friday night, and then appeared in Callaway Rock three days after, which *I* wouldn't know if you weren't there." He hesitated and then said grudgingly, "That O'Malley did a good job of hiding her."

And Jude had brought the hounds right to her door.

Goddamn it.

"And Romanov? What's he want with her?"

"Your guess is as good as mine. Fuck, marry, kill—with that guy, it's bound to be one of those three options. I mean that in the literal sense, not that stupid fucking game everyone seems to be playing."

None of those options were actually options as far as Jude was concerned. Sloan deserved better than to be a casualty in a war she thought she'd escaped.

As for fuck or marry...

Over my dead fucking body.

"Find out his plan."

"Jesus fucking Christ, Jude. I'm not a mind reader. If he has a plan, he hasn't written it down, and he sure as fuck hasn't put it somewhere as public as the Internet. It's not like this fucker has a goddamn blog."

"I'll pay double. Figure it out." He hung up. Stefan might play both sides against the middle when it suited him, but he owed Jude his life. Seven years ago, Stefan had stolen from the wrong man—who just happened to have been Jude's current mark. Jude had killed the man before he could kill Stefan, and the dramatic fashion of his demise had made an impression on the hacker.

It didn't prevent him from charging a shit-ton of money to provide his services, but it kept him more or less loyal.

Neither one of them had counted on Romanov finding Stefan.

The web kept getting more and more tangled. Maybe it'd be different if he hadn't given in to the temptation Sloan's hot little body offered, but the truth was that her fledgling strength attracted him just as much as her pussy. She had the makings of being a force of nature, and hell if he didn't want to stand witness and watch it happen.

He looked at the bag containing the pills and cursed. He might be attracted to her, but that was a long shot from wanting to bring a tiny person into the world with her— with *anyone*. He wasn't the settling down and starting a family type. With his history... Yeah, it just wasn't in the cards for him. It's not like he could cart a kid and woman around while he staked out marks and fucking murdered them.

Shoving the whole mess from his mind, he stalked outside and across the short distance to Sloan's house. He let himself in through the back door and was halfway across the living room when a dry voice said, "Young man, I don't suppose you're a strippergram here to celebrate my birthday. No? Then I'd take kindly to you explaining why you're in my house."

He turned slowly to find a shotgun leveled at his chest, wielded by a well-dressed, attractive woman in her late fifties.

Sorcha O'Connor was home.

* * *

Sloan heard voices and walked out of her bedroom to find Sorcha had drawn on Jude. Panic flared, but she managed to keep her voice calm and even. *If I startle her, she might pull the trigger.* "Sorcha, this is my friend Jude. Jude, this is Sorcha. She's the one who owns the house."

Sorcha didn't lower the gun. "Are you sure he's a friend, darling? He looks like a hired gun from where I'm standing. They all move like that, quiet as cats and twice as lethal."

Sloan blinked. "He's a writer." She didn't believe it any more now than she had when Jessica told her, but she wasn't about to let the older woman kill him out of hand. "I invited him over, so please don't shoot him." Frankly, she didn't particularly want to see him while she was still all twisted up over what had happened this morning, but she wasn't about to tell Sorcha that. And, judging from the brown paper bag in his hands, he'd successfully tracked down the pills for her. "Please."

With a sigh, Sorcha lowered the gun. "Next time, young man, knock. It's rude to just walk in." She shifted to face Sloan, the gun pointed carefully at the ground. "I'm going to wash the stink of travel off me. Deal with this Neanderthal and get him out of here. We're due for a dinner to get to know each other." She turned and walked into the primary bedroom, closing the door firmly behind her.

Sloan was *definitely* going to have a discussion with

Teague about expectations. He'd told her that Sorcha was a nice older woman who was a bit eccentric. After that encounter, Sloan was inclined to think she was off her rocker.

Though she couldn't fault the woman for mistaking Jude for a hired gun. He carried himself with confidence, and danger practically emanated from him. But a criminal? A *murderer*? It was too far-fetched, even for her life. She nodded at the bag. "I'll take that."

He didn't immediately move, a strange look on his face. "We need to talk, Sloan. Actually talk."

She knew that, but she didn't have the emotional fortitude to deal with it today. She shook her head. "We will, but as you heard—I have plans tonight. I get done at the diner tomorrow at two. We can talk then." She didn't ask if he was free.

Jude hesitated and then nodded. "Tomorrow, then." He set the bag on the counter and walked out without another word.

* * *

Sloan wasn't sure what to think of the woman sitting across from her. They'd driven up to Cannon Beach for dinner, and Sorcha had put on an album of show tunes so loudly, there'd been no way to attempt to hold a conversation. Not that Sloan minded. She'd relished the ability to sit and just think for a little bit.

Jude was…She didn't know how to put it into words. Jude was a problem, if only because he brought forth a side of her she'd never known existed. Being in the same room with him made her feel wild and bold and a thousand other things she couldn't afford. She wasn't those things. Not really.

And then they'd gone and broken a condom.

She'd taken one of the pills he brought her as soon as he'd left, but there were no guarantees. She could be pregnant. She shuddered at the thought.

"That boy is nothing but trouble." Sorcha eyed the glass in front of her and filled it with wine from the bottle she'd ordered as soon as they walked through the door. "Gorgeous, and most likely an animal in bed, but trouble nonetheless."

Sloan blushed and accepted the glass of wine. "With all due respect, ma'am, it's none of your business."

She narrowed brown eyes remarkably like Callie's at Sloan. "That's the beauty of getting old, my dear. I can say whatever I damn well please and you have to be respectful back. Now tell me, how is it you know my niece?"

"You don't know?" She'd agreed to have Sloan here without knowing a single thing about her? The thought was downright preposterous. "Surely Callie told you."

"Callista and I are just beginning to feel each other out. My fool brother never reached out to me when she was a child and so I didn't even know she existed until a few months ago."

"I…" What was she supposed to say to that? "I didn't know."

"I didn't expect you to." Sorcha sat back, looking like a queen who'd wandered into this part of the world. Carrigan did that, too. She owned every space she walked into, no matter what the situation.

But if Sloan could face down Jude, she could face down this woman. She straightened in her chair. "Callie is my sister-in-law."

"Yes, she did mention you're one of those O'Malleys."

"Why did you ask if you already knew?" Irritation made Sloan's voice sharp.

Sorcha smiled. "There it is. I was wondering if you had a backbone at all with how you cower so."

Irritation bled to anger. She'd been *testing* her? Sloan was so incredibly tired of being tested, played with, and manipulated. She'd come to Oregon to get away from that, not to jump through *more* hoops. "Why don't you tell me a bit about yourself, Sorcha, since I don't know a single thing about *you*?"

The woman idly swirled her wine. "Yes, let's get this silly small talk out of the way. I was born a Sheridan, and like yourself, I didn't much like the idea of being treated like chattel. I would have hoped those old fools had learned from their mistakes and realized us women have much better heads for politics and power, but my niece tells me little has changed. Idiots, all of them." She sighed theatrically. "I was young and in love with a beautiful man and, when my father and brother threatened to kill my lover, we eloped. I haven't been back to Boston since."

It sounded terribly romantic.

Except there was obviously more to the story. Sloan may have been wrong, but if Sorcha had been living in wedded bliss this entire time, without connection to any illicit workings, she wouldn't cart around a shotgun. *She's a lot like Callie, though at least Callie doesn't play the word games.*

Sloan sipped her wine, fought to keep her grimace off her face, and set the glass on the table. "You must have been very successful in whatever it was you chose to do if you're able to travel so much." She'd seen the photos of a variety of exotic locales scattered around the house. Sloan hadn't thought much of them at the time, but it was obvious this woman didn't stay in one place for very long. She had rest-less energy akin to Jude's, though he hid it better.

Sorcha laughed. "Oh, darling, that marriage didn't last. My sweet Rodger was killed in a factory accident not long after we moved to New York. I was wild with grief." She said it matter-of-factly, as if reciting from a book she'd read a long time ago. "Crazed, really. I almost went back and begged my father for mercy but, well, I don't beg. Pride, it's a horrible sin. That doesn't seem to be your issue, though." She turned a penetrating look on Sloan. "Then again, I may be wrong. Yours isn't the flashy kind of pride like mine, one that a person waves around whenever it suits them. It's more of a quiet thing, a martyrdom." She tsked. "Martyrs are boring, my dear."

"We weren't talking about me."

"Weren't we?" She smiled at the waiter who brought the food neither of them had ordered. Sloan frowned at her plate, but Sorcha didn't seem the least bit disconcerted. "Neill, darling, you look as dashing as always. How are the wife and kids?"

"Shelly is pregnant again, a boy this time." He smiled. "The girls are doing well. They're excited for a little brother."

"Good for you, though, goodness, Neill, give your poor wife a break. Four children." She shook her head, though her brown eyes twinkled. "You'll have to give her a spa day before that baby comes, because God knows she won't be resting anytime soon. My treat, I insist."

The waiter looked like he might argue, but finally nod-ded. "She'll appreciate that, Ms. O'Connor. Thank you."

"Us women have to look out for each other. Don't you agree, Sloan?"

Sloan made a noncommittal noise, but that didn't slow Sorcha down in the least. She chatted with Neill and then smiled as he walked away. "That right there is a good man." She arched her eyebrows. "And he most definitely isn't sniffing around for nefarious purposes."

So they were back to that again. She didn't feel like defending Jude, partially because she *wasn't* sure what he actually did for a living. She couldn't argue with Sorcha's disbelief, especially since that had been *her* first reaction as well. Instead, she asked, "How did he know your order?"

Sorcha smiled like a cat who'd gotten into the cream. "Neill has been here a long time, and he's a smart boy. He pays attention."

"And mine?"

She shrugged. "There's a standing order for any guest I bring with me."

Of all the... Sloan frowned. "Do you have something against ordering like a normal person?"

"Life is too short, darling. No reason to waste it." She speared a piece of her salmon. "Now, my niece has filled me in on the bare bones, but I'm going to have to insist you explain your circumstances to me in detail. I am sticking my neck out for you, after all."

Sloan wanted to brush her off, but the older woman was right. So she gritted her teeth, smiled, and began at the beginning. When Teague met Callie.

CHAPTER THIRTEEN

Jude couldn't settle down until he saw the headlights of Sorcha O'Connor's car pull into the driveway, and even then the tension riding him didn't relax until Sloan climbed out of the passenger seat. The whole situation was fucked. He should be planning his next step—how to remove the old woman—but all he could think about was the Russian offering money in exchange for Colm's death.

And the very real possibility that Sloan could be pregnant with his child.

She glanced his way as she walked up to the front door, but she didn't show any indication that she saw him lurking in the shadows—or that she wanted to talk to him. Jude silently cursed. His focus was shot, his mission was in shambles, and he didn't know what the fuck his next step was supposed to be.

Even now, he wanted her, the desire like a sickness inside him that he couldn't exorcise—that he wasn't sure he even wanted to.

She'd taken the pill. He'd watched her, disappointment and something almost like fear warring within him. Jude would make a shit father. He wasn't even sure he knew *how* to be a father. It wasn't like his mother, God rest her soul, had been a sterling example of parenthood. She'd done the best she could, and he loved her for that, but the thought of putting any child of his through what he went through growing up...

It didn't sit well with him. It didn't sit well at all.

Sloan had been taking care of herself for less than a month. And her parents weren't much better than his had been. How was she supposed to be a good mother when the only example she'd ever had had been content to sell her off into a political marriage to further her own power?

Damn it, that's not fair.

But then, he didn't much feel like being fair right around now.

He stalked into his house, but the walls were too small, the closed shutters only adding to the feeling. He needed to *move*. More than that, he needed to hunt something.

Someone.

He had his phone in his hand before he could think better of it. Stefan answered on the first ring. "What now?"

"Dmitri Romanov."

"Oh, fuck off. It's bad enough that I'm on that bastard's radar. I'm sure as hell not going to go *looking* for him. Owing you my life doesn't mean I'm going to get myself killed for you."

The fear in Stefan's voice almost made him reconsider, but there was too much on the line to be delicate. Still... He strode another circle around his living room. "I just need an address."

"You're not going after him."

He snorted. "I thought you didn't want to be involved."

"Newsflash, your contrary ass involved me when you had me hunting down information on that chick. And, to be perfectly honest, things were rather dull before you burst in and saved my life like some kind of psychotic superhero. If you die, that would be fuck-all for shit going forward."

"Stefan, sometimes I have no goddamn idea what you're saying."

"I'm saying going after Romanov is fucking suicide, and you're smarter than that."

Maybe two weeks ago, but that was before the stakes had been raised. Before Jude potentially had something to lose. Going after Dmitri, even in a roundabout way, was like stepping into a cage with a rabid lion and hoping for the best—it was risky as hell and not to be done if there were any other option. Unfortunately, Jude was fresh out of options. He had to ensure Dmitri didn't snatch Sloan, and there were only two ways to do it—keep Sloan on lockdown indefinitely... or go straight to the source. Since he knew how the former would go, that really only left him with one option. *Hate getting painted into a fucking corner.*

He moved to the window and stared out through the thin crack in the shutters. "The address, Stefan."

"Oh, for Christ's sake. *Fine.*"

"And I need a local doctor—someone who can do blood tests and is known for their discretion." The sooner he knew which way the pregnancy scare went, the better. Hell, he should have called Stefan before traipsing up to Portland, but he'd been too goddamn frazzled to even consider it.

Stefan was silent for a beat, and then another. "That will take longer to get ahold of than the address." He didn't ask why Jude needed a doctor with those credentials, and Jude didn't offer.

"By the end of the week." He hung up. It'd have to wait either way. He needed a chance to scope out the Russian's defenses and see just how suicidal a man would have to be to make an attempt on him. Hoping it wouldn't come to that was useless. Jude didn't rely on hope. All he had were cold hard facts, and the fact was Dmitri had threatened Sloan, no matter how carefully worded it had been, or how he'd done his best to pretend they were on the same side.

They might have similar goals when it came to Colm Sheridan.

They sure as fuck didn't where Sloan was concerned.

He wanted her for his own reasons, and Jude wasn't about to give her up *before* the condom broke. Now? Now he'd slaughter his way through every person in the Romanov camp if it meant keeping her safe.

Careful there. You're in danger of forgetting your mission.

He turned to stare at the picture of his family. Revenge had been the only thing keeping him going for a very long time. It was always the end goal, from the second his mother first pressed a .45 into his hands. All the hunts, all the kills, all the paydays—all to give him the resources he needed to fulfill his mother's dying wish.

Kill the Sheridans.

Make Colm pay for what he'd done to Jude's family.

He didn't know what he'd have if he didn't have that. Quitting when he was so close to seeing his endgame realized...He couldn't even wrap his head around the thought. It would be a betrayal to his mother, to the brothers and father who he'd never get to know because of what Colm Sheridan did.

But moving forward now, when he had Romanov on his ass and the potential that Sloan might be pregnant, didn't sit right with him, either. Was endangering the living worth fulfilling his promise to the dead?

One thing at a time.

* * *

He walked over to the O'Connor place. It felt weird to knock on the door, but he had no interest in being on the wrong end of a shotgun again. Sloan answered, shadows in her eyes for the first time since they'd had sex. She stared at him, but she didn't move back to let him in or do anything other than wait.

"I have to leave town for a little bit," he said.

"Thanks for letting me know." She started to shut the door.

He stopped it before she could close him out. "Sloan..." There wasn't much he could tell her without revealing everything—who he was, how he was connected to her without realizing it, the danger she was in because of him. "Don't call anyone. Don't go out at night. Keep a goddamn low profile until I'm back."

Some life flared in her eyes. "I don't need a keeper."

"Not a keeper." *Protector.* A hat he'd never had to wear—one he wasn't sure fit him. He huffed out a breath. "It's not safe."

"Life rarely is."

Damn it, he was fucking this up. Jude took a step back. "Come here."

"We've been through this song and dance before, and

considering the potential outcome, I don't feel inclined to go another round." She leaned against the doorframe. "I want you, Jude. I'd be a liar if I said otherwise, but this whole potential pregnancy thing is freaking me out, and I can't even look at you without thinking about it. I know you're scared, too, so please just give me some space until we know one way or another."

When it became clear she had no intention of closing the distance between them, he did it, taking her hand. "Baby or no, this thing between us is nowhere near finished."

"You were very clear about the expiration date, and after a pregnancy scare...I can't do this back-and-forth with you. It twists me up."

He traced a thumb over her inner wrist. If he were a better man, he'd tell her what was going on, what was at risk. He'd warn her to lose herself again and, this time, he wouldn't lead the dogs right to her door.

But Jude wasn't a better man, and he was nowhere near done with Sloan. Not yet. "You don't want this to end."

She looked up at him with eyes gone inky in the darkness. "Sometimes the pleasure isn't worth the pain."

"That's where you're wrong." He tugged on her wrist, and she allowed him to pull her against his chest. "The pleasure is *always* worth the pain. Life is too short for that to be anything but the truth."

"Where are you going, Jude?"

He couldn't tell her—not until he knew exactly what Dmitri Romanov had leveled at them. Not until he had a plan. "It's not important."

She arched her eyebrows. "Important enough to leave. Important enough that you're telling me to be careful."

She has you there.

He went with half the truth. "I have a complicated history. Someone interested in my past has made threats that I can't dismiss. Since you're close to me, those threats extend to you."

"That's incredibly vague." She frowned. "And we're not close. We're just sleeping together."

A shard of something like hurt went through him at her words, but he pushed it away and snagged the back of her neck. "We're not *just* anything." He kissed her, harsh and brutal. "Stay safe until I get back."

Sloan blinked up at him. "You still owe me answers. Real answers."

"I know." There'd be no escaping it once he returned.

There wouldn't be any escaping *anything*.

* * *

Life fell into a strange sort of rhythm with Jude gone. Sloan worked in the diner, did yoga with Jessica, and spent her evenings with Sorcha. She didn't particularly like the older woman, but she was nothing short of entertaining.

Through it all, Sloan worried about Jude, about the threat that had called him away, about the fact she hadn't gotten her period yet despite taking the morning-after pill.

Telling herself that every single thing she feared was beyond her control didn't do anything but deepen her anxiety. Jude was obviously capable, and just because he said there was a threat didn't mean it was a threat like *she* would have fielded growing up as an O'Malley.

Normal people didn't worry about urban warfare between mobs or drive-by shootings or convenient fires that showed up when people didn't fall in line.

She was just projecting her own issues onto him. Simple. But no matter how many times she told herself that, with each day that went by without word, her fear deepened.

A week into Jude's absence, she couldn't stand it any longer. She called Teague on one of the burner phones she'd hidden under her bed. It rang and rang and rang before finally clicking over to voicemail. Sloan hung up without leaving a message.

Her phone rang almost instantly, and she startled. "Hello?"

"What's wrong?"

She breathed out a sigh of relief. "Teague."

For his part, he didn't sound the least bit reassured. "Are you okay?"

"I'm fine. I just..."

"Then why are you calling?" He seemed to realize he sounded terse, because his tone gentled. "Not that I'm not happy to hear from you, but Aiden has his hounds out looking for you, and I don't want to do something to tip them off."

A different kind of fear rose at his words. She'd known her family would search for her, but Teague had been so reassuring when he said they'd never find her. He hadn't sounded worried through the entire planning and extraction process. He sounded worried now. She clutched the phone. "Does he know where I am?"

"We covered your trail too well. Even Cillian can't make progress with it."

Thank God. She took a deep breath, well aware that they were nearing the time limit for a potential wiretap. "Then I'll make it quick. I'm fine. Everything is fine. I just need some information."

"I'll do what I can." He always would. That was so very Teague of him. Of all her brothers, Teague was the one who'd bend over backward, putting himself in danger time and time again, to ensure the people around him were safe.

She wanted to ask him how everything else was going. Callie would be well into her second trimester now, maybe even showing. Cillian must have been okay because Teague mentioned him... *I miss them.* The realization staggered her. It shouldn't have. She loved her family dearly. Her siblings weren't the reason she'd left.

"Sloan?"

The concern in his voice brought her back to the matter at hand. "Do you know a man named Jude? He's big, long dark hair, short beard, dark eyes. He... He might be a hit man or hired muscle."

Teague was silent for a beat, and then another. "The name doesn't ring any bells, though if he's in that life, I doubt his name is really Jude."

"I know." She breathed another small sigh of relief. She hadn't really believed Jude was somehow linked to her life back home, but with everything going on, she couldn't help but be a little paranoid. *Maybe he's running from something, the same way I am.* It would explain the potentially fake last name. "Thank you."

"Don't thank me yet. Just because I haven't met the man, doesn't mean he isn't exactly what you fear. How do you know him?"

She clutched the phone tighter. "He's my next-door neighbor." *My lover. Possibly the man who got me pregnant... if I'm pregnant.* The longer she went without a period, the greater that fear grew—so great that she couldn't force the words into the open air, even when she was alone.

She'd bought a test, but technically she wasn't supposed to have her period for another week, and the information she'd found online said the pregnancy hormone levels wouldn't be high enough to be picked up by an at-home test until then. Taking one now wouldn't prove anything, because it'd likely come back negative regardless of whether she was pregnant or not.

Teague cursed. "I knew we should have put you somewhere else. Listen carefully, Sloan. Sorcha has enemies. Not just because she was born a Sheridan, but because of who her late husband was. We thought you'd be okay there because she's successfully kept both herself and her small staff safe, but..." He cursed again. "If you think for a second that you might be in danger, get out. Get out immediately. Take the money and run, and I'll find a way to get you a new identity, more money, whatever you need. Listen to your instincts."

What instincts? She fought down the helpless feeling trying to take root.

She wasn't helpless.

And she wasn't leaving.

"It's fine. I'll be careful. I promise." The same promise she'd made to Jude. Sloan took a deep breath. "Is there any way one of the other families could know I'm here?"

"No. If Cillian can't find you, I doubt anyone can."

The reassurance felt like a lie, though she couldn't say if it was because he thought there were better hunters out there than Cillian or because he was that worried. She forced a smile into her voice. "I'm safe. It will be okay. Take care of yourself and Callie."

"I will. Love you."

"Love you, too." She hung up and systematically dismantled the phone, removing the battery and tossing it into the wastebasket next to her bed.

Teague had offered little information about what was going on back home, but that was just the way she'd wanted it. She couldn't have it both ways. Her earlier realization rose up and choked her. *I miss them.* This was the longest she'd gone without seeing her siblings since she was born.

The longer she was away, the more she wondered if she'd been too hard on her sister Carrigan.

Sloan could attest to how being around Jude was turning her into a fool for him. She felt like an addict, craving his presence, craving his hands on her body and his lips against her skin, muttering the filthiest of words. And that draw was *without* the love her sister professed for James Halloran.

If Carrigan felt an ounce of the attraction for James that Sloan felt for Jude...

She suddenly understood her sister's choice all too well.

CHAPTER FOURTEEN

Jude knew he wasn't alone the second he walked into his apartment. It was one of three he kept in New York, all under different names that shouldn't have been connected to his real identity. He pulled his gun out of its holster and moved deeper into the apartment, bypassing the hallway that led to the two bedrooms and stopping just inside the doorway to the living area. It wasn't large by any means, but the floor-to-ceiling windows let in plenty of light to see the man sitting in Jude's favorite chair.

He pointed the gun at him, pausing when the stranger leaned forward and clicked on the light.

Dmitri Romanov.

Jude didn't holster his gun, but once he determined the other man didn't have a weapon pointed at him, Jude let his arm fall to his side. "Very dramatic. How long did you sit in the dark, waiting for me?"

Dmitri gave a small smile. "Ah, but that would be telling.

I have it on good authority that you're in the neighborhood to see me."

Goddamn it, Stefan. "I came to deliver my message in person, since you seem to have an issue understanding it over the phone. Sloan O'Malley is off-limits. Go find your petty revenge somewhere else."

"Petty revenge, is it?" Dmitri laughed softly. "What is that saying? Those who live in glass houses shouldn't throw stones. You of all people shouldn't dismiss revenge."

"It's different." He wasn't forcing anyone else to be part of his revenge. Jude had enough shit on his plate with the Sheridans. He didn't need to borrow vendettas and the trouble that came with them.

"Is it?"

He stroked the trigger of his gun. "Sloan has no part of this. You and I can reach an understanding in regards to Sheridan, but you'll keep her out of your plans."

"It's not your decision to make."

Jude considered him, pausing to look around the living room again. *No one else here.* "What's to stop me from putting a bullet between your eyes and ending the threat to my woman?" *My woman. Fuck, why the hell did I just say that?*

Dmitri, that crafty bastard, caught his slip. He raised his eyebrows. "Yours, is she? Now that *is* interesting."

"On second thought." Jude shifted his stance, sighting down his gun. "I think I'll just kill you and be done with it. I don't need your permission or your money to take out Colm Sheridan. I bet Aiden O'Malley would send me a Thank You card."

"With your dirty MacNamara hands all over his sweet and innocent sister? I think not." Dmitri laughed again, and this time it actually sounded real. "I doubt you can see the irony from where you're standing, but it truly is amusing in the extreme."

"I'm bored of your games."

"Then stop playing." Just like that, the amusement disappeared from Dmitri's face and he straightened, his hands carefully set on the arms of the chair and away from his sides. "You're a MacNamara. The O'Malleys might have been just getting started in the game when Colm Sheridan made the move to clear out your family, but the cruelties of your father are well-known. You're as bad as a Romanov in their minds—worse in some ways because you might actually have a claim to the power scheme in Boston if you were an ambitious man." He leaned forward, propping his elbows on his knees. "Are you an ambitious man, Jude?"

"I have my own plans. I don't need your shit fucking them up."

Dmitri's gaze flicked to the gun and away. "I'm an ally—currently—and you seem to have a shortage of those. Think about it. I'll even let you keep the O'Malley girl if that will sweeten the pot."

"How charitable of you." Jude knew what he was doing. The man wanted him for some purpose, and he was willing to bargain to get Jude on his side. He took a careful step back into the hallway, keeping Dmitri in sight. "I'll consider your offer."

"I'm not the enemy here. The O'Malleys may like to paint me the villain, but they put themselves in this position. *They* didn't honor their word. At the very first opportunity, they turned on me without warning."

And Dmitri was just an innocent? Doubtful. The man was a wolf who didn't bother to wear the sheep's clothing.

Jude holstered the gun. "If I see a single one of your men near Sloan, they're dead."

"I'm more than willing to grant you Sloan in return for Colm's death. I would think you'd be jumping at the deal."

There was no missing the threat that wasn't quite a threat. Dmitri might sweeten the deal with Sloan because he wanted Sheridan dead, but if Jude didn't fall in line like a good little soldier, the man would have no problem taking her. *I'd need an army to hold his people off—or at least a better hiding spot.* He'd consider his options once he was back in Callaway Rock—back with Sloan. For now, he knew damn well that Dmitri wouldn't let him walk without agreeing to this. "I already took your damn contract."

"Yes, you did. And breaking your word won't be without consequences." Romanov rose and buttoned his suit jacket. "You'd do well to remember that if you suddenly have a change of heart."

* * *

"Good job today."

Sloan smiled at Marge. "Thanks." Ten days since Jude had gone and she was finally getting to the point where she wasn't afraid Marge would fire her on the spot one day. She even sort of liked the gruff older woman. Marge told it like she saw it and, as a result, Sloan always knew where she stood with her—and her compliments were worth their weight in gold.

Marge eyed her. "I think we can set up a more regular schedule going forward. You good with mornings?"

"Sure." Sloan didn't have a preference either way, but she did enjoy the breakfast shift. She still didn't know most of the residents of Callaway Rock by anything other than their faces, but she was learning names as she went. They all seemed to come through the diner at least one day a week to take breakfast from Marge and catch up with friends. It was downright cozy.

"We'll have you working the eight-hour shift from six to two, Wednesday to Sunday. If you need time off, I need minimum of two weeks' notice. You sick, you better be *sick* or—"

"I'm fired."

Marge snorted. "Something like that. Now git. You look like you haven't slept in days."

Because the longer Jude was gone, the more difficult it was to drown out the little voice in her head saying that something terrible had happened to him. She lay in bed and tried to imagine what could have pulled him away. If he was really the hired gun Sorcha swore he was, had he left to take a job? The thought made her sick to her stomach.

She managed a smile, though, for Marge. "I'll see you tomorrow." Sloan raised her voice. "Bye, Luke."

"Don't forget your grub." He slid a foam container through the pass-through. For whatever reason, he seemed to think she needed to fatten up a bit, so he slipped her food at the end of each shift.

"Thank you." She accepted the food and headed for the door. It was well past the lunch rush hour, so there was no one about as Sloan kicked off her shoes and headed down the sandy beach for home.

Home.

She wasn't sure when the O'Connor house had become home, but it was. She still missed her siblings something fierce, but she had to admit she liked her life here. She liked her job, enjoyed the people who lived in Callaway Rock.

And Jude...

Well, Jude was something else altogether.

And he's still not back.

He hadn't even left her a number to contact him. Not that she'd call, because what was there to say? They didn't have a relationship, not really. He'd been very, very clear about what her expectations should be, and she'd accepted his terms the same way he'd accepted hers. Changing the rules now wouldn't be fair to either of them.

Except that broken condom might have gone and done exactly that.

Sloan had to make an effort not to press her hand to her stomach. She didn't *feel* any different. But then, the websites she'd looked up said it could be weeks yet for the hormones to build up enough to exhibit some kind of physical response in her body—which was right around the time she could actually take an over-the-counter pregnancy test.

Weeks of not knowing.

Anxiety rose in a tidal wave, threatening to send her curling up into a ball and waiting for all this to blow over. She fought the feeling. *That is not who I am anymore. I'm stronger than I used to be.* She would find a path forward, one way or another.

As she approached her house, a flash of movement in the window next door caught her attention. Her heart leaped into her throat, and she stopped, wondering if she should call the police. If her family—or their enemies—had found her, the local sheriff would be in over his head and she'd likely be consigning him to his death. *What do I do?*

The choice disappeared as the door opened. *Jude.* Relief made her sway, but as quickly as it had come, it vanished, morphing into anger. *Ten days. He's gone ten days and he doesn't bother to let me know he's okay.*

Has he been back and just didn't tell me?

The jagged feeling inside her spiked with every step she took, until she was nearly running. Sloan marched up the steps to his porch and kept going, only stopping when she was as in his face as she could be with their height difference. "You should have called."

"I was occupied."

Occupied...*occupied.* She pushed at his chest, hating that she couldn't move him even when she tried. "That's a pathetic excuse. You show up ten days—*ten days*—ago, telling me to watch my back and that you'd return as soon as you are able to, and then you don't bother to say a single thing until I'm walking past, minding my own business. No. Enough. I'm done." She started to turn, but he snagged her wrist.

"Sloan."

Her name. Not sunshine. She yanked on his hold, but she might as well have tried to fight a tidal wave. "Let go."

"Are you pissed I was gone so long, or that I didn't come crawl into your bed like a whipped dog the second I hit the town limits?" Nothing on his face but a faint smirk. Nothing. Not a hint of the feeling she'd gotten from him before.

She hated how controlled he was, hated even more how *out* of control he made her feel. *I know what to do to crack that mask.* She squared her shoulders and met his dark eyes. "I kept myself plenty *occupied* while you were gone." She enjoyed throwing that word back into his face.

"Is that so?" He pulled her toward him, inch by inch, closing the distance between them. "Because I think you went out of your fucking mind without my cock to keep you happy."

"Oh please." She rolled her eyes even as her body sparked at his words. "I lived my entire life without you and your dick. A week of sex isn't enough to ruin me for anyone else, no matter how highly you think of yourself."

His brows slanted down, and he looked downright murderous for the first time since they'd first met. "You know damn well that I've ruined you for any other man." He stepped into the house, towing her behind him, ignoring her gasp of outrage. "I think you stroked yourself to the memory of me a couple times a day the entire time I was gone. In fact, I don't think—I know."

She wanted to spit and claw and say *anything* to bring him down a notch, but fury stole her wits. "You have a high opinion of yourself."

"Nah, I know the truth." He sat down on his couch, yanking her forward to sprawl on his chest. His hands hit her waist the same time his lips brushed her ear. "And, sunshine, what you were doing before wasn't fucking living and you know it."

CHAPTER FIFTEEN

Jude had waited all goddamn day for Sloan to finish her shift at the diner—and even then he'd only gone home after checking to make sure she was there and okay. It had driven him out of his fucking mind not to walk in there and toss her over his shoulder, marking her as his for all to see.

His.

She wasn't. Not really. She couldn't be.

He'd worked too hard to extract any and all weaknesses that potential enemies could use against him. After his mother passed, he had nothing to lose—nothing that could be taken to hurt him. He'd liked his life that way. There was no room for anything beyond his mission, which he'd possibly just side-lined by allowing Dmitri Romanov to leave his place alive.

The fact that there was a MacNamara alive—that he was hunting Sheridans—was knowledge without price in the game they all played. Romanov might be currently an ally, but that didn't mean he'd stay that way.

And Jude just didn't give a fuck right now.

Sloan was here, she was safe, and she was pissed enough at him for leaving in the first place that she was practically spitting fire. He skimmed his hands up her sides. "I like that you missed me."

"Missed you? You must be out of your mind." But she grabbed his hair, tilting his head back and rolling her hips as if just realizing he was as hard as a rock. "Stop talking. You're just going to say something unforgivable and then I'll have to leave on principle."

"That's the dumbest fucking thing I've ever heard." He grinned when she jerked on his hair. "I like you when you've missed me."

"Stop. Saying. That." She kissed him, her fury evident in every stroke of her tongue, in the way she drew back to bite his bottom lip hard enough to hurt. He enjoyed the hell out of it.

Jude growled when she did it again, then flipped them, using his body to hold her in place. "If you're going to be mean, you're going to get tied down."

Her dark eyes flashed a challenge. "You wouldn't dare."

"You should know better. I think you'll find that there isn't a damn thing I wouldn't dare to do when it comes to you." He pinned her wrists with one hand and undid his belt with the other, his gaze never leaving her face. He watched her closely for something like fear or even that anxious little lip-biting thing she did when they first met. There was nothing but challenge written across her face. *Good.*

He whipped his belt through the loops and wound it around her wrists. Then he jerked the cushion off the couch and hooked the buckle to the bar of the fold-out bed inside it. The position left her head a little lower than the rest of her body, but that was just fine with him.

Sloan tugged on the belt, her eyes narrowing when she realized she couldn't get free. "I hate you."

"No, you don't." He sat back, appreciating the view. She'd worn a floral sundress today with a cardigan that would look at home on a kindergarten teacher. Innocent. Sweet.

Sexy as fuck.

"It's been too long since I tasted you." He pushed her dress up around her hips, revealing white panties. He didn't think she had any other color, and on anyone else that would be like they were trying too hard. It was just the way Sloan was. He spread her thighs, growling. "I like you in white, sunshine. I can see how soaked your panties are, how much you want me."

"Involuntary reaction."

She was wicked pissed. It might not stop her from wanting him, but...*Shit*. He couldn't take her like this, not with knowing what he knew and not with the current threat hanging over their heads—a threat he was solely responsible for. If he fucked her without talking to her about it, that would be as good as lying to her.

He couldn't do it.

Jude cursed long and hard, silently calling himself ten kinds of fool, but he reached over and undid the belt. "Another time."

"What?" Sloan sat up, confusion replacing the anger on her face, bleeding into something like embarrassment. She pulled her dress down to cover herself, and he could see her gathering her composure one shred at a time.

It fucking killed him.

He crouched down in front of her, knowing that there was no right way to go about this. There was no skirting the subject or breaking it to her gently. *But I can focus on the one thing she's expecting.* For now. "I've got a doctor coming into town to do a blood test for you."

* * *

Sloan stared at Jude, half-sure she'd heard him wrong. She must have. Her mind was still reeling—not to mention her pride—by his going from no-holds-barred sex to...this. "I'm sorry, what did you just say?"

"I'm bringing in a doctor. If you haven't had your period, we need to know if you're pregnant, and we need to know now."

The words didn't make any more sense the second time around. She pushed to her feet, straightening her dress. Jude didn't move from his position in front of her, and her dress swung forward just enough to brush his bare chest. God, he was so beautiful, even now when she wanted to smack some sense into him.

No. You're letting your emotions get the best of you. Think rationally, react *rationally.* She smoothed back her hair, holding herself tall. "That's out of the question."

"Your right to make decisions without me disappeared the second you may have become pregnant with my child."

He was such a...a brute. Her earlier fury rose, stronger than before. Sloan's voice was hoarse from trying to keep control of herself, but she didn't let that stop her as she very carefully enunciated. "Wrong, Jude. Even if I were pregnant—and that's a rather large *if* at this point—you don't get a single say in matters unless *I* say you do. I spent my entire life bowing to others' wishes, and I threw away my entire family for my freedom. Do not think for a second that I won't do the same to *you*." She made it almost to the door when his next words stopped her cold.

"Did you know that both the O'Malleys and the Romanovs are looking for you?"

The world did a slow turn, leaving her woozy. Sloan rotated to face him, part of her sure that she was in a hallucination as a result of orgasm deprivation, and he *hadn't* just said two names that he most certainly shouldn't know. "What did you say?"

"Sloan O'Malley." He said the name like he was tasting her. "I think we need to have a talk."

"How did you..." She moved back toward him, fear finally starting to take root. *What if Sorcha was right all along? What if Romanov sent Jude here to hurt me...to kill me*? "How long have you known?"

"That's irrelevant."

His dismissive tone rankled. She glared. "I don't think it is."

"The important thing is that I know where you come from, and I know what you're up against. You need me. I can keep you safe—keep you free."

She searched his face. "You must be joking. I don't know a single thing about you, which was perfectly fine when I was under the assumption that we were strangers. You've been lying to me this entire time, and now you're...What? Offering me an ultimatum? If I say no, are you going to hand me over to either my family or our enemies?"

"What? No." Jude cursed and shoved to his feet, towering over her. "You're missing the point."

"I don't think I am." She knew letting him into her bed was like playing with fire, but the pleasure had been worth the risk when he was just a man who happened to live next door to her. Discovering that he seemed to be something else altogether made her sick to her stomach. He'd set a neat little trap, and she'd blithely walked into it, fool that she was. She pressed her hand to her chest. "Did you orchestrate that condom being torn, too?"

His eyes went wide. "Why the fuck would I do that?"

"I don't know! Who *are* you, Jude? You know who I am, where I come from, but you haven't given me a single piece of information about yourself, other than this offer to keep me 'safe' which, forgive me, sounds like a crock of shit. Tell me the truth, or I walk out of here right now, and I'll be gone by morning." She didn't want to leave, but if Jude was somehow connected to her past, she had no choice.

"Sloan..."

She saw him searching for a lie, and took a careful step backward. "Good-bye, Jude."

"Wait." He cursed, long and hard. "Fuck, you don't make this easy, do you?"

The fact he was accusing *her* of being the problem was downright laughable. She started for the door. "Tell whoever sent you that I'm not going back. They should save us both a load of trouble and stop searching for me."

He stepped in front of her, keeping a careful distance between them. "I didn't want to do it like this."

Do what? Kidnap me? When I compared him to James Halloran, I thought I was reaching. I didn't realize how close I truly was. She fought to keep her voice from wavering. "Then don't."

He ignored her. "We've never been properly introduced. Sloan O'Malley, I can't say you were part of my plan, but it's been a fucking pleasure to meet you." He held out a hand, the move screaming arrogance. "Jude MacNamara."

CHAPTER SIXTEEN

Where were you?" Aiden made an effort to keep from massaging his temples, though he could damn well feel a headache starting. At this point, the pain was almost welcome. Anything to distract him from the bullshit he was currently dealing with.

His youngest sister crossed her arms over her chest and lifted her chin, the move so like Carrigan's that his heart actually ached for a moment. Keira narrowed her eyes. "Last I checked, I was over eighteen and can do whatever I want."

"And last *I* checked, one of our sisters is missing, and our enemies are multiplying by the second. Stop slipping your security detail or—"

"Or you'll lock me up?" She kicked her feet up onto his desk, her combat boots looking ridiculously massive on her thin legs. Everything about her was thin these days, to the point where he suspected she had more alcohol and coke in her system than actual food or water. Keira laughed harshly.

"Or are you going to shuttle me off to a nunnery? You can't hold me. None of those places can. You might as well just deal with it."

There was no *just dealing with it*.

Aiden already had blood on his hands in his efforts to keep the power base stable and his siblings safe. He didn't like it, but he'd do the same thing over again. A transfer of power, even to someone groomed for it, was fraught with potential difficulty. He couldn't afford to be weak.

Letting Keira have the run of the place and disappear to God knew where was fucking weak.

He steepled his hands, and then stopped the move when he recognized it for one their father used. "Keira, this isn't a game."

"You think I don't know that? Carrigan is gone, God knows who has Sloan, and Devlin is *dead*." Her feet hit the floor with a heavy thud. "You don't have to tell me a single fucking thing. Leave it alone, Aiden. We're all dealing with this shit the only way we can, and if you lock me up, I'll put a gun in my mouth and pull the trigger. Simple as that."

He stared. He wanted to tell her that she was being dramatic and threatening *that* sure as fuck wasn't the way to get him to back off. But as he looked at her, *really* looked at her, he suddenly wasn't sure if it was theatrics. Keira's eyes were a little too wide, her hands shaking at her sides. She looked half a second away from bolting out of the room.

"Keira—" He cut himself off as the door opened. "Get out. I'm busy."

Cillian poked his head in. "It's important."

Important could mean any number of things, none of which were good from the look on his brother's face. He drummed his fingers on the desk. Keira didn't look any more interested in whatever news Cillian had than she was interested in anything lately. He wanted to shake her, to yell in her face that she was still among the living and her lifestyle would put her in an early grave faster than being an O'Malley would.

He made an abrupt decision and nodded at Cillian. "Tell me."

His brother stepped into the office and shot a look at their sister. When Aiden didn't tell her to leave, Cillian shrugged. "A courier just delivered this."

The envelope was the size of a greeting card, the paper thick and their address written in a bold hand across the front. The return address was just an emblem, a stylized R that wasn't quite a family crest. *Romanov.* "What does that bastard want?"

Keira laughed, tilting her head back against the chair to stare at the ceiling. "What all evil bastards want—world domination with a side of death and destruction."

He opened the envelope and examined the card. It wasn't much to look at. Plain white, obviously expensive, but without any pictures or words on either side. Aiden cursed himself for stalling and flipped it open. It took his brain precious seconds to process the words, and when it did, he had to fight not to throw the thing in the nearest fireplace. Instead, he very carefully read it aloud.

I've found your darling Sloan. That old proverb demands an eye for an eye. By my count, you owe me both a wife and a sister. I'll be content with one of yours. Keira or Sloan, Aiden.
I'll be generous and allow you to pick.
The alternative is war.

"You've got to be fucking kidding me." Cillian looked ready to drive to New York solely to throttle Dmitri. "He has to know that you won't give up either."

"He *does* know." This wasn't about a wife, and it wasn't about Dmitri's half sister, Olivia, who was currently residing in the family home with Cillian. It was a power play, plain and simple. If they bowed to this demand, they might as well kneel and offer their throats for whoever wanted their territory.

Not to mention I'll give one of my little sisters over to him over my dead fucking body.

He'd let his father dictate Carrigan's marriage, had stood back while her desperation drove her straight into James Halloran's arms. He'd be damned before he let it happen again. "He wants war."

"No." Keira pushed to her feet, shaking her head. Her eyes looked clear for the first time since he'd had her hauled into his office. "Not that. Never that. I don't care what it takes. I'll do it."

"Out of the question." He nodded at Cillian, who instantly stepped forward to usher Keira out of the office. Only then did Aiden give in to the urge to shred the card into tiny pieces, each move controlled and contained. It didn't help. He could still see the words imprinted there, the silk-coated threat.

They had to do something about Dmitri Romanov—and they had to do it now.

* * *

MacNamara.

The name seemed to echo between them, and in the

silence that followed, Sloan half convinced herself that she'd misheard. "That's impossible." She wasn't foolish enough not to realize there had to be other people with that last name in the country. Of course there were. But for him to be *here*, to know the things he knew... She shook her head. "Impossible."

"I have no issue with your family."

Every word he said confirmed what she could hardly believe. Everyone knew what had been done to that family, though the details on why they'd deserved it were a little hazy, most likely because her brothers hadn't wanted to traumatize her. Sloan had met Callie's father. He might be as ruthless as her father—he couldn't have brought his family into so much power if he wasn't—but he seemed to actually respect the fact that his daughter had the skills necessary to take over their operations. Something he and Seamus O'Malley didn't see eye to eye on.

She'd thought the stories must have been exaggerated, but... "I don't understand. How are you here? Colm Sheridan... He..."

"Wiped out my entire family. Yeah, I'm aware." Nothing showed on Jude's face, but then, he'd had a very long time to come to terms with this truth. Sloan had had all of thirty seconds.

She shook her head again, the pieces clicking into place. "Your mother was pregnant." Then his other words penetrated. *I have no issue with your family.* Which meant there *was* a family he had an issue with. The Sheridans.

She started shaking. "That's why you're here, why you're in this house. You were waiting for Sorcha. But she's hardly a Sheridan. She hasn't been considered part of the family for decades. Callie only found out about her recently."

His eyes went hard. "Sorcha is no innocent. You can trust me on that—though I wouldn't expect you to understand."

Except she understood all too well. After Devlin had died, if someone had wiped out every single Halloran, she wouldn't have shed a single tear. It would have been *justice*.

But that was before her sister became a Halloran, in everything but name.

"You have some sort of vengeance scheme in place." She held her breath, waiting for him to deny it, to tell her that she was being dramatic.

He didn't.

Jude crossed his arms over his chest. "I would hardly call my life's work a *scheme*."

His life's work...

She ran her fingers through her hair, panic building with each heartbeat, a steady *whoosh-whoosh* sound that drowned out everything else. She couldn't do this. She got *out*. She'd worked so incredibly hard to make a life for herself that had no strings leading back to Boston.

And yet she'd taken a man into her bed who had more strings than she did. No wonder Jude had told her that he had no room for a relationship—no room for *her*. She'd allowed her needs—allowed herself—to be put last time and time again.

She wasn't going to do it now.

She lifted her chin, even though all she wanted to do was break down sobbing. "Please move."

"Sunshine...Fuck, just give me a chance to explain this." For the first time since he'd revealed who he was, he looked less than sure of himself. "I didn't plan on this—on you. I knew you had some connection to Sorcha, which meant you had some connection to the Sheridans, but I had no idea that you were an O'Malley at first." He scrubbed a hand across his face, half reaching out for her with the other before he let it drop to his side. "Fuck, Sloan, I like you."

She barked out a laugh. "At first. That means you knew at some point. When was it? When you came over and let me throw myself at you? When you agreed to sleep next to me? *Tell me.*"

"After we had sex that first time."

She waved a hand as if she could banish his words. "You should have told me. You *lied* to me."

"No, I omitted. I know that might seem like the same damn thing to you, but we were on the same page—you wanted my cock and I wanted you on my cock. Simple. This wasn't supposed to last, so it didn't matter who I was or who you were." He raised a single eyebrow. "And if we're on the subject of lying, you sure as fuck weren't offering up the truth to me, either."

"That's different."

"Is it?"

She opened her mouth to confirm that it was, but stopped. If the Sheridans knew that there was a MacNamara left alive—especially one as capable and filled with a need for vengeance as Jude—they would hunt him to the ends of the earth. The only way for him to pay Colm Sheridan back in kind would be to remove every living Sheridan from the equation.

Callie.

Sloan clenched her jaw to keep from asking him for details. Callie was pregnant and running the Sheridan empire with Sloan's brother at her side. If Jude meant Callie harm, that would put him directly at odds with Teague.

With Sloan.

She shook her head again, slower this time. "Callie is my sister-in-law. She is desperately in love with my brother, and she has fought too long and hard to survive to fall victim to something that happened before she was even born."

"There are no innocents in this game. If you think Callista Sheridan is one, then you're even more naive than I could have guessed."

She wasn't naive. She knew the stakes better than anyone. She'd lost a brother, same as Callie...

A slow dawning horror rolled over her. She looked up into Jude's face, as a part of her that had stopped praying a very long time ago began to pray. *Please no, please don't be true.*

"Did you have something to do with Ronan Sheridan's death?"

It was an accident. He drank too much and wrapped his car around a telephone pole. Please, please, please *don't have had anything to do with this.*

The tightening in Jude's jaw confirmed it even before he spoke the damning words. "He was a Sheridan, sunshine."

CHAPTER SEVENTEEN

Jude was losing her and he knew it. He couldn't lie, though, not now, not when there was so much on the line. *Maybe you should have thought about that shit before you set the bridge on fire while you were standing on it.* He didn't touch Sloan. She looked half a second from either going for his throat or for the nearest window.

If he pushed her now, she'd be gone, and then he'd have to track her down to keep her safe.

So he took a careful step away from the doorway, clearing a path for her to escape. "I don't expect you to understand." How could she? Even with the bullshit that came from being raised in a mob family, the woman had led a pampered life overall. It had been touched by the barest fingers of tragedy when her brother died last year, but what was one death compared to familial genocide?

One doesn't make the other okay. He didn't know what to think of the fact that it was *her* voice he heard, his long-forgotten conscience deciding to find itself now.

"I do understand."

He froze, his gaze flying to her face, taking in the steely glint in her dark eyes, the barely contained fury in her body. "What?"

"I know what it's like to want them dead—the ones who hurt you. But the difference is that I left it all behind instead of letting vengeance consume me." She tucked her hair behind her ears, not meeting his gaze. "Maybe you should consider it. Though if you're willing to kill a pregnant woman, I don't know that you can be reasoned with. Some things are unforgivable, Jude." And then she was gone, striding through the door, her shoulders back and her spine straight.

Callista Sheridan is pregnant.

The knowledge rocked him back on his heels. Jude stared blankly after Sloan, trying to process the knowledge, but his brain kept offering up a picture of his mother. She'd been pregnant and wouldn't have escaped the slaughter if Colm Sheridan had known. Rationally, he *knew* his mother and Callista weren't the same.

But he couldn't shake the comparison.

Killing her would make him worse than Colm Sheridan had ever been.

Jude moved to the window and looked out across the beach. The incoming storm had created a false twilight, leaving shadows where there'd been sunlight before. There was a chill in the late afternoon air that had driven people inside. With the knowledge of Sloan's parting shot riding him hard, he welcomed it.

He needed time and space to plan. To *think*. That had always been his strength—to detach himself from any situation and to implement a strategy guaranteed to succeed.

In all the years since he'd started down this path, he'd never had a problem taking that first step back.

But that was before Sloan.

Before his perfect plan had blown up in his face.

It was easier to focus on her and their present situation than whatever the hell he was supposed to do about the future. How the fuck was he supposed to stay calm and rational when she was marching out across the sand, without a weapon on her, *alone*? He moved before he made a decision to, throwing open the door and following her.

It didn't take long to catch up to her. She'd stopped just short of the waterline, her head tilted back and her hair whipping in the wind. She looked...Fuck, he didn't know. She looked like some kind of fey creature who'd wandered into their world by mistake. It made him hesitant to break the silence—what there was of it against the crash of the waves and the wind picking up to nearly a howl.

Storm will be here faster than I thought.

He wasn't superstitious by nature, but he'd have been a fool to think of the impending storm as anything other than a sign. "Sloan." He barely raised his voice, but she heard him all the same.

"I don't want to talk to you right now."

He started to argue but reconsidered. The woman had had everything she thought was true shaken down to the roots in the last hour. She needed time to process that. He could respect it. He glanced up and down the beach, searching for threats, but it was impossible. The sand was far from perfectly flat, and any hit man worth his salt could dig in a little bit and become nearly invisible in the twilight. "Then don't talk to me while you're in the house with the shades shut. It's not safe."

"It's not safe." She did a fair job of mocking his deep voice. Sloan spun on him, her eyes as wild as he'd ever seen them. "And whose fault is that, Jude? What else did you lie about?" Her voice caught, but she charged on. "I was *safe* here before you looked into me, leading us directly into *Dmitri Romanov's* web. Do you know what he does to his enemies?"

"Probably better than you do." The man was ruthless to a clinical degree, but he seemed to keep his word. It was more than Jude could say for others in the underground world.

"Of course you do—because you're a stone-cold killer." She moved closer, pushing him with both hands. He let himself fall back a step because otherwise she might shove *herself* back and land on her ass. Sloan closed the distance between them, fury written over her face. "Are you going to kill me, Jude? It would hurt the Sheridans, and that's all you care about, isn't it? Your goddamn revenge."

"Wrong." He caught her chin, forcing her to meet his gaze. "So fucking wrong."

She didn't so much as flinch. "Really? Because we both know the only reason you got close to me in the first place was to get your vengeance. It wasn't about me. It *still* isn't about me."

"Do you think for a goddamn second that this is *convenient* for me? You were a potential source of information, true, but I've told myself half a dozen times to walk the fuck away. Damn it, I just can't leave you alone."

* * *

A fury unlike any Sloan had ever known rose from beneath her skin. She wanted to attack Jude, to hit him, to shove him, to claw out his eyes. How *dare* he stand there and look tormented while her entire world was crashing down around her *again*? "Stop it," she hissed. "You have all the power and I have *none*."

"You don't think so?" Jude shook his head. "You've met me every single step of the way. You're not stupid. You knew the second you met me that I wasn't like the rest of them." He slashed his hand through the air, indicating the entirety of Callaway Rock. "You loved that I was dangerous—your rabid little pet who let you lead him around by his cock."

She took a step back. "That's not true." Except hadn't she liked that he pushed her, that she rode the line of fear like a wave about to crest, hoping like hell she wouldn't wipe out and feeling more alive because of that fear? But some things she couldn't get past, no matter how good he made her body feel. "I meant what I said before—some things are unforgivable. If you hurt Callie and my niece or nephew, that makes you a monster. A real one." It struck her that he wasn't in Callaway Rock for Callie. "And what about Sorcha? She's just an old woman."

"Sorcha isn't *just* anything." A muscle ticked in his jaw and, for a moment, she thought he'd leave it at that. "She and Ronan were planning a coup—a coup that might have very well left your precious Callista a casualty."

"No. I've heard Callie talk about her brother. He never would have hurt her." ... *Would he?* She tried to think past the emotions roaring through her, but it was nearly impossible. She didn't know a single thing about Ronan except that he'd been an heir and died—which was why Callie and Teague ended up engaged in the first place. Just because Callie wasn't a horrible person didn't mean that truth extended to her brother.

Sloan shook her head. "Even if that's true, it changes nothing." That was the life she left behind—for a good damn reason. It shouldn't have anything to do with her and Jude.

"I know."

She waited, holding her breath even though she told herself she was a fool for doing so. What they had might be earth-shattering to her, but that didn't mean he felt it on the same level. To turn his back on a vendetta that he'd obviously spent his life preparing for...It was too much to ask.

Jude scrubbed a hand over his face, looking tired for the first time since she'd met him. "I didn't know she was pregnant."

"Why would that change anything? Even if Ronan was planning a coup, you said yourself that Callie wasn't involved. You'd be killing a woman who's innocent."

He looked out toward the ocean. "Do you know I've never killed an innocent? Not once in a decade."

Part of her tried to soften, but she wouldn't let it. "I'm less concerned with what you've done in your past than with what you intend for your future." Not Callie. She couldn't let him do it. Or Sorcha, for that matter. Sloan might not particularly like the woman—and she might like her even less if what he claimed was true—but that didn't mean she was okay with her being cold bloodedly murdered.

He cursed, low and defeated. "Killing Callista would be like going back in time and killing my mother."

Hope rose, but it faltered when he said, "I make no promises for Colm, though. That man has been living on borrowed time for thirty-five years."

Sloan tried to hold on to her anger, but it slipped through

her grasp. She didn't know if she was supposed to be happy that he apparently wasn't planning on murdering her friend, or if she should try to convince him to walk away completely... She was just so incredibly tired. "I don't want to see you again."

"Bullshit."

She narrowed her eyes. "You *will* respect my wishes."

"I won't do anything of the damn sort, even if you're throwing a tantrum like a spoiled princess who didn't get her way." He moved forward, closing the distance between them until he towered over her. "There's more at stake than some wounded pride, and you're smart enough to know that if you'd stop reacting and *think*."

"I can't *think* with you so close." She grabbed the back of his neck and kissed him. It was more a sign of aggression than intimacy, a clash of tongue and teeth, with him meeting her every step of the way. Sloan pushed him, all too aware that he let her, and then rode him down to the sand.

More, more, I need more. Anything to keep from thinking a little while longer. She yanked his shirt off, dragging her nails across his chest as she went for the front of his jeans.

Jude's hands were rough on her, shoving up her dress and ripping her panties off, his mouth never leaving hers. As if he needed this as much as she did. He pushed a finger into her, testing her, and then there was nothing there but his hard length, ready and waiting.

He stopped her from descending, his grip hard on her hips. "Wait."

Sloan met his gaze, knowing in her heart of hearts that it didn't matter, that it was too late, and one more choice had been taken away from her. Even if it was too early for a test to pick it up, she would have had a period by now if the Plan B pill had worked.

She hadn't.

She gripped his chin much the same way he'd held hers earlier. "Don't you think we're beyond that? It's too late. It's happened." When he didn't say anything—for *once* not using that mouth of his—she continued. "I want to feel you, Jude. All of you, with nothing between us."

"It shouldn't be like this."

She laughed, low and desperate. "And how else should it be? Are you going to romance me with sweet words and tell me that you love me? That's not what this is—something you've told me from the beginning." He still didn't budge, so she aimed below the belt. "Take what I'm offering or I'll find someone who will."

"Find someone who will." He repeated it like he couldn't believe she said it. Jude's fingers tightened hard enough to bruise on her hips. "Do you think for a goddamn second that I'll let you fuck someone else?"

A thrill went through her at his words, but she fought to keep her face expressionless—a Herculean feat considering their position. "This is temporary, Jude. You told me so yourself."

"I changed my fucking mind."

She reached between them and notched him at her entrance, silently daring him to tell her to stop. "Maybe I don't want you."

"You want me, sunshine." He used his grip to guide her down, impaling her inch by glorious inch. "You want me so much it scares the shit out of you. No other man will do, and you damn well know it."

She rocked her hips, taking him deeper yet, and tangled her

fingers in his hair. The wind screamed around them, but she couldn't care less because all that mattered was the man inside her and the forbidding look on his face. He wanted her as much as she wanted him, even if a part of him hated that. Sloan didn't care. Everyone else in this world was taking what they wanted with no apologies. It was time for her to do the same.

She licked her way up his neck to bite his earlobe. "You can't get me out of your system and that pisses you off, doesn't it?" The sky opened up, rain falling in sheets, plastering her dress to her, slicking their bodies as she rode him. "You want to keep me."

"Yes." He lifted her almost completely off him and slammed her down. Jude kept one hand on the small of her back, preventing her from moving away—as if she were going anywhere—and reached up with the other to rip her dress down the front. "I'm keeping you. You had your chance to leave. You didn't. You're mine now."

She picked up her movements, not caring where they were or who might see them through the sheets of rain. "For good." It was a demand, not a request. If he wanted her, he was very well going to have her. She hadn't realized she had no intention of letting this man go, but sometime in the last hour it had cemented in her mind. Come hell or high water, they were in this together.

"For good." Jude palmed one breast, his mouth against her neck.

She leaned back enough to force him to meet her eyes. "And if you lie to me again, I will leave, and I will disappear to where you can never find me."

"There's nowhere you could run that I wouldn't find you." He shifted, gripping the back of her neck with one hand and stroking her clit with the other. "And that gets you off like nothing else, knowing that I'd rip myself apart to hunt you down, that I wouldn't rest, wouldn't eat, would go mad with wanting you until you were with me again. To know that you're fucking irreplaceable."

Sloan's orgasm exploded through her, brought on by his words as much as by what he was doing to her body. He kept her riding him until his strokes became jerky and he came, her name on his lips. She slumped against him, her mind slowly kicking back into gear despite her best efforts to keep the glorious post-orgasm fog around her.

What does it say about me that I find his threatening to hunt me down sexy? That's not sexy. It's deranged.

Except...Part of her felt the same way. She hated that he'd lied to her, hated that his looking for information instead of just *talking* to her had brought Romanov dogs down upon them, hated that he'd killed people...But she could understand, no matter how much she didn't want to.

She wasn't fierce, like Carrigan or Keira. She hadn't been willing to go to war when Devlin was killed. All Sloan had wanted was to curl in on herself until the pain passed enough that she could breathe through it. But Carrigan? What would Carrigan have done if her entire family was murdered by the enemy?

The exact same thing Jude has. She wouldn't have let something as simple as pain or guilt stop her from seeking vengeance.

She didn't want to understand, but she did all the same.

She lifted her head. "Jude—"

"Not yet." He helped her stand and fixed his clothing. There was no help for hers. Even if the rain hadn't made her sundress sheer, the rip down the center ensured there was no way she could cover herself effectively.

There was no one around to see, though it was entirely possible that Sorcha had gotten an eyeful if she'd happened to look out the window at the wrong time. Sloan glanced in that direction, but the rain created a haze that made it difficult to see more than the vague shapes of their houses. "I—"

"I said not yet."

He started to take her hand, but she jerked away. "If we're doing this, there's one thing you're going to have to come to terms with. You can't steamroll me anywhere except the bedroom. I won't stand for it." She'd been a doormat for far too long. She'd just finally gotten her feet beneath her, and going back to how things had been before wasn't an option. She refused to allow it to be.

For a moment, it looked like Jude might argue, but he crossed his arms over his chest and raised his eyebrows instead. "Yes?"

Right about then was when she realized they were both soaked to the bone and standing in the rain, and that it was downright foolish to have any kind of conversation out here when his house was a hundred yards away. Sloan shook her head. "No, you're right. We'll talk once we're inside."

CHAPTER EIGHTEEN

Jude shut the door behind them and stripped out of his wet clothes. He didn't give Sloan a chance to voice whatever was going on in her head before he was stripping her down, too. He led her into his bathroom and turned on the shower, his words from earlier echoing in his mind. He'd called her his. He'd told her that he'd hunt her down like some sort of madman if she left him.

He had passed the point of no return with this woman.

It didn't make a damn bit of sense. The sex was out of control, but it was sex. It shouldn't be enough to derail his entire plan. Then again, his plan hadn't counted on Callista being pregnant. Jude guided Sloan beneath the spray, ignoring her pointed look. She was playing along, and that was all he asked for right now. He needed time to process, to get his head on straight again.

If that was even possible at this point.

Already, he wanted her again, but they had shit to iron

out first. Fucking her until they weren't capable of moving might sound like a dream right now, but it wouldn't solve a damn thing. He shut off the water and handed her a towel. "Now we talk."

Sloan wrapped herself in the big fluffy towel, the sheer amount of fabric dwarfing her. It made her look younger, innocent, and even though he knew it was an illusion, it didn't stop a pang of something like guilt from going through him. She frowned. "Why are you looking at me like that?"

Because everything's changed.

He didn't say it. Instead, he grabbed a towel for himself and dried off. "You will take a pregnancy test tomorrow. It's not negotiable."

"Okay."

He glanced over, having expected her to argue, and she sighed. "While living in denial a little while longer wouldn't be a bad thing, it's also unrealistic. If I am, I need to know—"

"*We* need to know."

"—so I can plan accordingly."

"That sounds an awful lot like you making plans that don't include me." He should be grateful—he needed a kid like he needed another hole in his head—but the thought of her out in the world without him, let alone out in the world with his *child*, didn't sit well. He'd told her she was *his*, and it didn't matter that he'd said it while he was inside her. It felt like the truth.

Jude hadn't had anyone to call his own before. Not truly. He didn't know what to think of that.

Sloan toweled off her hair and stood there, gloriously naked and without so much as a blush. "I'm being realistic. It's only in the last twenty minutes that you've changed your tune, and that's on the heels of some rather large news I'm still reeling from. So forgive me if I don't take what you said in the middle of sex as the Lord's honest truth."

"I can protect you—both of you." If there was a baby. If there wasn't, well then, they'd figure that out, too.

She opened her mouth, hesitated, and finally shrugged. "It's all a moot point until I take the test. We'll know more once we have the results."

Which also sounded a hell of a lot like she was making more plans without him. He couldn't blame her. He had more than enough money to last several lifetimes, but what else did he have to offer a woman like Sloan? Sure as fuck not stability.

And there was his vendetta to consider. He might be pathetically relieved to have his options taken away when it came to Callista—and Sorcha, for that matter—but that didn't mean Sloan would forgive him for killing Colm. Taking that bastard out would hurt Sloan's sister-in-law, which might hurt *Sloan*. Something he never could have taken into account when he put his plans in motion—or when he took that goddamn contract from Romanov.

He'd laughed when Dmitri talked about him having a change of heart. Fast forward twenty-four hours and he couldn't help weighing his vengeance against the woman who stood before him. Even after such a short time together, could one really compare to the other?

Killing Colm might be enough to make her walk away from me for good.

For so long his revenge was everything. Now? Now he wasn't sure of anything anymore.

* * *

Sloan pulled one of Jude's shirts over her head and sighed. "I need to go get some clothes."

"You don't need clothes." He didn't look up from his laptop.

She crossed her arms over her chest. "Am I allowed to have a book? Or should I just quit my job and plan on being here and naked for whenever you're ready for me?"

He looked up at that, brown eyes so dark, they were almost black. "Don't tempt me."

"For goodness' sake, Jude, I have a life. It might not be a fancy one, and it might be changing dramatically, but it's still mine. You can't lock me up as a prisoner and try to tell me it's for my own good." She still had shifts for the next four days, and she wasn't about to jeopardize that when Marge had finally put her on a regular schedule. And there was Sorcha to consider. Though the woman would disappear for hours on end, she'd be sure to call Callie if a day or two went by without her seeing Sloan.

He looked like he wanted to do what she'd said and lock her up, but he finally gave a short nod. "Make it quick."

They were going to have to have a talk about the fact that she may like it when he was overbearing in bed, but she had no intention of bowing to his every whim when it came to the rest of her life. For now, she'd settle for some clean clothes, a book, and something resembling a plan for going forward.

Romanov found me.

How am I going to face Sorcha knowing Jude had fully intended to kill her?

Not to mention warning Callie that her aunt might be up to no good.

She was working very hard not to think too closely

about either thing, but they were there, lurking in the back of her mind. Her brothers finding her was one thing—the worst she had to expect was being dragged home, kicking and screaming, and thrown into an advanced sort of lockdown. Her brothers loved her, and while they might put the O'Malley family before her mental health, they wouldn't physically hurt her.

Dmitri Romanov?

He was a different kind of threat altogether. Sloan hadn't forgotten that he'd tried to have James Halloran killed, or that he'd bargained so coldly with her sister while planning that. He wasn't done with her family, and she was currently the weakest link, Jude's protection or no.

I have to get out of Callaway Rock.

Away from Sorcha. Jude might have said that he wasn't going to pull the trigger when it came to her—or Callie—but even in her limited experience, Sloan knew that things said in the heat of the moment couldn't be trusted. She *wanted* to trust him, but to walk blindly forward without reservation was beyond her. If Sorcha had truly done something to deserve death, she selfishly didn't want Jude to be the one to deliver it.

I have to warn Teague about Jude. Warn Callie about Sorcha.

She pulled Jude's shirt into place, nearly rolling her eyes when it hit her at her knees. The man was monstrously large. "I'll be back shortly." The faster she was out of Sorcha's house, the less likely it was that he'd change his mind.

"Sloan."

She stopped in the doorway and glanced back, finding him watching her. "Yes?"

"Be careful."

She wanted to laugh, to tell him that she was walking ten feet to the house next door, and that nothing bad could happen to her in the process. She didn't. She knew better. So instead she just nodded. "I will."

The rain hadn't abated in the short time they'd been inside, so she ran from his back door to hers. She unlocked the door as fast as she could and ducked into the house, only to find it dark and deserted. *Where is Sorcha?*

She moved through the house, frowning. There should have been at least a few lights on, despite the fact that it was early still, but there wasn't a single one lit. Her skin broke out in goose bumps that had nothing to do with the chill, and she hurried to her room. *The faster I pack, the faster I can get out of here for good.*

She threw what little she'd acquired into her bag and dug out the burner phones to toss on top of them. She was in the process of muscling the zipper closed when the creak of a board made her look over her shoulder.

Sloan froze. "You don't want to do that."

"On the contrary, I've lived a very long time by doing exactly what is necessary to survive." Sorcha had the shotgun braced against her shoulder with the ease of long practice. At this distance, Sloan stood no chance of avoiding getting hit if she pulled the trigger. The older woman took her in. "Going somewhere, my dear?"

"You know why I'm here. The people looking for me know where I am, and I need to leave."

"Do they?" Sorcha stepped into the room. "Or is that what that filthy MacNamara told you? Don't look so surprised—like I said, I've done what it takes to survive this long. I know a stone-cold killer when I see one, and it was child's play to discover who he really was."

"Or you were eavesdropping." She and Jude hadn't exactly been quiet earlier when they were fighting. *So incredibly foolish.*

Sorcha shrugged. "The how hardly matters. What matters is that he's here with one goal in mind—my death. It might make my fool brother's day to find out that I've finally kicked the bucket, but I have no interest in dying just yet." She jerked the barrel of the shotgun. "Up, my dear."

Sloan stood, her hands carefully raised. "We're leaving. He's not going to hurt you." She prayed she was speaking the truth, but in reality she'd say nearly anything to get that gun pointed away from her. "No matter how much you might deserve it."

"And you do." Jude's voice made Sloan jump, but Sorcha didn't so much as flinch when he pressed a gun to her temple. He was little more than a shadow behind the woman, but she could still see the fury on his face—and the flash of the pistol he had pointed at Sorcha's head.

"Like I said, I have no intention of going the way of the saints, yet."

"You're no saint, old woman, and we both know it. Now put that fucking shotgun down before I pull the trigger."

She smiled, not looking the least bit intimidated. "I've been around the block a few times, MacNamara. The second I put down this gun and your little lady is safe, you're going to snap my neck."

"The thought did cross my mind."

Sloan looked from one of them to the other. She could rush at Sorcha, but the woman would pull the trigger and that would be the end of her. If Jude shot her, she might still pull the trigger and shoot Sloan. There was a window behind her, but the glass was reinforced to withstand the winter storms that roared in off the ocean. The chance she had of breaking it, let alone breaking it without cutting herself to ribbons, wasn't good. Sloan tried to keep her fear out of her voice. "Think about this."

"I have." Sorcha turned and looked at Jude, ignoring the gun in her face. "Step back. Now."

Jude's mouth went tight, but he did what she commanded.

And then he slammed forward, jerked the shotgun barrel toward the ceiling as Sorcha pulled the trigger. Plaster rained down and Sloan hit the floor, trying to make herself as small a target as possible. She watched Jude yank the gun out of the older woman's hands, his face becoming a terrifyingly cold mask. "Did you think for a fucking second that I would let you walk out of this house alive after you threatened my woman?"

Sorcha didn't raise her hands, didn't flinch when he moved forward, into her space. "What can I say? I'm a survivor."

"Not anymore." He lifted the pistol.

"Stop!" Sloan shoved to her feet but didn't try to approach. "Jude, *stop*."

He didn't look at her. "She's a threat."

She couldn't pretend to argue that point. "You promised you wouldn't, or was that a lie?" Her breath hitched, but she powered on. "She's an old woman."

Sorcha shot her a glare. "Not *that* old."

"Shut up." She forced the panic out of her voice as much as possible. "Don't kill her."

"Did you forget what I told you earlier?"

That Sorcha was a potential threat to Callie. That she was as much a monster as everyone else in their world—

more so, since her target had been her own family. The thought made Sloan sick to her stomach. "Tie her up. Leave her for Teague and Callie to deal with. Let them decide." No matter how that fell out, at least it would be one less death on Jude's conscience.

For a long moment, she thought he'd ignore her. She fully expected him to. But he finally gave a jerky nod. "Get your shit."

"I'm packed." She finished zipping up her suitcase, hardly daring to take her eyes off them.

"Go to my house and wait for me." When she hesitated, he shot her an exasperated look. "Sunshine, trust me."

It was a moment of truth in a way. She could demand to know what in God's name he had planned, or she could obey him now and get her answers later. If she didn't trust him—truly didn't trust him—then she needed to walk out of this house, get in her car, and drive away without looking back. Without trust, they were doomed.

Sloan's hand went to her stomach, to where, even now, there might be a tiny person growing. *A baby. She could have killed my baby.*

She opened her house to me.

She might be planning something horrible for Callie.

She took a measured breath. "Remember what you promised me." *Leave her to Callie and Teague.*

He gave a short nod without taking his eyes off Sorcha. "I won't be long."

There was nothing to do but walk out of the room and pray that he kept his word.

CHAPTER NINETEEN

Jude found Sloan sitting on his couch, her suitcase beside her, a distant look in her big brown eyes. Something had changed back in the O'Connor house, though he was at a loss to know what it was. Even when Sorcha had threatened her, Sloan stood up to him and demanded he keep his promise.

Jude crouched in front of her, putting himself in her line of sight. "She's alive." He'd left her tied as Sloan requested, but he didn't like the woman's odds once Callista Sheridan got ahold of her. *Still doesn't put Callista on my list. Not anymore.*

"Thank you."

He didn't know what to say to that, didn't know how to deal with the way his entire world had changed the second Sloan walked into it. Really, there wasn't a damn thing to do but keep moving. He straightened. "It's time to move."

"Don't you need to pack?"

He checked her eyes for signs of shock, but they were clear and her hands didn't shake when she placed one in his.

"I'm ready." He'd packed everything up but the bare necessities the second he'd gotten back to Callaway Rock after meeting with Dmitri. Even if he hadn't, he was ready to leave on the fly as a matter of habit. "We're taking my truck."

She nodded, then looked away. "I have to call my brother to tell him about Sorcha. And before you say something scathing, I have several burner phones and will destroy them as soon as I hang up."

"I wasn't going to say anything." When it came right down to it, Sloan had a point. Sorcha's wrong hadn't been aimed at him—it had been aimed at her own family. It was up to her family to deliver justice.

And if they didn't... Well, he'd deal with that when the time came.

He wasn't going to forget that Sorcha had pulled a gun on Sloan, and had likely had every intention of using it.

"Come on." He kept ahold of her hand and grabbed her suitcase. It made it damn near impossible to get to his gun, but he didn't like the stiff way Sloan was holding herself. She was going to break down at some point, possibly in the near future, and getting her in his truck took precedence.

He headed out his front door, not bothering to lock it behind him. There was nothing to find, no evidence that he'd ever been there or where he might be going. If someone wanted in badly enough, a locked door was child's play to get past.

And a part of him wondered if he'd ever be back. He'd enjoyed being so close to the beach, and even the townspeople weren't *that* aggravating when it came right down to it. More than any of that, this was the place he'd met

Sloan. The exact spot that had sent him spinning from the path he'd been on since he could remember.

The place where everything changed.

Jude didn't usually waste time feeling sentimental about a house, but he was doing a lot of things these days that he didn't normally do. He tossed the suitcase into the bed of the truck and opened the door, taking in his surroundings. There was no movement from the O'Connor house, but he didn't expect there to be, and the rest of the street was deserted. The rain would keep people inside, which was a goddamn blessing in disguise because it meant he didn't have to worry about someone wandering over to make small talk the second he left his front porch. He slammed the door behind Sloan and wasted no time getting into the driver's side and gunning the engine.

With every street they passed, the tension wound tighter between his shoulder blades. There weren't any warning signs, no indication that someone was following them, and he'd scoured the truck for bugs before he'd gone to check on Sloan while she packed. But it was still too easy. There should be *something*.

As if on cue, his satellite phone rang. He cursed and yanked it out of his jacket. "What?"

"Going somewhere?"

How the hell did that Russian fucker know? Jude checked the rearview again, but there wasn't any other vehicle on the road. Then again, with the godforsaken trees trying to encroach on the highway and the way the pavement dipped and twisted, it was entirely possible that he had a tail just out of sight. There weren't many ways in or out of Callaway Rock beyond Route 101. He could go north toward Seaside and cut east to Portland and hope to lose them there, or head south toward California... None of them good options.

He kept his voice detached, ignoring the questioning look Sloan sent him. "I was under the impression that we were aligned and you were going to mind your own god-damn business in the meantime."

Romanov sighed. "Things have escalated, and we need to reevaluate."

"That's unfortunate. For you."

"We're in this together, MacNamara."

Except they weren't. Dmitri wanted Colm dead—hell, *Jude* still wanted Colm dead—but the Russian was more right than he knew. Things had escalated faster than anyone could have anticipated. With Sloan's potential pregnancy in the equation, gunning for Colm on someone else's schedule was too much of a risk to take. "The timeline has changed."

"Unacceptable."

He shot a look at Sloan. She was staring out the window at the dark trees as they flew down the road, but she would hear every word he said. *And why not?* She knew who he was now. She knew what he did—what he had planned on doing. He'd promised to leave Callista and Sorcha alive and unscathed, and he had no intention of breaking that promise.

But his chances of getting to Colm Sheridan without putting Callista in the crossfire could be complicated. He had to go back to square one and rework his plan from there. "You can say 'unacceptable' all you want, but you know better than to rush me."

"Colm and Callista Sheridan have dinner at their favorite restaurant every week. There's an apartment across the street with a perfect view of two of the three entrances. I expect you to make good use of it."

Jude white-knuckled the steering wheel. "I don't appreciate you doing my job for me."

"I wouldn't have to if you weren't about to go back on your word." Dmitri waited a beat. "You know what I do to people who break their word to me."

"I'm not breaking my word. I just need more time. In the meantime, however you're tracking me, fucking stop it. Or any *consideration* I have of working with you will disappear and I'll take my chances elsewhere."

"Do not cross me. You will be at that apartment with the appropriate weapons before their Sunday dinner—one way or another."

"What the fuck is that supposed to mean? Are you going to kidnap me?"

Dmitri snorted. "Please spare me the dramatics. Once your identity is out, who do you think is going to be blamed if both the remaining Sheridans are assassinated?"

Even if I don't pull the trigger, he's going to make sure everyone thinks I did.

The realization sat like a stone in his stomach. The Russian had effectively backed him into a corner, and he didn't know what the fuck he was supposed to do about it. He wouldn't shed a single damn tear if Colm Sheridan was taken out with a bullet from someone other than him. But Callista…

Knowing she was pregnant, he'd be no better than Colm if he sat back and didn't do anything to stop it. No better than Romanov.

Fuck. "I'll be there." At least then he could ensure the only person who died was the one who deserved it. *Don't know how I'm going to explain that to Sloan, though.*

"I thought as much." Dmitri hung up, leaving turmoil in his wake.

Sloan wasted no time, turning in the seat to face him completely. "Please tell me that wasn't Dmitri Romanov."

"It was Dmitri Romanov." There was no point in lying to her. Either she'd be able to handle everything or she wouldn't. It was better to know now than...What? He wasn't letting her go. He damn well knew it. She'd come into his life with her quiet strength and now everything he thought he knew was gone. It didn't make a single fucking bit of sense, but he was actually considering throwing everything he'd spent his entire life working for out the window if it meant keeping her safe.

More than considering it. He was damn near planning on it.

She smoothed her hair back, her hands only now shaking. What did it say about Sloan that she could face down certain death by shotgun and be relatively unaffected but that Russian bastard flustered her calm? *That she's a smart fucking woman.* Sloan took a deep breath, and he could almost see her counting to three before she released it. "Any kind of alliance with that man is out of the question."

"I don't remember putting you in charge of this operation."

"Well, you should if you're stupid enough to think that man won't stab you in the back the first chance he gets." Her voice shook and she made a visible effort to calm it. "He's a snake. Worse than a snake. He's not to be trusted."

"I don't trust him." Especially considering the threat currently hanging over his head.

"I don't..." Her breath hitched again. "I'm scared, Jude."

"I'll take care of you, sunshine." He just had to figure out how the hell he was going to pull that off without signing a death warrant for both of them.

* * *

"You're sure."

Liam sat behind the wheel of the sedan, his face unread-able in the neon light from the bar across the street. "As sure as I can be. She's John Finch's daughter—his only kid. It took some digging because she disappeared off the face of the earth four years ago."

Aiden studied the place. It looked like a thousand dive bars across the country—filthy and unassuming. The kind of place bikers and people up to no good would congregate. "There's more."

Liam nodded. "Charlotte Finch used to be a cop. She was a bright shining star of the NYPD and moving up the ranks pretty damn quickly—until she was accused of being a dirty cop and thrown off the force. There wasn't an official trial for some reason, but right after that she disappeared. Two years later, Charlie Moreaux shows up in this shitty lit-tle bar in New York City, running high-stakes poker in the back room."

"*Was* she dirty?" If she was, it would have broken her dear father's heart—and she'd be useless to him, because John Finch seemed the type to cut ties if he thought his daughter was on the wrong side of the law.

Aiden flipped through the file Liam handed him, raising his brows at the list of her accomplishments. She hadn't just been a cop—she'd been a *good* cop. Beneath that sheet was a short report about her time in the academy. Good grades, one hell of a shot, and adored by both her instructors and peers. *Must have been quite the kick in the teeth to have them turn on you at the flip of a coin.*

"She's not dirty." Liam hesitated. "Though I can't be

sure without more info. But if I were a betting man, I'd say that Charlotte stumbled onto something she shouldn't have and paid the price. Her former partner got a promotion. And there's this." He passed over a photo.

Aiden studied the two men. One he knew far better than he'd like to. Dark hair, lean build, predatory gaze—Romanov. The other... "This is her partner?"

"Yeah."

Which meant it was possible—probable even—that Romanov had some of New York's finest on his payroll and, when the starry-eyed golden girl had found out and refused to fall in line, he'd had her discredited.

It's what Aiden would have done.

Killing cops was bad for business. It was easier to have the ones who wouldn't take bribes framed and removed, since there was little that honorable cops hated more than finding out one of their own was dirty. No one would believe what a dirty cop said, and no one was going to be forming a posse to avenge them. It was a nice bloodless way to tie up loose ends.

I bet John Finch just loved that shit. "She still have contact with her father?"

"Hard to say. He spoke out in her defense at first, but after she left the force, he shut the hell up."

Aiden considered what he knew of John Finch. It was quite a bit these days. The man was from a long line of cops who firmly believed that the ends justified the means. He hadn't flinched at using Teague to further his investigation, and gave no regard to what the O'Malleys—or Sheridans or Hallorans, for that matter—would do to him if they found out he was a rat. They would have killed his brother—worse than killed him.

And John Finch would have just kept on living, doing what he did best—turning people against their friends and families. Part of him still couldn't believe that his little brother was a fucking informant to the feds. The O'Malleys did a lot of terrible things, but they held family above all others. To betray family...

He hadn't confronted Teague yet. He didn't trust himself to even see his brother's face without losing control. If Teague was still just his brother, it wouldn't have been an issue. But he wasn't just Teague O'Malley anymore. He was married to the head of the Sheridan family, which made any interaction Aiden had with him a potential political incident. They'd barely avoided a war up to this point, and *he* wasn't going to be the reason that changed.

But he was only holding off the inevitable and he knew it. Eventually he was going to have to see his brother face-to-face and tell him exactly what Aiden knew.

Anger tried to choke him, but he fought it, focusing on the man he *could* make pay. John Finch. If he simply removed the fed, another would take his place. No, Aiden needed leverage to get Finch to back the hell off of his own free will.

Aiden had no illusions about what kind of man he was. He'd do unforgivable things to uphold his family's power and keep those closest to him safe. He *had* done unforgivable things.

He was about to add one more to the list. "Let's go meet this Charlie Moreaux."

Approaching her on her own territory was a mistake. Even with Liam at his back, she would have home-court advantage. So they took up a spot just outside the door and waited. They'd timed their arrival to coincide with last call, and sure enough it didn't take long before a scattering of people filed out of the bar, some weaving on their feet.

Fifteen minutes later, a woman exited alone. Aiden didn't need Liam's nudge to know that this was Charlie Moreaux, formerly Charlotte Finch. Despite her white blond hair, painted-on jeans, and downright sinful good looks, her blue eyes were a cop's. She stopped when she saw them, taking both him and Liam in, in an instant. "If you're looking for trouble, you've got the wrong woman."

She shifted, and his gaze flicked to her right hand. "I suggest you don't pull that gun on me, bright eyes."

Charlotte frowned. "Who the hell are you?"

He weighed his odds of telling her the truth, and decided it was in his best interest to start things out correctly. "Aiden O'Malley. A pleasure."

"Wish I could say the same." She narrowed those gorgeous blue eyes. "I know that name...Isn't New York a bit of a jaunt from Boston? I wonder what Romanov thinks of your trespassing."

If he'd had any question about who she blamed for her downfall, the answer was in the way she practically spat the Russian's name. *Perfect.* His initial plan had changed the second Liam had mentioned her potential connection to Romanov—now, a new plan solidified. *Two birds, one stone.*

He kept his hands at his side, doing his best to be non-threatening, and went in for the kill. "Dmitri Romanov is no friend of mine, and with your help I can bring him down."

She snorted. "I've heard that one before."

"Maybe other men have promised. I can deliver."

She cocked her head to the side, her long hair spilling over one shoulder. The sheer lack of pigment in her hair drew his attention to her blood red lips. While she considered him, he returned the favor, taking in her fitted white T-shirt and jeans that hugged every curve. And then there were those heels, the same color as her lips. The woman looked like...Fuck, if he was going to be honest, she looked like sex, with her smoky eye makeup and her stillness and the way she watched him like she wasn't sure if she wanted to shoot him or fuck him.

"No."

Aiden took a step forward and caught himself, retreating immediately. Crowding her would only result in her doing something like going for the gun she must have in the back of her waistband. He couldn't bully her into agreeing. She had to do it because she wanted to or it wouldn't work. "Give me a chance to change your mind."

She hesitated, and he waited, giving her time to think about it. Charlotte finally glanced at the door to the bar and lowered her voice. "Look, I don't know what you think you know about me, but even if you had the ability to take Romanov down, I can't do a damn thing to help you. I don't have contacts in the force anymore. I'm just a woman with a gun who's better than average at poker."

"That's not all you are, and you know it." She was the daughter of a fed with a specialty in organized crime, and her record when she'd been a cop was downright impressive. Every sign pointed to her having a keen mind and the ability to think on her feet. The woman was practically built for undercover work.

And getting her to work with me will be a knife in her father's heart.

He set the thought aside, refusing to allow it to show on his face. He had to play this slow, because if she'd been a good cop, that meant she was going to want to check him out—which was a big fat black mark against him. There was no way she wouldn't equate him with Romanov, and getting into bed with one devil in order to take out another would reek of desperation.

Something he counted on.

Because if Charlotte Finch really wasn't a dirty cop, she'd do damn near anything to clear her name and punish the one who'd orchestrated the whole thing.

Moving slowly, Aiden pulled out a card and held it out. "If you want to meet up and talk someplace more…neutral…give me a call. I think you'll like what I have to say." He waited for her to take it, reaching out to snatch it like he was a snake who might strike at any time.

She read the card, her brows raising. "There's no such thing as neutral territory in New York. And I'm sure as hell not coming to Boston."

That's what you think.

Aiden gave a smile that made her take a step back despite his best efforts to be disarming. "The ball is in your court. You can toss that card in the nearest Dumpster, or you can call that number and let me help you right all the wrongs that Dmitri Romanov has done to you."

Her lips parted, and the tiny part of him not locked completely down and under control wondered if she'd taste as good as she looked. Charlotte hesitated. "I'll… think about it."

"I'll be waiting." He had her. She might not realize it yet, but he did. Now it was only a matter of playing his cards to maneuver her into exactly the right position to maximize her benefit.

And to maximize the knife to John Finch's throat once he realized his precious daughter was in bed with Aiden O'Malley.

CHAPTER TWENTY

Sloan's mind was awhirl as they drove. So much had happened in such a short time, and she didn't know where to start in order to wrap her head around it. Jude was a MacNamara—the sole remaining MacNamara. He'd killed Sheridans, and had fully intended on killing Sorcha and Callie before she'd come along.

She was reaching and she knew it, but she also didn't overestimate what he felt for her. Lust? Most definitely. But Jude was a cold and calculating man outside the bedroom. There was absolutely no way he would be swayed from his course—unless he hadn't wanted to be on it to begin with. Finding out Callie was pregnant was likely just the straw that broke the camel's back.

She wanted to know for sure, though. Sloan shifted to face him, studying the way his face was illuminated by the lights in the dashboard. "Why did it take you a year to track down Sorcha?"

"It wasn't because I was having second thoughts, if that's what you're hoping for." He drummed his fingers on the wheel. "Sorcha has spent her entire life avoiding being found by men like me—because she has a track record of crossing men like me."

Which was why Sloan really needed to call Teague and let him know everything that had happened.

She wanted answers first. "And Ronan? If you wanted Colm dead so badly, why not let his own son do it? That betrayal would cut deeper than anything you could do to him." She struggled to keep her tone even, as if she was merely curious. *What would Callie do if she knew Ronan might have put her in the line of fire?*

"You're right." Jude went still, his gaze never leaving the road. "But it takes a special kind of monster to plot the murder of his father. I don't give two shits about the other families in Boston, but Ronan would have made Brendan Halloran look like a lumbering idiot if he was in control of the Sheridans."

"You don't know that." She'd heard stories about Brendan Halloran. She didn't like thinking that someone like that could have been related to Callie.

Someone she loved. Someone she mourned.

"I know that. He hid it better than most, but he was his father's son." Jude finally tore his eyes from the road to look at her. "Which way are you going on this? Are you painting me as some kind of romantic vigilante? Or am I the monster that other monsters fear?"

She burst out laughing. She couldn't help it. He sounded so damn snarly at the thought that she might think either of him. "You're a man, Jude. You have a more colorful past than most, but I understand your reasoning for wanting Colm to pay. I just don't think you should run around murdering people."

"An eye for an eye."

"Leaves the whole world blind."

He huffed out a breath. "You're being intentionally difficult."

"Maybe." He might have changed his mind about Callie, and spared Sorcha, but he still wanted Colm's blood. Nothing she could do or say would turn him from that path.

She *did* understand, at least in theory. Colm Sheridan was the one responsible for killing Jude's family. Killing his relatives wouldn't make Jude feel better. Killing *Colm* was unlikely to assuage the loss he might never recover from. *Can you recover from losing something you never had?*

But then, this wasn't about his father and brothers. It couldn't be. The pain was too raw, too deep, too angry. It was like her plotting revenge for the death of the grandfather she'd never met. He might be related to her, but he was a stranger. People did not spend their entire lives orchestrating the downfall of someone who murdered a stranger.

But they would do it for a beloved family member—and Jude only had one living. "What happened to your mother?"

He was silent for so long, she thought he wouldn't respond. "She couldn't go back to the family home without fear of Colm finishing what he'd started with my father and brothers and their wives, so she ran. She had to resort to whoring to feed us, though she never let the johns near me." He shook his head. "Before my father and brothers were butchered, she was a happy woman. Carefree. Sweet. Or that's what I've discovered in the years since. One of the few boyfriends she had saw potential in me—in our situation—and trained me when he was around. I picked up skills in all the ways a disreputable kid does while growing up, all with the intent of providing for her so she wouldn't have to sell herself. It wasn't enough. Nothing I did would have been enough."

That wasn't quite an answer, though her heart ached for him. His mother may have been alive, but she wasn't living from the sounds of it. He'd been adrift and without any of the things she'd taken for granted—family, roots, security.

He looked at her and then back to the road in front of them. With the darkness now fallen completely and the trees blocking out what little moonlight there was, they might as well have been the last two people in the world. Jude sighed. "She took an entire bottle of pills when I was eighteen."

Eighteen.

He wouldn't take sympathy from her, and he certainly wouldn't take pity, but she squeezed his hand in silent support. *Eighteen.* He might have been legally an adult, but that didn't mean he was prepared to lose the only family he had in this world.

What a selfish choice to make.

She knew it was her growing feelings for Jude making her so angry, but that changed nothing. "She shouldn't have done that. She should have lived for you."

He squeezed her hand back and then slipped his free. "Call your brother."

She didn't want to. She wanted to keep talking, to deal with the fact that she was terrifyingly certain she was pregnant, to come up with some sort of plan. Perhaps an assurance that he wasn't going to change his mind, drop her on the side of the road, and continue pursuing his vendetta against the Sheridans, either getting himself killed or murdering the love of her brother's life. There was no winning scenario there. None.

I have to convince him to stop.

The sheer impossibility of that task made it hard to breathe. He had his entire life leading up to this plan, and they'd known each other a few short weeks. Yes, she was likely pregnant with his child, but that didn't mean much in the grand scheme of things. She was no stranger to the fact that a large percentage of the world's population were single mothers. Sloan would have to be living in a fantasy to expect things to work out between them simply because they might have created a life. That wasn't reality.

Reality was cold and heartless and brutal.

One step at a time. First, she had to ensure that Teague didn't send anyone after her, and ensure that Sorcha saw justice. She had no doubt that Jude would *remove* Teague's men who tried to track her down, and that would only antagonize the issue across the board. Sloan turned to look out the back window to where her suitcase slid around in the bed of the truck. "My phones are in there."

"Use mine. They shouldn't be able to trace it if you keep it short." He passed over the satellite phone that Dmitri Romanov had called him on. She didn't like thinking that they were on a familiar enough basis that they were calling each other. She didn't like that at all.

Sloan dialed her brother's number from memory and listened to it ring, part of her hoping he wouldn't pick up. Her hopes were in vain. "Teague O'Malley."

"It's me."

Instantly his voice changed, becoming less cold and more worried. "Sloan? Where are you calling from? This number's not one of the burner phones."

No point in denying it. "No, it's not." She watched their headlights cut through the darkness as Jude headed north, ever north. "I've left Sorcha's house. My location's been compromised."

"How do you know that? Are you hurt?"

"I'm fine." She said it calmly, firmly. She glanced at Jude, who held up a single finger. *One minute left.* "I've met someone. I'm safe. Sorcha was part of a plot to murder Colm Sheridan a year and a half ago, and I doubt she's changed her tune since then. Callie could be in danger. We left her tied and alive in the house for you to pick up."

"*We?* Sloan, where are you?"

Of course that was what he would focus on—where she was and who she was with—instead of the threat Sorcha represented. She sighed, considering telling him the truth. Revealing that Jude was a MacNamara might make Teague have a heart attack and decide to come after him to protect Callie...but it was likely Sorcha would try to use Jude's identity as a bargaining chip.

She couldn't let that woman have the upper hand. "I'm with Jude MacNamara. I'm safe."

"*MacNamara?*"

She charged on, all too aware of her time limit winding down. "I'm safe." Maybe if she said it enough times, he'd actually believe her. "Truly, I promise. Please don't look for me when you should be dealing with Sorcha. I'll call when I'm able to."

"Sloan—"

"Love you." She hung up and dropped the phone like it had caught fire in her hand, her brother's worried tone ringing in her ears. "I think I made things worse."

"It's a shitty situation. You're doing the best you can." He actually sounded like he meant it.

She tried not to let hope take hold, but it was impossible. God help her, but she *liked* this man. "What happens now?"

"Now we find a fucking pregnancy test and a place to hole up for the night." He slanted a look her way. "Tomorrow we'll come up with a plan."

* * *

Jude got them a cheap hotel in Seattle solely so Sloan wouldn't have to take a pregnancy test in some grocery store bathroom. He didn't like the idea of her facing that alone. Hell, he would have liked to go to a lab and get a blood test done to be sure, but she'd insisted on the over-the-counter test first.

He'd bought three boxes.

She raised her eyebrows when he dumped the bag on the bed's faded comforter. "Exactly how much do you think I have to pee?"

"We might get a false negative." He knew better than to say anything about a false positive. He'd done some research while he was considering which brand was best, and it appeared that false negatives were a whole lot more likely than the alternative. "It's been about ten days, so the hormones might not have built up enough to show up."

She stared. "Jude, I'm going to take these boxes and go into the bathroom now."

"Do you want me to—"

"No." She stood and gave him what she probably

thought was a reassuring smile. "I think I can manage without you hovering."

He muscled back the impulse to tell her to do a clean catch. She wouldn't appreciate it, and he would sound like even more of a fuckhead than he already did. Jude didn't like feeling out of control. Research usually centered him, but the things he did research on were normally things fully within his control.

There was nothing about the current situation that he could control.

Either Sloan was pregnant, or she wasn't. If she was, either she was keeping it, or she wasn't. Either the theoretical baby was healthy, or it wasn't.

Nothing he could do could influence any of those outcomes either way.

It made him wild.

He paced a loop around the bed, and then stalked back, pausing every few steps to glare at the closed bathroom door. *What's taking so long?*

It opened, revealing a pale Sloan. "Can you set a timer for three minutes, please?"

That, he could do. He set it on his phone and then dropped it onto the bed. Three minutes wasn't very long in the grand scheme of things, but it seemed a small eternity. "Sit down before you pass out."

She rolled her eyes, looking a little more like the woman he'd come to know. "There you are. I thought you were going soft on me."

"Don't know the meaning of the word." He kept close as she walked to the bed, but she only weaved a little as she sat next to the rapidly decreasing timer on his phone. Had he thought three minutes was forever?

It wasn't nearly long enough.

To distract himself, he crouched next to Sloan. "How are you doing?"

"About as well as can be expected."

He didn't know how to do this. Jude was so much better at destroying shit than comforting someone who was upset. And she was upset, even if she was doing a damn good job of hiding it. "You did well back at Sorcha's—getting out without breaking down." The second she frowned, he realized exactly how much of an asshole he sounded. "What I mean is—"

"That you fully expected me to curl up in a ball and require you to carry me out of there the same way you carried out my suitcase." She twined her fingers together. "I'm not okay, Jude. I'm not even in the realm of okay. I've been hit by one thing after another, starting with realizing that the life I actually really love has been jeopardized and ending with a gun pointed at my face. I might not be as strong as my sisters—"

"Stop."

She finally looked at him. "Excuse me?"

"That's not the first time you've said that."

"It's the truth—"

He checked the phone—two minutes left—then focused on her. "You uprooted your entire life and walked away from everything you ever knew. Has either of your sisters done that?"

"Well—" She bit her lip. "Sort of? I see your point."

"I don't think you do. It takes guts to remove yourself from the equation instead of just going along with the current. *You* did that. That's fucking impressive, let alone taking into account what you've done since. Marge wouldn't put up with you at the diner if you didn't work hard. Did you even have a job before you got to Callaway Rock?"

"No."

"Sunshine, you're a goddamn pillar of strength from where I'm sitting." He took her hands because being so close to her without touching her was just fucking wrong, and apparently it was the right thing to do because she clutched him like a drowning woman would a life raft.

"I am very, very afraid."

"Tell me who I need to kill."

She laughed, and then abruptly stopped. "Oh God, you're serious." Sloan stroked the back of his hand with her thumb, the kind of mindless action he didn't even think she realized she was doing. "I won't lie and say I'm not worried about my family's single worst enemy knowing my location."

"Your former location." He had no intention of projecting their whereabouts to Romanov again, though he couldn't be sure how the other man knew their movements in the first place. *No point in borrowing trouble.* Even if Romanov had their current location, Jude doubted he'd make a move until he knew one way or another how Jude would jump when it came to the Sheridans. The Russian wasn't the type to waste resources when it was likely Jude would do exactly as commanded.

She nodded, conceding the point. "But that's not what's freaking me out the most right now."

The baby. "We'll know shortly." In thirty seconds, to be specific.

Sloan gave a sad smile that was like a punch to the gut. "Jude, I think we both know exactly what that test is going to say."

Yeah, sometime in the last few hours, he'd let that

knowledge settle within him. It was entirely possible that they would look at that test in the bathroom and it would be negative, but he didn't think so. Apparently neither did she. And so he sat there, holding her hand and doing his damnedest not to say anything to make it worse. The timer went off before either of them could do anything resembling relaxing.

She blanched. "Jude, I can't look."

"I'll look for both of us." He stood, ignoring the way his instincts demanded he bolt from the room—from the truth that sat a few feet away. That was the coward's path, and Jude was many things, but a coward didn't number among them. He wouldn't leave Sloan to face this alone.

The walk to the bathroom seemed to take hours, but it was the sum of four steps. He paused in the doorway, and then cursed himself for pausing. It was a fucking pregnancy test, not the goddamn boogeyman. He stalked across the remaining distance and snatched the test up.

He'd read the instructions too many times to misinterpret the two blue lines showing in the little window.

"You don't have to say it. I can see the truth on your face."

He looked up to find Sloan leaning against the doorjamb, her arms wrapped around herself. He couldn't keep silent. He had to give the truth words. "You're pregnant. We're having a baby."

A baby. His *baby.*

CHAPTER TWENTY-ONE

Upon hearing that she was going to be a mother, Sloan went into a sort of strange shock. She was aware of Jude ushering her to his truck, where he then drove them...somewhere. She blinked and looked around, taking in the trees and lush greenness so similar to the area around Callaway Rock. "Where are we?"

"About to take a ferry."

She looked out over the water. It wasn't as open as the ocean off the coast of Oregon, and there were islands in the distance. "A ferry. You must be joking."

"I have a piece of property on Orcas Island with a private airstrip attached. It's easily defensible and has a built-in escape plan."

Her mind stumbled over that for a moment. "An airstrip. You're a pilot?"

"I don't like going into a situation without a way to get out of it if things go sideways."

So he'd learned to fly a plane.

She had to wonder what other skills he might have acquired because of that logic. It baffled her, though she found it comforting that he was so capable. She had a lot to learn to be able to take any situation without so much as a hiccup of stress because she had the skills necessary to survive. "If we were chased into the woods, could you keep us alive?"

"Yes." He gave a tight smile as he pulled into the line of cars leading to the dock, slowly making their way onto the ferry, which didn't look nearly large enough to dock them all. Jude waited until he'd paid and parked in between a minivan and a Prius. A couple got out of the Prius and wandered toward the door leading inside, but he made no move to get out of the truck. "Winter would be tough, but we could live off the grid indefinitely."

"That's impressive." She didn't know the first thing about what it would take to manage that, but it had to be difficult. More than difficult. And yet Sloan had no doubt that with the proper preparation he could keep them alive and as close to comfortable as possible.

Jude turned off the truck, removing what little light they'd had. There was a sole bulb shining from the door to the inside of the ferry, but it might as well have been on Mars for all that it illuminated them.

"Is that what you want to do? Take off into the woods with me?" He asked it oh so carefully.

He'd been doing that a lot since they left Callaway Rock, at least after her conversation with Teague. Everything was as close to hesitant as Jude was capable of. She appreciated that he cared enough to try to be gentle with her, but it felt awkward and strange, and not like the way they were at all.

So she did the one thing she knew would put them back on familiar ground.

Sloan slid across the bench seat and crawled into his lap. His hands settled on her hips, his face almost lost in the darkness. "I'm not in the mood."

"Really?" She reached between them to stroke him, finding him already hard. "How long is this ferry ride going to take?"

"Fifty minutes."

"Plenty of time." She kept stroking him through his jeans, never taking her eyes off his face. "Everything is changing and I know neither of us planned on this, and we're both terrified in our own ways, so I could really use some comfort."

He chuckled, and she knew she had him. Jude used his thumbs to inch her dress up. "You find my cock comforting."

"Very." She dipped her hands beneath his shirt, scraping her nails lightly across his chest. "I still want you." She unbuttoned his jeans, and then he was in her hand, hot and hard and ready for her. "God, I want you so much, it makes me wild."

"Trust me, sunshine, the feeling is more than mutual." He pulled her panties to the side, dragging his thumb over her, spreading her wetness up across her clit. She hissed out a breath, almost shaking with need. He knew. He always knew. "It's been hours since I had you, and I'm going to hell for this, but the feeling of you without a fucking condom is perfection. I want it again. Now."

Good. That was exactly what she wanted, too. "Yes."

"I'm clean. We had that conversation, but it's worth saying again. I can get you test results—"

"Jude, it's okay. I trust you." And she did. They'd already crossed over the one boundary there was no going back from. Not for her. It struck her that they hadn't had that conversation—*any* conversation. She froze, her desire temporarily derailed.

"What is it?"

"I...we..." She tried to catch her breath, but a band appeared around her chest, threatening to choke the life out of her. *What if he wants me to get an abortion? What if I want to get an abortion?* She couldn't say it. She couldn't even ask. "The baby..."

He went tense beneath her. "Tell me what you're thinking."

She didn't want to, but life was full of hard conversations and this wouldn't be the first or the last they'd have. So she braced herself. "Do you want to terminate the pregnancy?"

"Are you fucking kidding me?" She flinched and he immediately lowered his voice, but the tone was no less fierce. "Don't get me wrong. It's your choice. I might be a bastard and a half, but I would never take that choice away from you. But don't think for a second that I don't want that baby, no matter how new this whole thing is to me. I never thought I'd be a father. I never *wanted* to be a father, but I'll figure that shit out as I go."

She released a breath she hadn't been aware she was holding. "I see."

"So there's the real question—do *you* want to terminate the pregnancy?" He asked it with no inflection. No judgment or trying to persuade her to go one way or another on the decision. Just a simple question that wasn't the least bit simple.

She sat back, but she was still too close, too aware of him, so she slid off his lap and retreated to her side of the seat. And he let her. She stared into the darkness. "I've always wanted kids. That seems even more naive than you already thought I was, especially considering the fact that any child of mine would be a political player, because any *husband* of mine would be a political player. I'd almost resigned myself to that truth before Teague offered me a chance out, and that changed everything." She pressed a hand to her stomach, though she knew there was no change, no indication of the tiny life now growing there.

"And now?"

And now she'd gotten her first taste of freedom, and what a real life could be like, and she was well aware that a child would restrict her new freedom in a significant way. Not to mention the man beside her might not be her father's choice for a political match, but it was a political match all the same. *And just as likely to get both myself and any children we have killed.*

But still...

"I want this baby. I know it won't be easy or uncomplicated and I know that you and I barely know each other, but it doesn't matter. I want this baby, and I'll fight to keep it."

* * *

Jude reached for Sloan before he bothered to try to talk himself out of it. *She's keeping the baby.* He hadn't expected the relief her words brought. He'd told her the truth—he never planned on kids. But a kid with Sloan...Jude wanted that. He wanted that more than he could have anticipated. If anyone back in Boston thought to use their child as a pawn, he'd dig their grave himself.

He pulled Sloan back into his lap, needing to hold her, and rested his chin on the top of her head. "If you change your mind—"

"I won't."

"All the same. *If* you do, tell me." He wouldn't like it, but he hadn't been lying when he told her that it was her choice. The only way he could force the issue was to chain her up in a basement somewhere until she had the baby, and that was a level of sadistic that he would never resort to for an enemy, let alone to a woman he cared about.

"Promise me that you'll put an end to this unholy alliance with Dmitri Romanov."

He pulled back enough to look down at her. "No."

"What?"

"No. I don't like the man and I don't trust him, but I'll do whatever it takes to keep you and our baby safe. If that means I have to lie down with the devil himself and compromise what little honor I have left, I'll do it gladly."

Her lips parted in shock. "I would never ask that of you."

"I know." She didn't have to.

It was too much to ask for that any child of his would have a normal life. But if anyone was going to be making sacrifices, it would be him.

Not Sloan.

Sure as fuck not their child.

She shook her head, harder this time. "No. That's the whole point. We've become like a snake eating its own tail. Violence begets violence, and we have a chance to get out—truly get out." She twisted the hem of her skirt around her fingers. "I just...We barely know each other. I'm well aware of that. But what if the way to keep our baby safe isn't to compromise your honor or get into bed with Dmitri Romanov? What if the thing we need to do is to get on a plane and never look back?"

There was sense in what she said. He might not like it, but that was the truth.

His whole landscape had altered with the news that she was pregnant. While he grew up, there had only been him and his mother, and then she'd left him behind permanently and there'd been only Jude and his vengeance. *That* was his truth.

But what if it didn't have to be?

He looked at Sloan, trying to picture what the kind of life she suggested would even look like. He had no frame of reference. He just didn't fucking know.

"What if we did get to know each other better?" he said. What they needed most right now was time, and that might be the one thing they didn't have.

She twisted on her dress until her knuckles went white. "I would like that."

"Then why do you look like you're about to throw yourself out of my truck and try to swim for the shore?" He pointed at her knotted dress. "You're freaking the fuck out right now."

"What an astute observation, Jude. I *am* freaking out a little. I don't know how to be a mother, and I don't know how to be in a relationship—if that's even what you're talking about. You're being so incredibly careful with me that I have no way of knowing what in God's name you want— aside from our baby."

Our baby.

Would he ever get used to hearing those words? To *thinking* those words? It was beyond comprehension that some nine months from now, she'd be bringing their kid into the world.

So he didn't focus on that.

Jude rotated to face her fully. "So let's take a week. There isn't a damn thing that needs to be decided before then." Except he needed to figure out what the hell he was going to do about Romanov's threat. It might be a matter of delving into the file he had on the man and figuring out something to use for leverage to buy himself a bit more time.

"A week." Sloan blinked. "You can't get to know a person in a week."

"You sure about that, sunshine? Because I know your body as well as my own and we've barely been fucking more than a week." He squeezed her knee, sliding his hand up her thigh. "I know that you like it when I push you to the limit and beyond. I know exactly where to touch you to make you go soft and wanting." He reached the apex of her thighs and cupped her, stroking her softly over her cotton panties. "Tell me, what other man knows as much about you?"

Her lips parted, even though she didn't look totally convinced. "If I wasn't a virgin when we met, there would be others who knew that."

"That's where you're wrong. Fucking is the lowest common denominator. Just because some little shit has had his cock inside you doesn't mean he knows your clit from your big toe—and it sure as hell doesn't mean he knows how to get you off." He snagged the band of her panties and dipped his hand inside, sliding a single finger into her. "Not like me. You could have been with a hundred assholes, and that would still be the God's honest truth."

She hooked a leg over his, opening for him, and let her head fall back to rest against the seat. "You're unbelievably arrogant."

"I know my strengths." He stroked her with one hand and used the other to tug her dress off one shoulder, baring her breast in the faint light. "And I know you. I might not know your favorite food or your favorite book, but I know that you're stronger than you give yourself credit for. I know you've been kept cooped up, your wings clipped, and that freedom is a heady thing. That you'll fight tooth and nail to keep from having to give it up."

Jude leaned down and tongued her nipple, lightly raking his teeth over it until she gasped and her hands came up to dig in his hair. "I'll never cage you, sunshine. It's not my way. I'd rather watch you learn to fly instead."

She shuddered, her hips rising to take his finger as he slowly slid it in and out of her. "You seem to think you know a lot."

"Tell me I'm wrong."

Sloan covered his hand with her own, guiding a second finger into herself. "You're not wrong."

Jude smiled against her skin. "I know."

CHAPTER TWENTY-TWO

Sloan stepped out of the truck and looked around. The ferry had deposited them onto Orcas Island, and they'd left the quaint little town around the dock behind, driving into the thick trees. It had almost been possible to forget they were on an island at all, but Jude had taken a turn and suddenly the Sound was there, the water dark and fathomless, and similar enough to the ocean at Callaway Rock to make her heart ache.

She forced her gaze away from the water to take in the house. It wasn't extravagant by any means, but there was something charming about it all the same. The thick wooden timbers created a worn look that could have been built five years ago or a hundred, and the front door was oversized with a giant iron knocker. She shot a look at Jude, only to find him watching her. "What?"

"I've never brought anyone here before." He led the way to the front door and unlocked it, holding it open for her. "Stay here."

She started to ask why, but then it hit her that he was likely going to sweep the house. Sloan nodded and wrapped her arms around herself. She knew how to shoot—in theory. Teague had dragged her and their other sisters out to a range a few times, but the gun he'd tried to convince Sloan was a good fit for her had felt cold and alien in her hands. She didn't like guns. They were part of the world—of *her* world—but she didn't want anything to do with them.

She wished she'd paid more attention now.

Standing there while she listened for Jude's footsteps, she felt worse than useless. She took a step farther into the hallway, looking around. The place didn't seem like a house that had been abandoned for months on end. There was no dust, and the whole room smelled faintly of evergreen. She inhaled deeply, taking in the big leather couches arranged around a massive river rock fireplace. The mantel looked like driftwood and sturdy enough for her to use it to scale the wall if she was so inclined.

Large windows took up the walls at the front and back of the house, giving a plain view of Jude's truck and of the water. There wasn't a beach, the ground dropping off sharply, though she wouldn't know what kind of drop it would be without going outside to investigate.

"Sloan."

She turned to find him at the bottom of the stairs. "It's clear?"

"No one's been here but the local woman I have come in every couple of weeks to clean. Her family has lived on the island for a couple generations and she's got no ties to any of my enemies, though I monitor the situation."

He would. Even without taking his family into account,

being a hit man would generate enemies. It had to. "How does it work?" She motioned in a general direction. "The killing people thing."

Jude raised an eyebrow. "'The killing people thing'?"

"Don't do that. Don't patronize me. It's a perfectly legitimate question."

"I didn't say it wasn't." He rubbed a hand over his face. "It's a business transaction. I have an in-between man who accepts the jobs, and then I double-check the target and the information—no innocents under any circumstances. If I'm satisfied, I accept payment—seventy-five percent up front, the remainder after the kill is confirmed."

It seemed so cold, but then she supposed it'd have to be. A hit man was the very definition of distanced and icy—to be any other way was to invite mistakes and an inevitably short lifespan as a result. "How many?"

"Do you really want to know?"

She started to say yes, and then stopped and thought about it. Would it make a difference? The facts of their meeting and the gray area that represented their future weren't affected in the least by how many people he'd killed. It felt almost like asking a lover how many partners they'd had—something she most certainly would *not* ask Jude. The past mattered only in reference to the present. "I suppose it doesn't matter."

"I've killed enough people to get good at it. I'm one of the best."

"Do you like it?"

"I won't spin some bullshit fairy tale about how they all deserved killing. Some did, some didn't, but they all did something to earn the contract on their lives. I don't love it, but I don't lose sleep at night, either. I'm not a good man, sunshine. I'm one of the worst the world has to offer. Don't try to make me some hero."

Was that what he really thought?

She lifted her chin. "Well, I'm not exactly a blushing innocent, either. If I were the precious good girl you seem to think I am, I would have done something to stop all the hurt my family caused, even if it meant turning them over to the authorities. I know where the books are kept. I know where some of the bodies are buried. I could have. I didn't. Sitting passively by might not make me a full-fledged monster, but I'm not a saint, either. So stop expecting me to flinch away from you or faint into a dainty puddle at your feet."

"Strip."

She blinked. "I'm sorry, what?"

"You've convinced me." He didn't grin; his expression didn't so much as give a flicker of warmth. "Take off that tease of a sundress or I'm going to rip it off like I did the last one."

Her body went warm and then hot, her legs shaking a little, her nipples pebbling against the thin fabric of her dress. One sentence was all it took and her body readied itself for him. She pressed her lips together, considering. "How much property around the house do you own?"

"I own half the island." He narrowed his eyes. "Why?"

Maybe it was the darkness making her bold, or the fact that he was here and sharing bits of himself in a way he never had before. Or maybe she was just a little wilder than she could have dreamed. She took a step back, and then another, shrugging her dress off one shoulder.

He tracked her movement, his whole body going still like a predator about to pounce. "You're playing games."

"Yes." She inched her dress off her other shoulder and it

fell to her hips. A slight shimmy and she was left in only her panties. She reached the door, hooking her thumbs in the band and pushing them down. "I am."

And then she ran.

* * *

Jude gave Sloan a five-second head start—not because he was being generous, but because he couldn't believe she'd just stripped and then run away. He made it to the door in time to catch sight of her pale skin disappearing into the trees surrounding the house. His cock went so hard, it was a wonder he didn't pass the fuck out.

He'd never stuck with a woman long enough for her to figure out what made him tick. He'd never wanted to. He was more than capable of getting off whoever he was with and getting himself off in the bargain. Doing more—wanting more—had never entered into the equation.

Fuck, if someone had asked him if he got off on the idea of chasing a naked woman through the woods, he would have said no—said *hell no*. But then, he'd never put much thought into that sort of thing.

Now he was.

Jude stalked after Sloan, purposefully letting her get a little distance on him. He knew these woods. This was one of the places he came after a job to unwind and center himself before he was fit for polite society again. He had a house in Florida and another in Maine, but this was the one he preferred. It was quiet. Peaceful.

He didn't feel the least bit peaceful right now.

Sloan let loose a breathless laugh and he started to jog, loping after her. He half expected her to pause and taunt him, but she caught sight of him over her shoulder and picked up her pace. *She's going to make me work for it.*

Good.

He raced after her, closing the distance easily despite the fact she was moving at a good clip. "Little tease, aren't you?"

She dove sideways, his fingertips barely brushing her long hair as she changed directions. He grabbed a tree trunk, using it to slingshot his way after her, not losing any momentum in the process. Jude snagged her around the waist, rolling as they fell so she landed on top of him.

Sloan wiggled and fought, getting half out of his grasp before he rolled again, pinning her against the forest floor. Her dark eyes were alight with mischief and she let loose a laugh that made his heart actually skip a beat.

"Submit, sunshine."

"Never." She bit his shoulder.

He wrenched her arms over her head and shifted his hips until he was between her thighs. "You're not going anywhere, you little hellion." He thrust against her, liking the way her eyes slid half-closed. "But you don't want to, do you? You want me to fuck you right here in the dirt like an animal."

She thrashed and a little moan slipped free. "That's not what I want."

"You sure about that?" He shifted her wrists to a single hand and reached between them with the other to stroke her. "You're awfully fucking wet for something you don't want." Jude dragged his mouth up her throat. "I like this game. So unless you tell me to stop right this fucking second, I'm going to take you here."

He lifted his head to find her lips pressed together, her

expression daring him to put his money where his mouth was. She knew he'd do it. He'd bet she was counting on it.

"That's what I thought." He kissed her, thrusting his tongue into her mouth and groaning when she met him every step of the way, kissing him so hard, their teeth clinked together. It didn't matter. Nothing mattered but how hot and sweet she was in his arms and the fact she was *his*.

He stopped fucking her with his fingers to unbutton his jeans and work them off his hips enough to free his cock. He dragged the head through her wetness and up over her clit, watching her face the entire time. "You like that. Fuck, you love it. You love that I chased you, that anyone could be walking in these woods and see that hot little body of yours, to see me about to fuck you until you scream for me." He circled her clit with his cock.

"Yes." She arched her back, shoving her breasts against him. "I love everything you do to me."

He liked that she didn't even try to deny it. In fact, he fucking loved that Sloan had no qualms about meeting him every step of the way from their very first time. Jude notched his cock at her entrance and shoved into her, sheathing himself to the hilt. He took her hard, thrusting until her breasts bounced and she moaned every time he slammed into her cervix. Nothing else mattered but the woman beneath him and the pursuit of their mutual pleasure.

Can't get enough of her.
Don't even want to try.

He let go of her wrists and put his hand on the ground to get better leverage and cursed when a rock damn near sliced the shit out of his palm. Jude froze. *What the hell was I thinking?* He sat back, taking her with him, already touching her back before he got settled, feeling for any cuts. "Are you okay?"

"Don't you dare. I'm fine." She lifted herself almost completely off his cock and slammed down. "I'm about to come, Jude. Don't stop."

Holy fuck, this woman is something else.

"Leave you wanting? Never." He looped an arm around her waist and captured her left nipple in his mouth, flicking it with his tongue in the way he knew she liked. She shuddered and picked up her pace.

"Harder." She yanked on his hair, pulling him closer.

He lifted his head and *looked* at her. Her eyes were wild, her pale skin streaked with dirt, her dark hair tangled with leaves. She was like a forest nymph, more at one with the nature around them than with the civilization they'd left behind. He tightened his grip, preventing her from moving over him. "Harder."

"That's what I said." She tried to roll her hips and hissed out a breath when he wouldn't let her. "If you're not going to do it, at least have the decency to hold still and let *me* do it."

He pinched her nipple, just enough to hurt. "You're not in charge here, sunshine."

"Then *act* like it."

Enough. He lifted her off him, took a quick glance around, and stood. He didn't give her a chance to snarl at him again, pulling her half-off her feet and slamming her hands onto a nearby tree. "You want me to fuck you. Hard."

"Yes."

He pulled off his shirt, needing to feel her skin against his, and covered her from behind, his chest against her back. There were scratches there, just like he suspected. He ignored them. "You want me to fuck you hard."

"Stop saying it and *do it*."

He grabbed the back of her neck and bent her forward. "To make it hurt. To make you feel alive." He slammed into her, hard enough that she had to catch herself on the tree, her fingers digging into the bark. She moaned, so he did it again. "I love the sound you make when my cock is buried deep inside you. It's helpless and needy for something only I can give you." He slammed into her again, reaching around to stroke her clit, alternating the little circles with a pinch that made her entire body go tight. "Your tight little pussy makes me wild. *You* make me wild." He thrust deep, timing it with another light pinch of her clit, and she went wild around him. "That's right, sunshine. Come for me."

"*Jude.*"

He lost it, releasing her clit to grab her hips and fuck her until his balls drew up almost painfully and he came long and hard. And still he moved behind her, unable to stop. "Fuck, I could take you again right now."

Sloan moaned, clenching around him. "You make me as wild as I make you."

"Good." He forced himself to withdraw from her, to do up his jeans, and hand her his shirt, even though a dark part of him wanted nothing more than to keep her naked and wanting until they were too exhausted to move.

Sloan pulled his shirt on, wincing a little. "You may have been right about the change of positions." He scooped her up, ignoring her squeal of surprise. Sloan smacked his chest. "What are you doing?"

"I'm wearing shoes. You aren't. I'm making sure the bottoms of your feet don't take any more damage." And hell if he didn't want to just hold her for a few minutes.

That was new, too.

CHAPTER TWENTY-THREE

Sloan woke to the sunlight on her face. She opened her eyes and squinted at Jude sitting in a chair across the room, a screwdriver in his hand as he worked on something she couldn't see. She sat up and rubbed at her eyes. "Do you ever sleep?"

"Not often. I never have." He looked tired, though; the lines around his mouth and eyes deeper than they had been when she'd met him.

"What are you doing?"

"Repairing my roofing coil gun. Some of the shingles on the roof were blown off since I was here last, so I'll need to get up there and replace them sometime today."

Was there no end to what this man was capable of? He was deadly, could survive off the grid for who knew how long, and he was handy, too.

She resisted the urge to tell him to come to bed. If he did, the last thing they'd be doing was sleeping, and right now talking was more important. So Sloan tucked the sheet more tightly around her and propped her chin on her knees. "We need some sort of plan when it comes to the future. I don't expect you to marry me." He sent her a sharp look, which she pointedly ignored. "But there are things to consider. If you plan on being part of the baby's life, then there needs to be some sort of schedule worked out. I need a job—"

"I can more than provide for anything you need."

She ignored that, too. "All the same, I will be getting a job." As he was so fond of telling her, Jude was no white knight. He might be willing to take care of her, but she wanted more than that for herself. Even if she didn't, their relationship—such as it was—was already too unbalanced in some ways. She needed her independence, and if he didn't respect that, this was going to end before it had a chance to begin.

For a moment, he looked like he might argue, but then he gave a short nod. "You want to work out the semantics."

"Exactly."

Jude paced a lap around the room and then stopped at the foot of the bed. "Tell me something. I get that you value your ability to hold your own, and that's a respectable thing."

She tensed. "I'm sensing a 'but' coming."

"But because of who we are, our kid will be in danger from the moment he or she is born. Fuck, sunshine, the baby is in danger *now* and it's barely the size of a lima bean. So you might as well give up on any dream involving white picket fences and the kind of lifestyle that involves deep roots. That shit doesn't exist for people like us."

"Why not?" She hated the look on his face when she asked the question, the look that said she should really be smarter than to challenge his assumption. She lifted her chin. "The world is a big place. Yes, I know it's smaller than it used to be, but there's no reason we couldn't go somewhere where no one has heard of either the O'Malleys or the MacNamaras. It would require cutting all ties, but it's still possible." She pressed her lips together against the need to ask him why he couldn't just leave it all behind. It wasn't that simple. She *knew* it wasn't that simple.

Except it was for her.

Sloan sighed and climbed off the bed. She dug through her suitcase and came up with a pair of yoga pants and a tank top. "My point is that *I* have a plan, fledgling that it is. You're the one who appears to still be clinging to the past. Which is fine. I understand that some things are impossible to leave behind. But a future with me and a future where you're still hunting down Colm Sheridan are, unfortunately, mutually exclusive."

If he killed Colm, Callie would hunt him to the ends of the earth, just like he'd been doing to her family. She loved her father—apparently whatever issues Ronan had with the man, she hadn't inherited them. Even with a baby on the way, Callie would be fierce in her need for vengeance. Jude would be fanning a flame that was almost out.

"You're offering me an ultimatum."

He would see it that way. She waited until she was dressed to continue. "No, I'm telling you the truth. You say that you'll do whatever it takes to keep our child safe. In what world would creating another powerful enemy go hand in hand with his or her safety?" He still didn't understand, whether willfully or genuinely. She took a breath. "You're out. Whether you're responsible for Ronan Sheridan's death or not, whether Sorcha thinks you're a danger or not, you're *out*. As far as anyone is concerned, he drank too much and wrapped his car around a telephone pole, and no one is going to believe what that old woman says now that they know what her plans were. No one is hunting for an enemy to kill. If you hurt Colm, they will be. What did your family do to make Colm so mad all those years ago?"

"It's not important."

"Isn't it?" She wanted to shake him until he saw things her way, but that would only make him dig in his heels deeper. She couldn't force him, no matter how much she wanted to.

But that didn't mean she would stand silently by. She'd done that most her life, and there was more at stake than there ever had been before. "Your father was the reason Moira Sheridan died. Think about that for a second. He hurt her, and Colm committed acts beyond forgiveness in retribution. Callie might be leaning toward making their power base as legal as it can be, but she's just as ruthless as her father when she's cornered—and, for all his faults, she loves him. He's a good father to her. Do you think for a second that she won't burn this world to the ground hunting down his killer? You'd be starting the cycle of vengeance over, and it would be the next generation that pays for our sins." She headed for the door.

"Where are you going?"

"I'm incredibly tense and angry right now, and arguing more will accomplish about as much good as beating my head against a brick wall. I'm going to do yoga." A pang went through her when she realized she'd never do yoga with Jessica again by the ocean. Another life left behind, this one just as bittersweet as Boston. She looked at Jude looming in the doorway. "Please move."

He stepped aside without a word. *Good.* She was a fool and a half for thinking Jude would suddenly set aside everything he'd worked for just for *her.*

I set out planning to be alone. Now I'll just have to plan to be alone with a baby.

What was she going to do as a single mother?

* * *

Jude changed into a pair of shorts and tennis shoes and went running. He couldn't stand to be pent up in that house any longer, not with Sloan's words ringing in his ears. She was asking him to change. No, that wasn't right. She was very careful about *not* asking him to change. But she was demanding it of him all the same. He picked up speed, weaving between the trees.

Give up revenge.

Let Colm Sheridan have his happy life while my mother is rotting in the ground.

The thoughts didn't bring their usual tidal wave of rage. He was...tired. So goddamn tired. The path lay before him, as clear as day. Dmitri Romanov was playing hardball and trying to force his hand in killing the remaining Sheridans. Several months ago, that wouldn't have bothered him in the least. He would have shown up, killed Colm, and left Callista alive. Simple.

Now it sat like a rock in his gut.

He couldn't stop seeing Sloan, standing there unflinching in the face of his sins. She understood him. She...Fuck, he didn't know. He'd been telling the truth when he said that they would be hunted if it was found out that she was pregnant with his child.

But she was right, too, in a way. No one knew he was responsible for Ronan's death. Sorcha might suspect what he was about, but she couldn't confirm it—and she had more important things to worry about if Callista was half as ruthless as Sloan claimed. He could leave, could take Sloan and their baby and...What? He couldn't settle down in one place indefinitely. The thought made him feel like he was drowning, the sheer number of future years in the same place a weight on his head pushing him under. That wasn't him. Kids needed stability, though. He didn't know much about them, but he knew that.

It just didn't fit.

If he had half a brain in his head, he'd write her a check and leave. It'd be the best thing he could do for that kid. Sloan was strong. She'd be okay.

Fuck that.

It might be the most selfish thing he'd ever done, but he couldn't let them go. They were *his*. He'd never let anyone close enough to be his, not since his mother went the way of the angels. Who was to say they had to figure out all the dirty details now? He'd tell Sloan that he was in. He had to go to Boston to deal with Romanov's threat, because if he was going to sacrifice his vengeance for Sloan, he had to make sure he wasn't implicated in any murders in the meantime.

If he wasn't going to kill Colm, he'd be damned before someone else did it in his name.

He didn't know if Romanov realized Callista was pregnant, but he couldn't hold his breath and hope the man would have enough morals not to kill a woman with child.

So he'd go to Boston and make sure he and Romanov were on the same page. Jude would have to find somewhere safe to stash Sloan for that—and he had no illusions about how difficult it would be to convince her to stay there—but he'd figure out a way around this mess.

And after...After, they'd find somewhere to hunker down—maybe here—for the next nine months. See if they could really make a go of it without wanting to kill each other. After she had the baby, *then* they'd come up with a plan for their future.

His revenge had waited over thirty years. It could wait one more.

Maybe it could wait forever.

He turned for the house, taking the road back and looking for signs that someone else besides he and Sloan had passed. Last night it had been hard to tell. The house wasn't tampered with, and he'd let himself get distracted with fucking Sloan instead of doing a perimeter check. He'd dropped the ball then, but he wasn't about to make a habit of it.

The bushes lining the middle of the dirt road had been beaten down, but it was hard to say if that was from his vehicle or another. His housekeeper took a different route, something he'd specifically requested. If a stranger was on this island looking for him, they'd come this way, not the little path only known to locals.

Sloppy. Just fucking sloppy all around.

He'd have to do a more thorough check after he talked to Sloan, but the problem with not trusting anyone enough to tell them where his residences were located was that he didn't have anyone he could call in as backup. He'd never needed help before. He was the very definition of a lone wolf, and that was a strength when it came to his business and his plans. There was no need for extra muscle because the only one he had to worry about was himself.

That wasn't true anymore.

He picked up his pace, damn near sprinting down the road. There was no reason to think Sloan was in danger, but he couldn't shake the belief that if he didn't get her in his line of sight immediately, something terrible would happen.

Jude burst out of the trees and ran around the side of the house, slowing only when he saw Sloan doing some weird-ass pose with her head on the ground and her legs posed carefully on her elbows. He looked around, but no threat burst out of the surroundings.

You are freaking the fuck out.

The idea of going completely off the grid was suddenly appealing. He could provide for them indefinitely, and he wouldn't have to worry about Stefan giving away his location to Dmitri if there wasn't some sort of grid to connect to.

Sloan carefully touched her feet to the ground, slid seamlessly into downward dog, and then stood. "Is something wrong?"

Everything. He'd always had a plan, had his feet firmly on the ground and his head on straight. Now up was down and down was up. Nothing made sense anymore. Jude scrubbed a hand over his face. "I think we should leave."

Instantly, she was on alert. "Did someone find us?"

"Not yet."

She frowned. "I don't think I understand."

"I don't trust anyone to keep you safe but me, and this place has too many ways in to be totally secure." Even if he could secure it, he couldn't leave her here alone while he went to Boston. Not only was it impossible to lock down, but if she needed help, she was too isolated for it to get to her in time. *Didn't think this through.* "We need to find a better one."

"No."

"The fuck do you mean, 'no'?" He sounded furious and he knew it, which only served to piss him off. "You said you wanted a plan—"

"And I do. A realistic plan. And the reality is that I'm pregnant." She touched her stomach, and his heart stuttered a little. Sloan visibly braced herself. "Going off the grid is impossible. Even if this is a textbook pregnancy and nothing goes wrong requiring ultrasounds or other tests, are *you* planning on delivering this baby and providing aftercare? What if the baby has a health condition requiring a hospital? What if *I* do? No." She shook her head. "Going off the grid is out of the question."

She presented valid points. They didn't change his desire to wrap her up and take her somewhere where nothing bad would ever touch her. He lifted his hands, and then let them fall to his sides. "Well, fuck. You have me at a loss, sunshine. I want you. I want *this*. But hell if I know how."

"We'll figure it out." She crossed to him and slid into his arms. "Together."

CHAPTER TWENTY-FOUR

A ringing brought Sloan out of sleep. She looked around, but Jude was nowhere to be found. *Typical.* She stumbled out of bed, searching for the source of the ringing. She frowned. It was one of the remaining two burner phones. She frowned harder at the sight of Teague's number on the screen. "Hello?"

"What side of the house are you on?"

She rubbed her face, trying to shake off the last bit of sleep. "What are you talking about?"

"The house on Orcas Island. The one owned by Jude MacNamara, a hit man who has a reputation to keep even me up at night. That house, Sloan—the one you're currently in."

Slow dawning horror made her spin to stare at the window. "What did you do, Teague?"

"What it takes to keep you safe. So tell me where the hell you are. Now."

She shook her head, belatedly realizing that he couldn't

see the motion. "Just leave. We'll pretend this never happened and it won't ruin everything."

"I don't know if you're suffering from Stockholm syndrome or just a shitty decision, but you don't understand what's at stake. He's dangerous."

Yes, he is. She set the phone down carefully and pulled on the first clothing she laid hands on—jeans and a tank top—before picking it up again. "Please don't do this, Teague."

"It's too late." There was no mercy in his voice. None for her, and certainly none for Jude.

He thinks he's doing the right thing. She'd underestimated her brother's reaction when she told him who Jude was, but she hadn't thought he'd track her down after securing Sorcha, let alone so quickly... Sloan turned and cast a suspicious look at her luggage. "How did you find us?"

"That's not important."

Shock temporarily stole her words as she realized what he'd done. "You didn't. Tell me you didn't put a tracker in my things."

"Where. In. The. House? Tell me or get under a fucking bed, because my men are coming in."

Jude. She slid through the door and headed for the stairs, nearly stumbling over Jude as he walked up them. He took one look at her face and went from relaxed to on guard. She held up a finger. "I'm begging you, Teague. Don't do this." She hung up and dropped the phone to the ground. "We're in trouble."

"How much time do we have?" Glass splintered somewhere downstairs, and Jude nodded to himself. "None. Got it."

"I'm sorry."

"You couldn't have known. I should have." He glanced over his shoulder and then he was on the move, ushering her into a room she hadn't been in before. It appeared to be an

office of sorts, massive bookshelves framing the windows
and a large desk on the other side of the room. He stalked
to the bookshelf against the inner wall and pulled, the entire
case sliding out to reveal a doorway.

"You've got to be joking me."

"This house used to be owned by a smuggler. He wasn't
as famous as some of the ones back east, but he made sure
there was an exit strategy in place. Several, in fact."

She hurried through the gap after him and waited while
he closed the bookshelf. The fit was so close, there wasn't
even a seam of light to give its position away. Jude touched
the small of her back, his breath ghosting against her ear.
"The walls are fucking thin, so be as quiet as you can."

"Okay."

He took her hand, leading her down a set of narrow
stairs and then to a second set that seemed to go beneath
the house. It was hard to say, but when she pressed a hand
against the wall, it was far colder than she expected. *We're
below the ground.* She shivered.

"We're almost there." Jude sounded tense. Focused. But
not angry.

He should be. It was her stupid naïveté that had led her
not to check her things for a bug. Not that she'd know what
one would look like if she found it. She should have considered that Teague would have a way to track her if things
went sideways, or if she decided to flee from where he'd
placed her.

At the very least, she should have talked to Jude about it.

"Here." He let go of her hand long enough to open a
door, letting the barest light filter in. Outside. She stepped
into a cave and looked around. It was just tall enough for
her—Jude had to hunch over to get through the doorway

and shut the door behind him. They stood on a small rock shelf barely an inch above the water, and there wasn't any exit readily apparent.

"Jude?"

"You're not going to like this next part." He shucked off his shirt and boots. "The ledge out into the Sound is too low for a boat, so we have to swim. It'll be cold, but not life-threatening."

"*Swim?*" She looked back at the doorway they'd just come through. "You're serious."

"Sorry, sunshine." He dropped his boots on the rock shelf and cocked his head to the side. "They might not find the passageway down here, but we can't take that chance. They're going to rip that house apart trying to find you."

"I'm sorry."

"Don't be." He slid into the water and felt around. "There's a spot here. You aren't going to want to stay in the water longer than necessary, August or no." He paused. "Shit. You can swim, can't you?"

"Yes." She shimmied out of her jeans—they would only weigh her down—and followed him into the water. The cold shocked a gasp out of her, but she did her best to focus. "Where are we swimming to?"

Something like approval flared in Jude's dark eyes. "There's an inlet if you follow the coastline north. You'll know it because there isn't a damn way out of the water until then. Be careful. The currents are a little strange around here."

His phrasing wasn't right. Unless... "You're coming with me, aren't you?"

"Yes. Eventually." He cast a look up. "There's something I need from the house first."

She started to demand to know why he hadn't grabbed it

when they first fled, but the truth hit her. He'd put her first. Getting her out and safe had been his first priority.

Sloan warmed despite the ice-cold water. She wanted to tell him to forget whatever was back there, but some things were worth compromising and some weren't. Jude had taken a step toward putting his vengeance aside and creating a future with her. If he felt strongly enough to go back for something, she had to grit her teeth and deal with it, despite her fear for his safety.

So she nodded. "Be safe."

"I will." He hesitated. "I'll try not to kill any of your brother's men, but I can't make any promises."

"Thank you." She pulled him in for a quick kiss. "But do what you have to in order to come back to me safely." She pushed off before she could think too closely about the danger he was going back into, swimming for the gap in the rock leading out into the Sound. She stuck close to the rock ledge, but she had to stop for a moment in awe as Jude shot past her, more seal than human, his strong arms cutting through the water. He grabbed the edge of the cliff and pulled himself out of the water, scaling it fast enough to steal her breath.

He's magnificent.

She pushed forward again, all too aware that she wasn't in any sort of shape to be able to swim indefinitely, even with the exercise she'd been getting since living in Callaway Rock. Already, her muscles cried out in protest, her breath coming in short gasps.

She almost sobbed with relief when the inlet came into sight. She swam harder, fighting her way to the tiny rock beach. It took a few minutes to figure out where Jude had hidden the boat—it was cleverly disguised as a boulder beneath some shrubbery—and uncover it.

Then she sat down, cold and shivering despite the relatively warm day, to wait.

* * *

Jude hated knowing Sloan was alone in the water, but there
were things in that house he couldn't leave behind. Not even
for her. He moved through the trees, more ghost than man despite his soaked pants. He expected some sort of resistance, but
the fools had been so focused on getting into the house, they
hadn't set a perimeter. An amateur mistake and not one they'd
have made if they really understood the threat he was.

He climbed a tree with perfectly placed notches. It was
one of the only ones he'd allowed close to the house, exactly for this reason. He moved across the branches to the
roof. The widow's walk on the third floor appeared only
decorative, but there was a narrow staircase leading down
directly to the first-floor pantry. It was the perfect place to
hide valuables—something the original owner of the house
utilized. Jude had taken a page from his book and stashed
his bag in this room every time he stayed here. The worst
that could happen was a fire, and even if it did, he could
grab his shit and escape into the trees.

The bastard who'd built the house had been a paranoid
fuck, something Jude appreciated, especially considering
his current circumstances.

He could hear the O'Malley men moving through the
house below him, their frustration evident. They'd trash the
place before they were through. A pang went through him
at the thought. He might only come here a few times a year,
but this was one of the few places in the world he considered safe. It never would be again—and not just because

he'd never set foot in the place after today. It was being defiled by the men below him, tearing the place apart and leaving their imprint everywhere.

He should have known that nowhere was truly safe.

The truth was that there would always be someone gunning for him—gunning for *her*. *Should have considered that her brother would put a tracker on her.* He hadn't considered a lot of things when it came right down to it. That was his fuckup. She was new to the game. He'd been living it his entire life.

Jude slipped through the small door and worked his way down to the first floor. He was in the process of sliding the pantry wall back into place when footsteps sounded at his back. He twisted as the enemy's gun came up, grabbing his wrist and pointing the pistol away from him.

Then he saw the man's face.

Micah Jones.

This wasn't an O'Malley man. This was a motherfucking *Sheridan.*

Micah opened his mouth, likely to call for help, and Jude let go of his wrist long enough to punch him in the gut. Warring thoughts slammed through his head as he punched Micah again.

I promised Sloan I wouldn't kill anyone.

He's not an O'Malley.

He's also barely more than a kid. He wasn't even alive when my family was killed.

That stopped him. He pocketed the handgun and shoved Micah to the ground. The idiot kept trying to stand, obviously not recognizing a losing battle when he saw it. It would be so fucking easy to just put a bullet in his brain and be done with it.

He pistol-whipped Micah, and this time the man lay still. *Finally.* Jude headed for the back door, looking to get the fuck out before he had to kill someone. It wasn't only because of his promise, though he was just getting used to the idea of maybe being worthy of a woman like Sloan. Murdering his way through her brother's men wasn't the way to go about putting them on the right path forward. He was past the point of thinking that it shouldn't matter what Sloan thought of him. It did. He cared about her, and fuck if he'd do anything to hurt her if he had any other choice.

Killing her brother's men would hurt her.

Killing *Colm Sheridan* would hurt her, if only because it would forever cut her off from part of her family.

Painted myself into a goddamn corner with that one, didn't I?

The only warning he got was a slight exhale behind him and a shift in the air. Jude threw himself sideways, slamming into the wall as none other than Teague fucking O'Malley flew past him. The man barely missed a beat, drawing his gun on Jude. "Where is my sister?"

Jude measured the distance between them. Close enough that he had a chance at disarming the man before he got a shot off. Far enough that it wasn't a guarantee. Jude looked up, tracking the sets of footsteps searching. Another six men at least. He could throw himself out the window to his right, but he'd leave a trail of blood straight to the boat that any fool could follow. The back door was a better bet, but he had to go through Teague to get there.

Shit.

"Your sister made her choice."

Teague shook his head. "Forgive me if I don't take your word for it. I'd like to hear her say it herself."

"You did on the phone not too long ago. Who's to say you'll listen any better a second time?" Jude inched toward the door. He could rush the other man and hope for the best. He might get a bullet for his trouble, but as long as it didn't hit anything vital, he had a better chance of covering the blood trail from a single wound than he did if he went through the window. *Best chance I'm going to get.*

"If you're who you say you are, I know what you're here for. I don't even blame you." Teague followed him with the gun, the barrel not wavering in the least. "But the fact remains—if you're looking to hurt my sister or my wife, I'll bury you."

Jude could respect that, though hell if he wanted to. It was so much easier to hate everything about the Boston under-world before he started meeting the players one-on-one. Be-fore Sloan. Jude took another step to the side. "I would never hurt Sloan."

"Holy fuck." Teague's eyes went wide. "Don't think you can play that card with *me*. I know my sister. She would never choose someone like you—not willingly."

"Guess you don't know Sloan as well as you think." He rushed the other man. The gun went off and fire exploded in his side, but he didn't stop. Jude kicked Teague's knee out, then slammed a fist into his face. He didn't go down, but he was stunned long enough for Jude to run through the door and into the trees. Each step hurt like a bitch, but he didn't stop, didn't slow down, didn't do anything but keep one hand on his side to keep the blood blossoming there from hitting the ground.

The pain didn't matter. The fucking wound didn't matter, either.

All that mattered was getting back to Sloan.

CHAPTER TWENTY-FIVE

Sloan nearly screamed when Jude rushed out of the trees, covered in blood and panting. "Oh my God!"

"I didn't...kill...anyone." He stumbled a little, but shook his head when she rushed to his side. "Boat. We have to...go."

"Sit down right this instant." She bit her lip and went to the boat. "I can get it into the water." *Probably.* She didn't wait for his response, digging her bare feet into the rocks and pushing with all her might. The boat moved a few inches, not nearly as heavy as she'd expected. She'd gotten it another few inches closer to the water when Jude appeared next to her. "Sit down."

"Don't have time." He shoved the boat, sending it halfway into the water. "Get in."

There was no time to argue, not with the steady stream of blood trailing down his side. *He's been shot.* Her stomach lurched, but she muscled the reaction down. Her having a meltdown wouldn't do anything but add to their trouble. He wouldn't let her help him until they were away, so she needed to ensure they got somewhere safe where she could patch him up as best she could.

Sloan climbed into the boat, her heart in her throat as he pushed them the rest of the way into the water and rolled over the side to lie in the bottom. "Pull the cord on the engine. Takes a few tries."

She braced herself and yanked, and then again. On the third try, it caught, roaring to life. Sloan tested the handle, quickly discovering the basics of driving. "Where are we going?"

"Sloan!"

She twisted to see Teague standing on the shore, several of his men behind him. She recognized that man who always guarded Callie, Micah, nursing what looked like a broken nose, but the rest of the men were only vaguely familiar. Gauging the distance between the boat and where her brother stood, she gave it a little more gas so he'd have to swim if he came after her. "Go home, Teague."

He shook his head slowly, as if he couldn't believe what he was seeing. "You know I can't do that."

She didn't throw a fit. Didn't scream. Didn't do any of the things she could feel rising in her chest like a trapped bird. Sloan looked at Jude, lying there so pale and with a hole in him that had come as a direct result of her brother not listening to her. He'd never truly listened, not even when he got her out.

Because I wasn't really out. He still had a string attached to me that he could reel in whenever he felt like it.

Betrayal lay hot and thick in the back of her throat. "Then I guess you're no better than our father." She turned and powered the boat out of the inlet, doing her best to ignore the burning of her eyes.

Crying wouldn't solve anything.

It never had.

"I don't know where I'm going."

"Sunshine…" Jude hissed out a breath. "North. Keep to the coastline."

She obeyed and then looked down at him. "What do you need from me? I don't suppose you have some sort of first-aid kit in that bag of yours?"

"Yeah." He huffed out a laugh. Jude levered himself up until he leaned against the front of the boat. "It was a through-and-through. I'll live if I don't bleed out."

She wasn't a doctor, but he looked like he'd lost a significant amount of blood. "Do you have someone we can call?"

"Not on the island." He moved like a man three times his age, carefully pulling out a little white box with the familiar red cross on it. "Second inlet you see is…" He gritted his teeth as he pressed a gauze pad to his side. "Where we're headed."

"I can stop and help."

"No."

Arguing would waste time and energy, and he was right. They hadn't gone that far yet, and if Teague was truly determined to find her and bring her…wherever he intended…then they couldn't afford to be caught. Not when Jude was clearly injured. *But not helpless. I'd never make the mistake of assuming he is helpless.*

She watched with a critical eye as he seemed to slow down the bleeding. He was pale beneath his summer tan, but he didn't seem in danger of passing out like he had been when he first appeared at the boat.

Her attention turned to the bag at his feet. There was something in there—something worth potentially dying for. Curiosity bit her, hard and quick, but it wasn't her business. Not really.

She'd already pressed him hard in the last few days. If she kept it up, it was possible he'd snap back, out of sheer instinct.

He was alive. He was with her. It was enough.

For now.

The inlet was barely more than a sliver between the cliffs that had been getting higher the farther north they went. She would have missed the gap completely if she hadn't been searching for it. She scraped the sides of the boat several times trying to maneuver in, but as soon as she did, she understood why Jude had chosen this place. The top of the cliffs curved inward, creating almost another cave. She found an outcrop of rock to loop the boat tie around, keeping them close enough to the edge that someone above would have to actually climb into the area to be able to see them. "Now what?"

"Now we wait until dark."

She turned to find him trying to get medical tape on with one hand. "Let me help." Sloan didn't give him a chance to argue, taking the tape from his hands and ripping off several tabs. She took the opportunity to look at his injury. It was hard to tell with all the blood, but the entry wound didn't appear too large. "What are the chances it hit something vital?"

"If it had, I'd be dead."

She jerked back in shock, but then resumed taping the pad to him. "I see."

"No point in pussyfooting around the truth." He didn't flinch as he sat up so she could do the same to his back, but she saw the way the muscle tightened in his jaw. "That brother of yours is a dick."

"I'm not arguing with you at the moment." She finished taping him up and carefully sat back. "I knew he was overprotective, but this was way too far."

She'd *told* Teague she was fine, and he completely disregarded her, so sure that he knew better than she did. She loved her brother, but she could no longer trust him. "What's our exit strategy?"

"I don't know." He closed his eyes, looking exhausted. "We can't circle back and hope the plane hasn't been tampered with. They'll be watching the ferries in. This boat can island-hop to a limited degree, but we won't make it far beyond that—and it would still require a ferry back to the mainland."

No easy answer, then. She smoothed back his hair, taking comfort in the simple fact that he was alive and she could touch him to her heart's content. Jude had carried them both since they left Callaway Rock—even before, if she was being honest.

It was time for her to return the favor.

"Do you have a phone in that bag of yours?"

"Yes." He didn't open his eyes. "Are you going to call in the cavalry?"

She hesitated, but he left it at that—just a question. *He trusts my judgment. He trusts me.* That realization shouldn't have been so novel, and it said something truly sad about her history that it was. *Not to mention my seriously dropping the ball with the tracker situation.* Sloan cupped his jaw. "I'm going to try."

"Front pocket."

She found the pocket he'd indicated and pulled the phone out. Truly, there was only one person she could call.

Carrigan.

Sloan closed her eyes, took several deep breaths, and then opened them. *What are the chances that Carrigan hasn't changed her number?* Not likely. Still, she dialed it all the same, reaching out to her older sister for the first time since she'd learned that Carrigan had forsaken the family for James Halloran.

No one else would understand where she was coming from, not about Jude and not about her plans.

No one else would be the least bit sympathetic to her plight.

No one else would stop to consider that she might be perfectly rational about the decision she'd made.

"Hello?"

Her throat tried to close at Carrigan's familiar voice on the other end. "Carrigan...It's me."

"Sloan?"

"I...I'm in trouble. I need your help." She held her breath. She felt like a terrible person for refusing her sister's calls over and over again, and *now* reaching out when she needed something. Carrigan would be well within her rights to rip Sloan a new one and tell her to deal with the mess she'd made.

Instead, she said, "Anything."

* * *

Dmitri climbed out of his town car, motioning the driver to stay where he was. While he couldn't be anywhere in Boston without a degree of danger, he was willing to take his chances for the time being. The building looked like every other warehouse in the district, nondescript and windowless. The street was almost deserted, though he caught the rustling of someone in the shadows. A place for ill deeds.

He stalked to the door, staring at the man standing there until the guy backed off. And then Dmitri was inside, bodies pressing in from all sides, a deep music that he couldn't place rolling through them. The place stank of drugs and sweat and sex, and he wanted little more than to turn around and leave.

It wasn't an option.

He spotted her almost immediately, her thin body draped over a throne on a dais in the center of it all. A couple fucked on the throne next to her, but she paid them no mind, surveying the chaos around her like a queen with her subjects.

He knew the second Keira spotted him, because the leg she had hanging over the throne's arm started bobbing. Dmitri waited, fully expecting her to approach, but she didn't move.

Cheeky.

He made his way through the crowd, and those who didn't part on their own were tugged out of the way by their friends. Dmitri stepped onto the dais, raised an eyebrow at the couple still in the midst of their frenzy, and moved to stand in front of Keira.

She twisted a length of hair around her finger. "You're blocking my view."

"And you have something of mine."

She finally looked at him and smirked. "Considering you didn't cancel your cards, I took that as tacit permission. They're at the bottom of the Charles now."

He hadn't canceled his cards because he'd been curious to see what she'd do. She'd maxed out his cash withdrawals, which she shouldn't have been able to do without him there, and then she'd gone on a shopping spree. "One woman should not need ten thousand dollars' worth of lingerie."

"Shows what you know." There went her foot, bobbing again.

He took in her clothing. "How much of what you're wearing did I purchase for you?"

Keira gave him a wicked grin that didn't reach her eyes. "I guess you'll have to strip me down to find out."

It was all too easy to picture doing exactly that. Her black tank top was more holes than fabric, showing long slices of skin and a flash of black lace covering her breasts. Her pleated skirt was the traditional schoolgirl plaid, but that's where the similarities ended. The thing was as much of a tease as her shirt; what little fabric was there was riding up and making no effort to hide the tops of the fishnet thigh highs and garters she wore. "We covered this during our last encounter."

"You don't fuck children. I remember." She arched an eyebrow. "Tell me, Dmitri, do I look like a child to you?"

What she looked like was a woman in need of a thorough fucking, rough and uncontrolled—the kind of fucking that caused property damage.

He gave himself a shake, forcing his body back under control. "You look like a spoiled brat."

"That's rich coming from you." She laughed and shifted, giving him a glimpse of red lacy panties as she righted herself on the throne and leaned forward, her face at the same height as his cock. Keira eyed him. "Tell me something."

"I'll consider it." He stared at her sinfully curved lips, doing his damnedest to remind himself why he was here to begin with. He turned, finding the man he'd had following Keira in the first place, and nodded.

Mikhail strode up to the dais and grabbed Keira, tossing her over his shoulder and marching for the door. Dmitri followed, staring down anyone who looked like they might protest. There weren't many. An entire crowd full of people and exactly two appeared as if they weren't okay with witnessing a kidnapping. *These are the people she surrounds herself with. Unforgivable.*

His driver had the door open and waiting, and Mikhail

deposited her in there and shoved her back when she im-mediately tried to claw her way to freedom. He glanced askance at Dmitri, but he wasn't in the mood for an audi-ence. "Go."

Mikhail shoved Keira back one last time and slammed the door shut. Dmitri strode around the car and slid into the backseat, listening for the driver to engage the locks once more and for the car to lurch into motion. Satisfied they wouldn't be interrupted, he turned to Keira. "Now we can have a conversation."

She shoved her hair out of her eyes. "I know kidnapping worked out well for James Halloran, but he actually had the decency to fuck my sister before he took her."

"I—"

"Don't fuck children. You keep saying it." She took a slow breath and he could actually see the walls come back up, the panic disappearing and being replaced by arrogance. Keira leaned back against the seat and crossed her long legs, making her skirt ride up even farther. "You want to know what I think?"

He found that he did, which didn't suit his purposes one bit. "No."

She tossed her hair over one shoulder. "I think you can chant that I'm a child all you want, but we both know that I'm not. For fuck's sake, I haven't been a virgin for years."

The thought of some sweating teenager fumbling at her panties wasn't one Dmitri relished—and the thought of a grown man taking her in that way before she was eighteen made him downright murderous. He knew himself well enough to recognize that for the warning sign it was. "The fact remains."

"Does it?" She leaned over, taking his hand and sliding

it up her thigh to cup her. He hissed out a breath to find her panties soaked. Keira met his gaze. "Take me home and this is yours."

She's bargaining her body for her safety.

He jerked his hand away, though he could still feel her against his fingers, the barest barrier of lace between them. "I am taking you home."

She frowned. "I never pegged you for a liar. Murderer, yes. Torturer, most definitely, but not a liar."

"I don't lie."

Her gaze cleared and he realized for the first time that she was startlingly close to sober. "It's a power play. You're going to dump me on my family's doorstep to make a point that you can get to their dearest baby sister whenever you want to." She crossed her legs. "Are you going to rough me up a bit first? Or—"

"No." He shouldn't have let her take his hand. It was a mistake. Now all he could think about was how close she sat and how few barriers there were between them. He glanced out the window, checking their progress. *Not fast enough.*

"Some criminal mastermind you are."

He turned and pinned her with a look. "I would think you'd be relieved that you'll be left unharmed." It was the memory of her on his fingertips that had more words escaping, words he had no intention of giving voice to. "Or would you rather I rip off that pathetic excuse for panties and take what you've been waving in front of me since we met?"

Her eyes went wide and her breathing picked up. "You've said that you wouldn't."

"And you've pointed out that my primary defense is inaccurate." He touched her knee, the barest of pressure causing her thighs to spread. She watched him the way a

deer watches a hunter, all wide-eyed and frozen with inde-
cision on whether she should run or fight or welcome him.

Dmitri shifted, sliding his hand higher. "I could stroke
you like this and have you coming on my hand before you
decided if you wanted it or not." He cupped her, not bypassing the lace, his entire being focused on her reactions. Her
quick breaths, her gaze focused on his mouth, her hips sub-
tly arching up to meet his touch... All of it indicated desire.

I'd be a right bastard to take what she's offering.

He didn't care in the least.

He leaned in, his lips touching the shell of her ear with
each word. "Or I could hold perfectly still and let you ride my
fingers. Would you like that, Keira? The control you desperately crave would be in your hands and your hands alone."

Her hand closed around his wrist, holding him in place.
"Dmitri, I—"

The sound of his name on her lips broke the spell. "But
unfortunately neither is an option." He sat back, taking his
hand and leaving her splayed across the backseat, blinking
at him. "I don't fuck my enemies."

He said it to remind himself as much as to remind her.
In her presence, Dmitri was having an increasingly difficult
time cleaving to his own personal code. Keira might be
more woman than child, and she was an asset of his enemy's, but the true reason he couldn't take her up on the
offer she kept waving in his face was that she was a broken
thing. Walking wounded. She'd fuck him and then she'd
hate herself all the more for doing it, and he refused to be
party to her self-destruction.

More the fool he was.

CHAPTER TWENTY-SIX

J ude woke up without realizing he'd been asleep. *Not asleep. Passed the fuck out.* He immediately looked for Sloan, only relaxing when he saw her manning the engine of the little boat. Then he noticed that they weren't in the inlet any longer.

"Where are we?"

He started to move, and stopped, nearly cursing at the pain that shot through his side. He checked the bandage, breathing a little sigh of relief to find that while the gauze was soaked, the bleeding had slowed to a mere trickle. *Won't be bleeding out today.*

"Getting help."

He twisted enough to see that they'd left Orcas Island behind. He couldn't immediately place the island looming a few hundred yards away, though. "How long was I out?"

"Long enough for me to worry." She was paler than normal and shivering in her shirt and panties.

Goddamn it. It had been morning when they left and now it was twilight, so he'd been out a hell of a long time, leaving her to her own devices. *Goddamn it again.*

He kicked the bag closer to her. "I have some shorts in there and a sweatshirt."

He should have told her before. Hell, he shouldn't have let himself slip into unconsciousness until he knew she was taken care of. He'd fucked up across the board today, and it didn't look like that was going to be changing anytime soon.

Sloan let go of the throttle long enough to pull the sweatshirt from the top of the bag. "I think you need this more than I do. You're half-naked and you've lost too much blood."

He was fucking freezing, but he'd suffer that and worse before he sat here while she was shivering like a damn leaf. "Put on the goddamn sweatshirt."

She leveled a look at him, but pulled it on. "You're being stubborn."

"Yep."

Sloan shook her head. "It won't be much longer."

Thank Christ for that. He eyed her. "How are you holding up?"

"As well as can be expected." She tucked her legs beneath the sweatshirt, her eyes on the island they approached. "I'm angry and hungry and cold, but I'm not the one who was shot. There will be a doctor in the extraction party."

Extraction party? "Who did you call?" He remembered her getting the phone, but he must have passed out after that. He'd told her that he trusted her—and he did—but he didn't trust anyone else. "It could be a trap."

"It could be." She guided them to a small dock and worked to loop the lead over one of the tie-offs. It took her a couple tries, but she managed, and she tied a passably good knot while she was at it. "But we don't have many options, and I'm not willing to gamble your life on hoping you did a good enough first-aid job. This is the only choice we have."

We.

He managed to climb out of the boat, though he had to lean on her to do it. His weakness disgusted him. If he'd just taken Teague out when he first had the chance, the bastard wouldn't have gotten a shot off. *And I would have killed Sloan's brother.* The same brother who got her out, which is the only reason Jude met her in the first place.

Fuck, if it weren't for Teague, Sorcha would be dead and he'd be gunning for Callista.

Strange how things play out.

Jude thought he'd accounted for every possible outcome. He hadn't planned on Sloan.

"I'm sorry. We're going to have to climb." She hoisted the backpack firmly onto her shoulders and tucked herself beneath Jude's arm. "There's a flat space at the top of this hill—or so I'm told. The helicopter will meet us there."

Whose chopper? She still hadn't said.

But he didn't have the breath to demand answers as they started up the incline. It wasn't as heavily treed as Orcas Island, but they still had to weave back and forth to avoid trunks. By the time they reached the promised flat area, Jude was lightheaded and doing his damnedest not to pass out again. He slumped against a tree as Sloan peered at the sky. "We're right on time. They should be here shortly."

They waited, the minutes stretching into damn near an

hour. Every instinct he had demanded that he get her back on the boat and the hell away from here, but she was right—he needed a doctor. He'd survive the gunshot wound—he'd survived worse—but if he had stitches and a professional wrap job, it'd keep him from having to slow down more than strictly necessary.

The familiar sound of a chopper's blades cut through the relative quiet of the night. She touched his shoulder and they both looked up as a sleek black machine landed in the middle of the clearing. Sloan didn't move from the treeline until a woman hopped to the ground, her dark hair whipping around her face. She turned unerringly to face them.

Only when she was a few feet away did Sloan step forward, putting herself between the woman and Jude. By then, she was close enough for him to peg her as one of the other O'Malley daughters. She had the same dark hair as Sloan, though she carried herself like a queen despite her surroundings. It didn't take the blond monster at her back to place her identity. Carrigan O'Malley.

She didn't hesitate, ignoring Sloan's tense posture and pulling her into a hug. Jude was close enough to hear her say, "God, I missed you."

He watched Sloan relax, little by little. He'd known her relationship with Carrigan was complicated—there was no way to avoid that, considering her sister had chosen James Halloran over her own family—but he hadn't quite understood how deeply the issue had run until now. Sloan had obviously been the one to put the distance between them, but it had hurt her to do it.

She does a lot of things that hurt her when it comes to her siblings.

Carrigan caught sight of him over her sister's shoulder

and her eyebrows shot up. "Holy shit, you weren't kidding. That's no puppy you're bringing home."

"I'm not going home." Sloan pulled away. "We can't, for a variety of reasons."

"Which we'll discuss." Carrigan glanced back at James Halloran. "I'm not going to throw you in a trunk the way *some* people handle issues, but if you believe I'm going to let you just flit off somewhere, you have another thing coming. We'll talk somewhere safe, get your man patched up, and then we'll see what we can do about this mess."

Sloan hesitated, but finally nodded. "You brought a doctor?"

"Yes." Carrigan motioned imperiously to James. "Doc Jones is in the helicopter."

"How did you manage *that*?"

Her sister laughed. "Come on. You know she's always had a soft spot for me. All I had to do is tell her we were headed to Washington." James cleared his throat, and Carrigan rolled her eyes. "And offer to pay her double."

"You're right. That does sound like Doc Jones."

It still smelled like a trap to Jude, but then, Sloan had asked him to trust her, so that was what he'd do.

And if these two crossed them, he'd get his woman out and he'd ensure they didn't have a chance to do it again.

* * *

Sloan didn't know what to do with herself. Her sister had taken charge of the situation like she seemed to in *any* situation, no matter how hopeless the odds against her. Sloan had expected that. What she hadn't expected was to find herself sitting next to James Halloran.

She'd never met him before, never even seen him. It was strange to realize that a person she'd hated so intensely was one she didn't know by sight. Oh, there was no mistaking him—not by his big build, his blond hair, or the fact that he watched her sister like he wanted nothing more than to drag her back to some fortress to keep her safe.

It was the same expression she saw on Jude's face sometimes when he didn't think she noticed.

Doc Jones looked much the same as she had the last time Sloan had seen her—tall and redheaded and capable of hauling around injured people twice her size. She raised her eyebrows and barely waited for Sloan to get her headset on before she said, "When your sister told me *you* were in trouble, I hardly believed it. I thought you were smarter than that."

Sloan thought she was, too. But she didn't have it in her to deal with the woman's attitude when Jude was being strapped to a stretcher. "Take care of him. Please."

"This brute?" Doc Jones shook her head. "You O'Malley women sure like 'em big, don't you? Women after my own heart." She turned away, effectively dismissing Sloan, which was just fine because she was focusing on Jude.

It removed her distraction from the man sitting next to her, though.

Jude didn't flinch, didn't so much as deign to notice the woman bandaging him up, his gaze tracking James Halloran, and the distance between him and Sloan, and the pilot, who hadn't taken off his helmet.

"I told her this was a mistake."

Sloan went still and looked at the blond giant across from her. They all had a set of headphones on, but no one else seemed to have heard him. "Then why did you come?"

"Because your sister loves you and you getting yourself killed would break her goddamn heart." His blue eyes gave nothing away. "Not that you give two fucks, since you've been breaking her heart from the time she chose me, but *I* care. I'll break you before I let you fuck with her further."

"Stop it." She didn't want to hear how she'd hurt her sister. Carrigan was a warrior in high heels, the fearless one. How could *Sloan* hurt her?

She knew he spoke the truth, though. She'd known the endless unanswered calls wore on her sister, because they came less and less often as the months went on. She hadn't relished that knowledge, but she couldn't pretend she was the wounded party.

Not anymore.

"You're going back to Boston, Sloan. I don't care if you go back to the O'Malleys or the Sheridans or stay with us, but you're going back. That Russian bastard will skin you alive if he catches you, and—"

"That would break my sister's heart. I understand." She wanted to hate him for it, but she couldn't. Of them all, James was the one willing to put Carrigan first and let the world burn if that was what it took. He was entitled to his anger.

"But I'm not going back to Boston." Her going back to Boston would cause more problems than it'd solve. It sounded like a simple solution to everyone involved—get her somewhere safe where no one could hurt her. But things would become unforgivably complicated once they found out she was pregnant.

She wouldn't let her baby be used as a political pawn.

She *refused*.

A muscle ticked in his jaw. "We'll see."

The rest of the flight passed without anyone attempting conversation, the helicopter setting down gently on the top of a building in Seattle. James was the first to jump down, holding out his hand for Carrigan. He pulled her against him for a quick kiss, the casual intimacy of it making Sloan's chest ache. Her sister truly was happy with this man, no matter how deplorable Sloan and the rest of their family found him.

But then, she could no longer throw stones—not when she was living in a glass house by being with Jude.

She hopped down without assistance and waited for Doc Jones and Jude. He still looked pale, but that terrifying glazed look in his eyes wasn't there anymore. *Thank God.*

They followed her sister and James through a door and into an elevator that only had one destination. "The penthouse," Carrigan explained, punching the button. "We'll iron out the next step and go from there."

"I'm not going back to Boston." She shot a look at James, who pointedly ignored her.

"After that shit our darling brother just pulled, I don't exactly blame you." Carrigan shot a look at where Jude tried to shrug Doc Jones off and got smacked upside the back of the head for his efforts. "MacNamara, huh? I thought your lot was all killed off."

"Not all of us." His voice gave nothing away.

"I can see that." She turned back to Sloan. "I need to speak with you without all the overwhelming masculinity smothering us." Her practiced smile flickered, just a little. "It's been a long time."

"It has." Sloan pressed her lips together. "Jude, will you be okay?"

"Go. I won't die in the time it takes for you to talk

with your sister." He saw too much, just like he always seemed to.

"Not for lack of trying," Doc Jones muttered. "Now hold still or I *will* have Thing Two tie you down."

Sloan hesitated for a moment longer, but the truth was that she wanted to talk to Carrigan, and not only because she needed to convince her sister not to strong-arm them into going to Boston. Keeping Jude away from the Sheridans was paramount—more important than the chance Dmitri Romanov might hunt her down.

No, not might. He *would*.

It was only a matter of time.

CHAPTER TWENTY-SEVEN

Carrigan led the way into an en suite that was downright ostentatious. The bed looked big enough to sleep six people, and the doorway leading into the bathroom was more like a massive arch into another world.

Her sister flopped down onto the bed and cast a critical eye on her. "You haven't slept in a couple of days."

"Something like that." She perched on the edge of the mattress. "I...I'm sorry for the way I treated you. I was unforgivable in acting so holier-than-thou. I'm starting to understand now everything you had to go through."

"I see that." Carrigan rolled onto her side and propped her head on her hand. "Unlike some of the men of our family, I'm well aware that you know your own mind. You got out, Sloan. You took that step, and I'm seriously proud of you for doing it."

Hearing her sister's words warmed her more than she could have thought possible. "Teague got me out."

"Wrong. Teague offered you the chance. *You* are the one who took it. That was incredibly brave." Her lips twisted. "Braver than I was. I almost married Dmitri Romanov rather than leave the family behind."

Sloan hadn't spent much time wondering how a talk like this would go with Carrigan—mostly because she'd done her best not to think too much about her sister at all. They had always been so incredibly different, but she'd never doubted that Carrigan loved her.

Not even when she'd run off with a Halloran.

"He loves you, you know." Sloan didn't realize she was going to say the words until they were out. "James."

"I know." Her sister smiled. "The feeling is excessively mutual. But we're not here to talk about my gorgeous specimen of a man—we're here to talk about *yours*. I find it too much of a coincidence to believe that you fled across the country and magically happened to fall into the arms of the last remaining MacNamara. Did he gun for you?"

Of them all, she thought Carrigan might understand and let her get out the whole story without jumping to conclusions. The woman had, after all, fallen for a man who had thrown her into the trunk of his car and taken her to an almost-certain death at the hands of his father. Compared to that, Jude was almost tame.

No, he's not. And you're stalling.

"Not for me, not like that. I was staying in a house owned by Callie's aunt."

"I didn't realize Callie had an aunt." Carrigan's eyes went wide. "Holy shit, he was gunning for *her*—because she's a Sheridan."

It didn't surprise her that her sister caught on so quickly. Carrigan had always been a force of nature with a deadly sharp mind. If their father had seen that from the beginning, he wouldn't have wasted her in a political marriage. But then, she was a woman, so in the end it wouldn't have mattered to Seamus O'Malley. Sloan forced herself back to the topic at hand. "An O'Connor now, but yes."

"Can't say I blame him. If someone did to our family what Colm Sheridan did to the MacNamaras, I would hunt every last one of them to extinction." There was no amusement in her eyes, only ruthless determination. "And if someone laid a hand on James, I'd skin them alive."

"I know." Sloan was beginning to understand that fierceness, if only a little. She wasn't ready to declare war on her brother for *shooting* Jude, but she wanted to...she didn't even know. Punch him, at the very least.

"So that begs the question—what the hell are you two going to do?" Carrigan sat up. "If you say you're going to help him keep up murdering Sheridans, I'm stepping in. I know you care about him—I'd have to be an idiot not to see that—but Callie is family now. Teague is our *brother*."

"He shot Jude."

She froze. "You're serious?"

Just thinking about it made her angry all over again. Before she'd left Boston, she didn't think she'd had a temper. Now? Now rage seemed to be her gut instinct. It was slightly terrifying. She pressed her lips together, trying to rein it in. "He put a tracker on me and hunted me down despite my telling him that I was more than capable of deciding for myself what I wanted."

Carrigan watched her through narrowed eyes. "I'm not siding with him."

"But you're about to say something I won't like." She crossed her arms over her chest. "Say it."

"Teague can be an insufferable martyr at times, but he'd die for us. For Callie and their baby? He'd kill the world. Your needs have nothing to do with it. He just found out that you're shacking up with a MacNamara, a man who has every reason to hate his wife's family and want them dead. I can't say I'd react any differently." She gave a half smile. "Though I'd make sure my shot actually hit something vital."

Her sister was downright terrifying at times. "I'm not pretending that Jude isn't a threat, but he cares about me." Maybe if she could make her sister understand, Sloan could persuade the others. "He put his plan for revenge on hold. He promised that he wouldn't hurt Sorcha or Callie." *Unless he's suddenly changed his mind after what Teague did.* "We just wanted nine months to figure out if we could make a life work together."

"Nine...*No.* Sloan, tell me you're not saying what I think you're saying."

She hadn't meant to let that slip. She looked away, and then back, well aware that the truth was written all over her face. "It was an accident."

Carrigan pinched the bridge of her nose. "Let me get this straight. You are knocked up with a little MacNamara baby, your baby daddy is gunning for the Sheridan family—who your brother, occasional idiot or not, is now a part of—and this guy obviously cares about you if he's carting you around to his safe houses when he could have just disappeared into the night."

"That pretty much sums it up." Though it felt strange to hear it laid out in such bald terms.

"Do you love him?"

"I...I don't know." She cleared her throat. "I'm like a different person with him, stronger, fiercer. I...I like it. I crave him with an intensity I never imagined possible, and I like *him*. He's overbearing and high-handed, but he only steamrolls me in the bedroom. I don't know what kind of life we could lead, but I want it all the same."

Carrigan's eyes went wide. "Shit, Sloan. That sounds a whole lot like love."

It did, didn't it? But she couldn't let it go, not now that she had someone who might understand to talk to. Sloan grabbed a throw pillow from the mountain piled on the bed and hugged it to her chest. "But how do I know for sure? You know I was sheltered before I left the family. I didn't date, didn't do...anything. It's entirely possible that I fell for the first man I slept with simply because I slept with him, and now pregnancy hormones are coloring my view. How am I supposed to call this love when I have nothing to compare it to?"

Her sister laughed. "That, at least, I have an answer for." She picked at one of the tassels on the pillow nearest to her. "You know. I've been with enough guys that I can tell you that for sure. It's not the cocks that matter, as enjoyable as they can be. It's the person attached to them who makes the difference. That said, if you're not sure of Jude, then don't jump into anything with him. Go slow, figure your way through it."

There were a lot of elements of their current situation that Sloan wasn't sure of—her family, her future, Jude's vendetta—but the man himself wasn't on the list. "What if I am sure of him?"

Carrigan shrugged. "Then nothing you find after him is going to compare. Life is too short, Sloan. If you want the man, then fight for the man." She finally smiled. "He's a beast in the bedroom, isn't he? You can tell just by looking at him."

She laughed like Carrigan obviously intended for her to. "I'll never tell." But as soon as her amusement appeared, it faded. Sloan stared down at the intricately woven pillow and then finally raised her gaze to her sister's knowing dark eyes. "It does sound a whole lot like love, doesn't it?"

* * *

"They'll never accept you."

Jude took the beer James passed over, careful not to jar his side. As he'd suspected, his wound was a clean exit. It would hurt like a bitch for a while, but he'd feel more like himself by morning.

He looked at the man across from him. A threat to be sure, though it was his woman who had cold eyes. This man might beat an enemy to death, but it wouldn't be without provocation. Carrigan O'Malley would gut an enemy before they had a chance to hurt her or those she cared about. He'd only done passing research on the O'Malleys, but nothing in that report had prepared him for Sloan's sister. Her family had lost a major asset when they drove her into Halloran's arms.

She and Dmitri Romanov would have brought the East Coast to its knees.

Thank Christ *that* marriage hadn't happened.

"I'm aware dealing with the family won't be easy." As he found out a few hours ago, Teague O'Malley wouldn't hesitate to pull the fucking trigger. He doubted the rest of the O'Malley family would be any different.

"I'll tell you what I told Sloan—the safest place for her is in Boston."

Jude couldn't stay in Boston for more than a few hours

without essentially calling down the dogs of hell on his head. Take his woman and his child away from him? Over his dead fucking body. "Not gonna happen."

"I suggest you think really fucking carefully about your next step." James took a long pull from his beer. "The Hallorans, O'Malleys, and Sheridans are tied together tighter than ever. You can't take on one without dealing with the other two."

James had no idea the Romanovs were involved now, too, and Jude had no intention of telling him.

"You don't know the whole story." Though it could be argued that Jude didn't, either. He had only the scant details of that night from his mother. The official report had been buried by the Boston police.

"Maybe not." James shrugged. "And, trust me, I understand the need for retribution. I'd be on the warpath in a heartbeat if someone took Carrigan from me. I might not live to see the next dawn, but I'd ensure that those responsible paid dearly." His blue eyes narrowed. "Could you say you'd do any different for Sloan?"

I would kill them, burn their house to the ground, and salt the earth behind me.

James nodded like he'd answered even though he hadn't said a damn word. "Yeah, I thought so."

Jude knew Sloan had enemies. Fuck, she had almost as many as he did, through sheer accident of birth. Romanov had given his word not to harm her, but she'd have an even bigger target on her back once it became known she was pregnant with his child. If someone took her, hurt her, used her or their child against him...

Yeah, he could see James's point.

Fuck.

"Don't cross Callista Sheridan. She is her father's daughter, and she won't react any differently than you are now."

He had no intention of harming Callista. Not now, not when he had a living, breathing reason not to. But if he took out the one person truly responsible—Colm—she might retaliate and this cycle would begin again.

Which is exactly what Sloan warned me about.

Jude rubbed a hand over his face, suddenly exhausted. There was no way out of this where he wasn't either betraying his mother's memory or hurting the woman he had come to care about. The mother of his child.

Footsteps had him lifting his head as Sloan walked into the room, her sister on her heels. She looked like heaven. It didn't matter that she was wearing his sweatshirt, the huge size of it making her seem younger than she was. Or that there were dark circles under her eyes and she was paler than normal.

She looks like home.

She held her hand out to him, much the same way he'd done to her during their time together. "Let's go to bed."

He stood with some effort and took her hand, allowing her to lead him through a different door than the one she'd just come out of. It was decorated much the same way as the rest of the penthouse—ridiculously overdone—but the bed actually looked inviting.

"Doc Jones said no shower for the time being, but I could offer a sponge bath." Her smile was a shadow of its former self.

He used one hand to pull the sweatshirt off her, and her T-shirt and panties quickly followed. "Help me get out of these jeans."

It took some work to get them off, but then he stood before her, both of them naked. She licked her lips, but even that was half-hearted. She was practically weaving on her feet, and he wasn't much better. "Come to bed with me, sunshine."

"You don't sleep."

"I'll make an exception this time." The events of the day were catching up with him, his side one big ball of fury and pain, his head pounding in time with his heart. And he'd been unconscious for part of it. He hadn't had the emotional toll on top of the physical one like Sloan had. She needed sleep, not sex. Comfort.

He was shit-all for giving comfort, but he'd do his best.

Jude pulled back the covers and half sat, half fell onto the mattress. He cursed, but managed to get settled without too much trouble. Sloan slipped in next to him, carefully adjusting herself so she wasn't touching his injured side. He propped his chin on the top of her head and just held her. "I'm sorry about your brother."

"He's doing what he thinks is best. It doesn't make it okay, but... I do understand."

Jude understood, too.

Which was the crux of the problem. Her sister aside— and even that was in question—there wasn't a single person in Sloan's life who would sit back and allow her to ride off into the sunset with Jude. They would all fight it, for one reason or another.

Stop letting emotions fuck with your head and come up with a plan. That's what you're good at. Figure out the options and do what it takes to keep Sloan and the baby safe.

No matter what the cost.

CHAPTER TWENTY-EIGHT

Sloan stared down at Seattle as the rain lashed the windows. She'd woken in Jude's arms and the sheer joy that had suffused her at the realization that they were together and whole was staggering.

Carrigan's words from last night echoed through her head. *You're in love with him.*

Yes, she wanted a chance to see if they had a future together. Yes, the idea of being with anyone else left her cold. And, yes, she'd essentially chosen him over her family. But...love?

Love seemed a very large word in the face of such a short time of knowing each other.

He will leave. It might not be today, it might not be tomorrow, but eventually he will leave.

She pressed a hand to her chest, hating the ache that blossomed there, an insidious weed she wanted nothing to do with. She couldn't change Jude. She'd be the worst sort of fool to even try.

Then you have to be okay with him leaving.

An even more difficult task.

Was it better to have him for a finite amount of time? Or should she cut her losses now so he could continue his suicidal mission to eliminate Colm Sheridan? Doing so might honor his dead mother's memory, but it would be a death sentence for Jude.

No. I won't allow it.

She sighed. He'd been willing to give them the length of her pregnancy to figure things out. But now? Would things change once he woke up?

Make sure they don't.

Fight for him.

There was only one way to reach him, the one thing they had in common beyond a shadow of a doubt. She turned back to the bed, padding across the carpet on silent feet.

His dark eyes opened the second her knee touched the bed. "What's got that look on your face?"

"Don't leave." The words came out low, fierce. "Stay with me. Live. Be a father to our baby and be *my* man."

His eyebrows rose. "I think I must be dreaming."

"You're not." She climbed onto the bed and knelt between his thighs. "I'll do whatever it takes, Jude. If you go after Colm, you'll die." Her breath came out in a sob. "Don't you see? This never ends. They hurt you, you hurt them, and round and round it goes until the world ends."

He reached for her, but she grabbed his hand and pressed it against her stomach. "*This* is what matters. Not them. Not the past. Not a war that will start another war and another and another. *Us.*"

She held her breath as he looked at her, giving nothing away. "It won't stop. Even if I was willing to leave it all behind—and I'm getting to that point—there is another element in play."

The pieces clicked together in her head. "Dmitri Romanov."

He hesitated, and then said, "If I don't honor the deal I made with him to take out Colm, he'll just kill him—and Callista—anyway. And set me up to take the fall. It won't take much to create a convincing frame job. Everyone will think it was me anyway."

"No." Horror wrapped around her, making her sick to her stomach. "He can't do that." She didn't know how she was going to stop him, but she'd find a way.

"Fuck, you're killing me." He pulled her down and kissed her until her head spun. "I want to believe the fairy tale. I want to think that we can take off to some far corner of the world and they'll leave us the fuck alone. But even if the Sheridans don't know I exist, your family won't stop coming after us. They think you're brainwashed and that I'm your captor. Do you believe for one goddamn second that your brother will sit back and let you disappear?"

No, not when he put it like that. Teague would feel responsible that he didn't protect her enough and he'd hunt her to the ends of the earth, thinking he was saving her.

She closed her eyes, but she couldn't block out the truth. *No easy answers, no easy outs.*

Jude was right. But she was right, too. She didn't think for a second that she could deal with the Romanov threat... but he could. That wouldn't take care of the problem of *her* family, though.

She rubbed a hand over her face, hating the conclusion that arose. "We have to go back to Boston."

"What?"

"You have to stop Dmitri." She didn't like him putting himself in danger, but if anyone could deal with that threat, it was Jude. And Carrigan would help...maybe. Which left the O'Malleys to her. "I'll talk to Teague and Aiden. If I do that of my own free will, neither one of them can argue that you're keeping me trapped." As much as she'd like to keep the conversation to just her and Teague, she knew Aiden was looking for her, too.

Jude's arms tightened around her. "What the fuck makes you think that your brothers will let you walk out of Boston once you're back there?"

It was a gamble and, to be perfectly honest, not even a good one. If Teague didn't lock her in a room and throw away the key, Aiden certainly would. "It's worth the risk. And, really, *you're* the one in more danger." She didn't like thinking about that. They were between a rock and a hard place, and were out of good options.

"I don't fucking think so."

She pressed her face against his neck and inhaled deeply. He smelled crisp and clean like the sea, something she could live her entire life with and never get tired of. "We can't live on the run indefinitely, Jude. They will catch up to us again and, this time, someone might die. *You* might die." It made her shake simply thinking about it. "We can't let Dmitri hurt Callie. If you think Teague is after us now, imagine what will happen if he thinks you killed his wife and unborn child."

Jude cursed long and hard. "You crossed the country to get away from your family and now you're willing to walk back into that vipers' nest—"

"For you." She lifted her head and met his gaze. "For us."

* * *

Us.

Sloan kept saying that fucking word and, every time she did, it was a sucker punch Jude couldn't avoid. Because it was the truth. Even before they'd found out for sure that she was pregnant, it had been them against their enemies. Them against the whole damn world.

And she wanted him to sit on his goddamn hands and let her put herself in certain danger. *Not sit on your hands. Take out the enemy the way you've trained your whole life for.* He just hadn't anticipated the enemy being Romanov instead of Sheridan.

He held her as tightly as he dared, ignoring the flare of pain in his side. "I don't like it, sunshine."

"You don't have to like it... but you have to trust me to do this—just like I'm trusting you to walk away from Romanov alive." She took a shuddering breath. "Don't think for a second I like that you'll be in danger, too. But we don't have another choice."

It had nothing to do with trust and everything to do with wanting to keep her safe. He wanted to haul her ass out of here, hop the first flight to anywhere but Boston, and set up a little house for them. Maybe it would be enough. It wouldn't be easy to set his shit aside and tear his gaze from the past wrongs done to him, but he could give it a shot. They'd have...

A window. Not a future. Maybe a day or maybe a couple years, but eventually that window will close and she's right—someone will die.

It would likely be him this time.

The thought of death had never bothered him quite as

much as it did now. Everyone died. He hadn't thought about a life after his vendetta was finished because he hadn't really thought he'd get out alive. The odds had been against him even before the Sheridans knew he existed.

And if Dmitri Romanov framed him for Colm Sheridan's hit, the odds would be even worse.

He didn't like the thought of not being around to see Sloan get big with child. Of not being there to hold her hand and see if she'd actually curse at him during the labor. Of missing out on the rest of her fucking life and seeing what new curveballs she'd throw once she had six months, a year, five years away from her shitty-ass family.

And the kid. There were so many firsts that he never had considered until now. First steps, first words, first day of school, watching the baby grow into a real person. Seeing what kind of adult he or she would be. He'd miss all that.

Would that kid grow up wanting revenge for my death? Would it start the cycle all over again?

No. Sloan was too smart for that. She'd raise their kid right.

She wouldn't be alone forever, either. She's too fucking special not to attract other men like flies to honey. Eventually, she'd let one close enough to capture her heart. She'd let another man into her bed and into her life, and he'd be the lucky bastard who got to wake up every morning to her, who got to raise my *child.*

No fucking way.

He took her hand and pressed a kiss to each knuckle, not taking his eyes from hers. "We'll go back to Boston." He kissed her wrist. "I will take care of Romanov, one way or another, and you'll convince your brothers to call off their dogs. But if one of them hurts you, I will kill every last one of them."

"Jude—"

"It's the truth." He brushed his lips against hers. "I wasn't shitting you when I started calling you sunshine. You're *my* sunshine, and my world is fucking bleak without you. So, yeah, if something goes sideways in Boston, I'll make Colm Sheridan look like a fucking amateur."

He felt her sigh more than he heard it. "Is that a twisted way of you trying to convince me not to go?"

"No." He stroked a hand down her side, wanting her despite his pain. Needing her. "That's the God's honest truth."

She caught his wrist as he moved to her thigh. "You were shot. Yesterday."

"It'd take a whole hell of a lot more than being shot to keep me from wanting you." He shifted fully onto his back. "But if you're so concerned, you can ride my cock so I don't move too much."

She laughed softly. "You just want to watch me."

"Guilty." The rain muted the light, giving the whole room a dreamlike quality. "I'll never get enough of you, sunshine. Never."

She straddled him, casting a suspicious look at his bandage. "You'll tell me if it hurts."

No, he fucking wouldn't, and they both knew it. Jude stroked her lightly between her thighs. "You had a look of intent on your face when I woke up. Tell me why."

"I…" She hissed out a breath when he pushed two fingers into her, sliding them lazily in and out. "I was going to convince you to let me go to Boston and to not kill Colm."

"How?"

She rolled her hips, her eyes slitted. "I was going to give you head."

Jude's cock strained at her words said in that desperate

voice. He withdrew his fingers, sliding his hands down her thighs to spread them farther. "You can do that when we get back from Boston. The second we come through the door, hit your fucking knees and take my cock out for your pleasure. Do you like the picture I'm painting, sunshine? Because your face says you do."

"Yes." She reached between them and stroked him, dragging his cock across her clit the same way he'd done before.

"But not today. Today you're going to sink that tight little pussy onto me."

She notched him at her entrance and did exactly as he'd commanded, her eyes never once leaving his while she did. Only when she was impaled to the hilt did she lean back, propping her hands on his thighs, and start to move. She rolled her body, slow and sensuous, her breasts rising and falling with each breath.

Jude gripped her hips, allowing her to lead. "You are the most beautiful thing I've ever seen, sunshine. Nothing—no one—compares to you."

"You're mine, Jude MacNamara, and don't you forget it." She leaned forward and shifted up to grip the headboard over his head, picking up her pace, fucking him the way she knew he liked. He captured one of her nipples in his mouth and she let go of the headboard to cup the back of his head, pulling on his hair a little.

"Take what's yours, sunshine." She swiveled her hips in a move that made his eyes damn near cross. "*Fuck*."

"God, Jude, I'm never going to get enough of you." She grabbed his hand and pressed it between her legs, waiting until he gave her clit a stroke to let go. "Touch me."

"You don't have to ask twice." He made a V of his fingers and positioned his hand so her clit would ride up against him with every move. It didn't take long for her strokes to become wild, frantic.

He loved that. He loved seeing the calm mask she wore to face the rest of the world go up in smoke, replaced by wanton need that she looked to *him* to provide. She was stronger than she gave herself credit for, stronger than he'd given her credit for at first, but hell if she didn't keep surprising him.

Her orgasm hit her, her pussy milking him, her mouth parting in a gasp that hit him right in the chest. Fuck, he loved that sound. He let her carry him over the edge, pounding into her until he couldn't take the pleasure or the pressure anymore. "*Sloan.*"

CHAPTER TWENTY-NINE

Sloan didn't talk to Carrigan on the flight. She barely looked at her sister, her mind wrapped up in the man who was making his separate way back to Boston. If Dmitri Romanov didn't know they were both back in the area, Jude didn't want to announce it. *Not separated forever. I won't let it be forever.*

Jude hadn't wanted her to go. She'd seen it written all over his face before he'd shut down. She bet he'd even considered hauling her off to God knew where and chaining her to a radiator or something while he dealt with Romanov. Though, knowing Jude, he likely had some well-appointed cell where he'd sex her into submission before flying off to face the danger alone.

We're both facing danger. That's what has to happen to make a clean break.

"I know I said you needed to come back to Boston, but are you sure about this?"

She turned to find Carrigan had dropped into the seat across from her. Sloan had never flown on a private jet before—she hadn't flown *at all* before her escape—but Carrigan looked right at home in the luxurious setting. Sloan crossed her legs, still feeling a little tender from what she and Jude had done earlier. "No, I'm not sure."

"Damn, Sloan. Just...damn." Carrigan shook her head. "I don't know what you have planned, but I can only help so much. I'm already riding the line by showing up to help, though it was worth it."

She didn't deserve her sister. Once upon a time, she'd privately thought Carrigan was selfish, but she couldn't have been more wrong. *Sloan* was the selfish one. Her throat burned, and she swallowed hard. "I'm sorry. I was such a terrible person and I'm sorry, and—"

"Stop." Carrigan crossed to her seat and put her arm around her. "We're all just ships in the middle of a hurricane, doing our best to survive. For me, that meant breaking with the majority of the family. For you, that meant something different at the time. It's okay."

"How can you say that? I should have returned your calls."

"Maybe. I understood why you didn't, even if it hurt." Carrigan shrugged and gave her a squeeze. "But you called me when it counted. You trusted me enough to get you out of that situation without trying to haul you somewhere, insisting I knew what was best for you. That means something."

"Still." She pressed her lips together, though the burning in her throat had now reached her eyes. "I'm sorry."

"You're forgiven."

Just like that. Nothing more to it. She caught James

watching them over Carrigan's shoulder and fought back a shudder. *There is more to it than that. It doesn't matter that Carrigan's forgiven me*—James *hasn't forgiven me for hurting her.*

She liked him a little bit because of that.

Needing to focus on anything but what she and Jude were about to do—to risk—Sloan said, "Tell me what you've been doing since we last talked."

Carrigan's eyes sparked. "It's been a wild ride. James and I have set up a nonprofit foundation to help sex-trafficking victims find a new home. I won't lie and say I don't absolutely adore talking those rich assholes out of their money. It's for a good cause, and they have more than enough dollars to go around." She practically vibrated as she went on to explain how they were setting up stings, of sorts, tipping off the FBI when it suited them, and working their way toward the top supplier of human trafficking on the East Coast.

She's so incredibly happy.

It sounded dangerous. If one meet went wrong, or one person found out that they were working with cops, even distantly, it would bring the fury of both Sheridans and O'Malleys down on them.

And that wasn't even getting into the *other* enemies they had.

If Sloan had learned anything over her life, though, it was that every one of her siblings needed to find their own way—herself included. If she wanted the freedom to make her own choices, she'd be a terrible person to curtail Carrigan's choices. Even if her sister would allow it.

By the time their plane descended into Boston, it almost felt like old times again. If Carrigan had stopped partying, her stories had only gotten wilder now that she was moving through the upper crust of Boston. The rich had more secrets than they had money to bury them, and Carrigan had always been effective at getting people to talk when she wanted to.

As the plane taxied to a stop, her sister's smile fell away. "I'll see you to O'Malley territory, but I can't go farther without risking an incident." She glanced at James. "I'd fight for you, Sloan. Never think I wouldn't. But there's more at play than just us now, and I have to think about the people who rely on me and James for protection—and the girls who don't have anywhere to go and no money to get there. I'll try to help in any way I can, but—"

Sloan covered her sister's hand with her own. "I understand. I'd never ask you to go to war for me." She hesitated. "But I'm not going to O'Malley territory. I'm going to the Sheridans."

* * *

"Tell me again." It took every bit of Aiden's not-inconsiderable willpower not to yell the words. The week had gone to shit after he'd tracked down Charlotte Finch. Her not telling him to get lost permanently was the *only* thing that had gone right. He'd have to follow up with her before too long, but he could read people well enough to know that she'd stew on his offer until he forced her hand. The issue was getting the timing right to prevent her from digging in her heels through sheer instinct.

But that wasn't the problem right now.

His *problem* was sitting right in front of him, head hanging, her hair a tangled mess from the fact Liam had pulled her out of bed. He looked over Keira's shoulder and Liam gave a short shake of his head.

She wasn't telling the full story.

Keira blinked bloodshot eyes at him. "We've gone through this—three times. I was minding my own goddamn business and he showed up. Next thing I know, his thug hauled me to his car and tossed me into the backseat. Then he drove me here. End of story."

It was possible that was all there was to it, but Aiden had seen the footage of the front of their townhouse. She'd climbed out of the backseat, her clothes a fumbled mess, and the look on her face as Romanov had driven off...

Aiden didn't like it. He didn't like it one bit.

But he couldn't do a single damn thing if Keira wouldn't talk to him. "Did he...Did he hurt you?"

"Hurt..." She blinked those hazel eyes at him, and then laughed. "Oh my God, are you asking if he raped me? Does that word bother you, big brother? *Rape*."

He gripped the edge of the desk, trying to keep his temper and figure out if she was attempting to provoke a response because she was pissed at him, or because she actually *had* been hurt. "Answer the fucking question, Keira."

She pushed to her feet and shoved her hair back. "No, he didn't *rape* me. Fuck, Aiden. Stop trying to pretend that you're this ultimate protector, Seamus 2.0. You're not. You're worse than our father is." She shoved past Liam, but stopped in the doorway. "And Dmitri Romanov didn't lay a hand on me, though I would have gladly fucked him just to wipe that goddamn look off your face."

She slammed the door shut, leaving him staring at her, her accusation ringing in his ears.

Fuck. Just...fuck.

He sat back. *I have to do something about Romanov,*

sooner rather than later. That, at least, was a problem he could theoretically fix. He didn't know how to fix his sister, how to fix his broken family.

She was right. He wasn't their father. He didn't know how to be.

Things would be easier if he could detach the way Seamus did. If he were more ruthless, he would have brought Sloan back into the fold by now, would have ground out the last of Keira's rebellion, would have eliminated their enemies one by one until no one stood strong enough to threaten them.

Instead, he'd chosen to go about things in a less direct way. He motioned to Liam. "What have you got?"

"Your brother didn't manage to bring Sloan back. He went to Washington with eight men, and he's coming back with eight men, but several are injured."

Judging from what they'd discovered about Jude MacNamara in the time since Sloan told Teague who she was running with, he didn't find that surprising. The man had to be good at what he did if he'd survived as long as he had. Mediocre hit men didn't last long before someone put them out of their misery.

Aiden drummed his fingers on the desk. "It's time I had a conversation with my brother." Teague wouldn't like hearing that they'd tapped his phone, but that was too fucking bad. Aiden didn't like that Teague was informing for the goddamn FBI. It was time to address that, too.

"There's more."

Of course there was. He raised his eyebrows. "Yes?"

Liam gave a tight smile. "Carrigan and James Halloran just landed on a private airstrip north of the city—with Sloan."

He should have known Sloan wouldn't call *him* for help—especially when it appeared Teague was trying to do the noble thing and retrieve her despite her wishes. She wouldn't trust Aiden. But she apparently *did* trust their sister. The irony wasn't lost on him.

He drummed his fingers faster, considering the implications. Sloan wouldn't have come back here without a reason. As great as it'd be to think that she was coming home, he knew better. This had to do with the man she'd chosen for her own. *First Carrigan and now Sloan. God only knows who Keira is going to fall for when the time comes.*

"I think it's time MacNamara and I had a chat."

"I figured you'd want to eventually." Liam pulled a card out of his jacket pocket. It was blank except for a number scrawled across it. "I took the liberty of tracking down his contact information."

"I don't pay you enough."

"You're welcome to give me a raise."

He snorted. "Consider it done." There was no point in waiting to contact MacNamara. If Sloan was back in Boston, he doubted the man was far behind her. They wouldn't have extracted themselves from Teague's grasp just to go their separate ways.

He dialed, half expecting the man not to answer. Instead, a gruff voice came onto the line. "Who the fuck is this?"

No point in beating around the bush. "Aiden O'Malley."

"Jesus Christ, you O'Malley men are like cockroaches. How'd you get this number?" Jude cursed. "Scratch that. I don't give a fuck. What do you want?"

"Tell me why you're in Boston."

"Or what?"

He pinched the bridge of his nose. Aiden had known it would come down to this. Sloan had left of her own free will, even if she'd had Teague's help. Aiden wasn't Teague. He didn't see the best in people, and he sure as fuck didn't have a white knight complex. Which is why he believed his sister when she said she chose Jude MacNamara. Sloan might be sheltered, she might be as innocent as one of their family could get, but she'd sounded *alive* for the first time since Devlin died.

He had a feeling this man's presence in her life had something to do with that. "My sister chose you."

A hesitation. "You tapped Teague's phone."

"Wouldn't you?"

Jude snorted. "I would have whupped his ass for going behind my back and stealing my sister."

He should have. But then, Aiden's life would be a lot simpler if that was *all* Teague had done. "Answer the question."

"You didn't ask a question. But yeah, your sister chose me. I'm not letting her go without a fight, and I'm willing to bring that to your front door if you fall in with your idiot brother."

He wasn't who Aiden would have chosen for Sloan. But he'd done his homework. Hit man or not, Jude MacNamara had an honorable streak. "They say you never kill someone who doesn't have it coming."

"You seem to know a whole hell of a lot for someone I've never had a fucking conversation with." The background noise seemed to indicate he was in a city, which only supported Aiden's suspicion that Jude had followed Sloan back to Boston. *They're planning something.*

The question remained *what*.

Before he could ask again, Jude spoke. "If your sister

told you that she chooses me—that she wants to leave the life she had with your family behind—and that she's happy with me, would you believe her?"

His first instinct was to react the exact same way Teague had—instant denial. But Aiden took a step back and tried to think beyond his instinctive desire to protect Sloan. She'd come back to Boston on her own. She was outside this man's influence, and even if he didn't see eye to eye with Carrigan and James, Aiden had no doubt they were more than capable of protecting Sloan if the situation called for it. "If she tells me face-to-face that she chooses you, I'll believe her." He'd read the truth on her face, one way or another.

"Then you better leave pretty fucking fast. She'll be at the Sheridan house within thirty minutes. If you let her walk, then we'll talk."

Aiden hung up and stood. "Get four men. We're going to the Sheridans', and we're going now."

It was time to get his house in order.

* * *

The Sheridans had a decent perimeter set up and regular patrols who mostly managed not to look like patrols, but Jude had been casing the territory for years. He knew how to get in and get out without being seen. The house whose window he watched from had been earned with the blood of his first hit. He hadn't visited it more than a handful of times over the years, not wanting to risk drawing attention to himself.

A car pulled up to the front of the Sheridan house, expelling a nervous-looking Sloan. Oh, she looked calm on the outside, but he could recognize the set of her spine and the way she clenched her hands. She was scared shit-less, but hell if she'd let them see. Pride warred with fear, one wanting to kiss her, and the other wanting to charge down the street and scoop her up, taking her anywhere but here.

She trusted him to do the job and not get killed.

She'd asked him to trust her to get in and out of Sheridan hands without issue.

He was going to respect that.

But he was also going to follow through on his threat if he thought for a second that one of those bastards she called brothers so much as touched her.

Aiden, at least, sounded like he was willing to hear her out, and wasn't that a strange turn of events? Jude hadn't expected a call from the oldest O'Malley brother. He knew the man was perceptive from his reputation, but apparently he'd underestimated him. *Maybe he's perceptive enough to be an ally instead of an enemy.*

There was only one way to tell for sure.

A grand total of ninety seconds later, two cars slammed to a stop in front of the house, immediately expelling Aiden and five of his men. He paused and looked up and down the street, which only went to show he had good instincts. Jude wouldn't let himself be seen, but it said something that Aiden sensed his presence at all.

His phone rang as the O'Malley group walked into the Sheridan house, and he answered without taking his gaze from the door they'd disappeared through. "What?"

"You've traveled to Boston earlier than we discussed."

He silently cursed. "Aw, Romanov, did you miss me? It's only been a week. You should have said something. I would have come back sooner." *No reason to let him know that the plan changed.*

"Charming." A careful pause. "I truly hope you're not planning on double-crossing me, Jude."

"And let Colm walk? Not likely." He clenched his jaw, determined not to say more. In order for this to work, Romanov couldn't know his intentions, which meant playing along.

"Perhaps you should add some of the O'Malleys to that list you have of dead men walking."

Even though he knew better than to get drawn into a conversation with this man, he said, "And do your dirty work for you? I don't think so. You can't afford me."

"All evidence points to the contrary. I'm paying you to remove Colm Sheridan—something you'd do well to remember."

"I have certain criteria. The O'Malley men don't meet it."

Romanov chuckled. "Not yet. But when they decide to keep your precious Sloan from you? They will. She's the sweet little sister and you're a vicious killer. In what world would an O'Malley give their blessing?"

"Funny, but Carrigan gave her blessing. She says 'hi' by the way."

Silence for a beat, and then two. "You're a clever one, aren't you?"

He moved to the window and looked out, but nothing had changed. "I like to think so."

"Then tell me what the O'Malley men will do when they find out Sloan's carrying your child." He'd recovered from the Carrigan jab far too quickly, regaining his unruffled tone. "They'll keep her from you, and they'll remove the child. You know it's the truth."

Jude gripped the phone so tightly, the case creaked. "You're a motherfucker, aren't you?" They might not push her to have an abortion—bastard or no, he didn't think Teague would go to those lengths—but they would keep her under lock and key and then push her to give the baby up for adoption. *No. I won't allow it.*

"As you said, you're a smart man. Which is why you will be in that apartment with your finger on the trigger in an hour, won't you?"

"I'll be there." Jude was already moving, hustling down the stairs and onto the street. He could get to the apartment across from the restaurant in twenty. As much as he wanted to stay here and ensure Sloan got out okay, he didn't trust Romanov's timetable any more than he trusted the man himself. *Guess I'm going to get to find out the hard way if Aiden was serious about taking Sloan's word for it.* "Don't get any funny ideas, Dmitri. You fuck with me and I'll kill you." Jude disconnected before Dmitri could respond.

Sloan's brothers wouldn't hurt her, not in any permanent way. But Teague was already convinced that Jude had brainwashed her, twisting her will into his own. She was outmanned and outgunned, and she would be helpless if the tide of her family turned against her.

A slow burning started in his gut, working outward, scorching away every tendril of humanity Sloan had worked so fucking hard to bring out in him. He wouldn't let them take her away from him. Wouldn't let them decide the fate of *his* baby. He'd already lost too much. He wouldn't lose her—*them*—too. Every instinct he had demanded he turn around and rush back to defend them, the Sheridans be damned. Up until a week ago, he'd been planning on killing

Colm. What did they matter when weighed against the life of the woman he loved and their child?

I promised Sloan.

That he wouldn't hurt Callista—or let her be hurt. That he'd stop Romanov. That he'd trust her to do what she needed to do. If he went back now, he'd be breaking her trust and potentially doing irreparable harm to their relationship.

Jude hesitated, torn, and then gritted his teeth and charged forward. He would keep his promise.

But that didn't mean that he couldn't weigh things a bit in his favor in the meantime.

CHAPTER THIRTY

Sloan couldn't breathe. She stood in the middle of Callie's living room, watching her older brothers snipe at each other like rabid junkyard dogs. Teague looked half a second from pummeling Aiden, and Aiden was right there with him. The *only* saving grace was that they'd sent their men away and closed the doors, so it was just the three of them.

"You betrayed the family."

Teague rocked onto the balls of his feet. "I did what it took to protect our sister." He was sporting a black eye that she suspected was courtesy of Jude, and it made him look like a completely different person. Or maybe it was the wildness in his dark eyes. "Something *you* haven't even tried. Not with Carrigan, not with Keira, and sure as fuck not with Sloan."

Aiden took a slow step to the side like he was sizing Teague up for weakness. "And how's that protection working out? She's here, looking like shit, and it was *Carrigan* who brought her back. You had your chance. You fucked it up. She's leaving."

"The fuck she is." Teague's fists clenched and unclenched. "She's staying right here. You have no idea what's going on."

"Wrong. I know a whole hell of a lot more than you bargained on." Aiden crossed his arms over his chest. "Or were you just going to slink away and hope no one noticed you were informing to the fucking feds?"

"*Stop it!*" Sloan screamed, her hands going to the sides of her head as if she could contain the massive headache sprouting there. "I am not staying in Boston. I came back of my own free will. I was *not* retrieved like some naughty child. Stop acting like I'm not standing *right here.*" She wasn't even going to touch Aiden's comment about Teague informing on the family. That wasn't why she was here, and it wasn't her problem. She didn't want it to *be* her problem.

Though that explains why Aiden is here so quickly—he's been watching Teague.

They looked at her like she'd grown a second head. Teague took a cautious step toward her. "You don't know what you're saying. I know you think—"

"Don't you dare." She backed up, wanting to scream again in frustration. "I am an adult, though I've allowed you to treat me like an invalid up until this point. That ends now. When I leave Boston this time, I'm leaving for good. You will stop looking for me. Just...let me go."

Aiden narrowed his eyes. "You choose this?"

"That's what I've been saying all along."

Teague spoke over her. "She was targeted by Jude motherfucking MacNamara. He preyed on her and now she thinks she's in a relationship with him."

Aiden shook his head, looking disgusted. "When you

fuck something up, you *really* fuck it up, don't you, Teague? You're so damn sure you know better than everyone else that you stomp all over what *they* want."

Sloan was losing them. "Will you just *listen* to me?"

"It's okay. We aren't judging you for any of this." Teague took another step closer, approaching like she was a wild animal. "You couldn't have known."

"You are not listening to me. You don't know him." She realized her mistake as soon as Teague looked at her like he wanted to sedate her and lock her up until she came into her right mind—like she was certifiable. *Oh God, I was so wrong to come back here.* "I am turning around and walking out of this house. You are going to let me."

Teague shook his head. "We can't do that, Sloan."

"The fuck we can't. You're not listening to her. Again." Aiden's fists were clenched, and he looked half a second from punching Teague in the face.

"The fuck I *can*. I don't answer to you anymore, and you're standing on Sheridan territory. If you aren't willing to do what's right for our sister, then I am."

Her throat tried to close, but she forced the words out despite that. "You can't be serious. You're threatening *Aiden*. What is wrong with you?" Jude had been right, and she'd been a fool for thinking the best of her brother—for thinking she could reason with Teague. He'd always see her as the sweet little sister who needed to be protected, who couldn't think for herself.

If Cillian were here...

But it wouldn't matter. Teague was half of the head of the Sheridan family, and though Aiden now appeared to run the O'Malleys, they weren't on O'Malley territory. Teague outranked Aiden. He outranked *her*.

She lifted her chin. "This is your last chance. I'm leaving." She turned for the door, but Teague stepped in front of her.

"Don't make me call my men. This doesn't have to come to violence."

Behind her, a phone rang. She turned as Aiden took it out of his pocket and answered, his gaze never leaving her. "I'm with her right now. We're having a...difference of opinion with my brother."

"Is that fucking MacNamara?" Teague raised his voice. "Tell him to run. If he sets foot on my territory, I'm going to hunt him down like the mad dog he is."

No.

Sloan marched across the room and shoved Teague. "Teague Patrick O'Malley, I swear to God, if you don't stop acting like a Neanderthal, I'm going to call your wife. *She* will listen to me."

He took a step back and glared at her. "Callie and I are of the same mind when it comes to this."

"Liar." She knew Callie, and so she knew better. The woman could be fierce, but she didn't let Teague steamroll her—and Sloan doubted she'd take too kindly to him doing the same to his sister.

Except there's Jude to consider.

Aiden cursed. "You should have told me that to begin with."

Sloan turned, starting to respond, but the words died on her lips. Aiden wasn't talking to her. He was talking to Jude. From the determined set of his face, he had just discovered that Dmitri Romanov intended to murder Callie and her father. "Aiden—"

He held up a hand and put the phone on speaker. "I have men in the area. You know where he'll strike from?"

"There's a small apartment across the street from the restaurant. That's where I'd hit from." Jude paused. "But it's entirely likely that he'll have a backup location—several."

"We'll set up a perimeter. You take the apartment."

Sloan glared. "You just gave him the most dangerous task."

Aiden glared right back. "He seems to think that you two are going to ride off into the sunset together. You choose him? Fine. So be it. But he's got to prove himself."

"You are so *ruthless*." She sank as much disgust into the word as possible. Aiden was knowingly putting Jude in a situation where he might be hurt—or worse—and he didn't have the grace to so much as pretend he was sorry.

"Sunshine."

Her throat burned at the nickname, and she wanted nothing more than to snatch the phone out of her brother's hand. There wasn't time. "Jude."

"Are you hurt?"

He was going to do it. It didn't matter that her brother might have an ulterior motive for allying with him—temporarily or not. He would go into that apartment and do what needed to be done.

And there wasn't a single thing she could do about it. "I'm fine."

"I'm keeping my promise, sunshine. I'm tying up this last loose end, and then I'm coming for you, whether your brothers give their blessing or no. You know what will happen if they get in my way."

She knew.

Aiden cleared his throat. "I gave my word, MacNamara."

"We'll see if you keep it." Jude hung up.

"What the fuck was that?" Teague looked at Sloan and then Aiden. "Explain. Now."

When Aiden didn't immediately jump in, Sloan wrapped her arms around herself. "Dmitri Romanov is going to try to kill Callie and Colm—and he's going to make it look like Jude did it."

Teague was already moving, throwing open the door into the hall. "Micah. Call the men on Callie. Secure the entrances to the restaurant. Double the team in the restaurant."

Callie.

Just because Jude thought he could handle the situation alone didn't mean he could. If her family's dealings with Dmitri Romanov had taught her anything, it was that the man had a nasty habit of doing the unexpected. If he was as smart as everyone said, he had to know Jude was having second thoughts about finishing the Sheridans.

If he thought Jude would break his word...

If he knew that Aiden was working with Jude...

Oh God. What if it was a trap designed to take out multiple enemies in one fell swoop? She looked at her brothers. They didn't care about Jude...but they would move heaven and earth to keep family safe. "We have to go to them."

Teague shook his head. "You're not going anywhere. Our men can handle it."

"Like they handled things at the house on Orcas Island? You don't understand. Jude's better than all of you combined. This is what he's been training his entire life for."

The confusion cleared from Teague's face, leaving only fear in its wake. "He's going after Callie?"

"Colm." He already hated Jude. Telling him who he was gunning for wasn't going to change that. But maybe it *would* ensure they took her with them.

Teague already had his phone out. "*Triple* the men on her. I don't care if it's rush hour. I'm on my way." He pointed to Micah without looking up from his phone. "Put my sister in one of the guest rooms. Do *not* let her leave."

"Aiden, you said you gave Jude your word!"

Her oldest brother shook his head as he typed a number into his phone. "Teague's right on this one. You'll be safest here until this is over. If your man is still alive at the end of it, we'll talk."

She barely got a cry of protest out when Micah did Teague's bidding, hauling her up the stairs none too gently. Aiden's last words all but confirmed her suspicions. He might not want Jude dead the same way Teague did, but he wouldn't necessarily step in to save him if something happened.

I have to be there. I have to fight for Jude.

No one else is going to.

* * *

Jude used the cover of pedestrians to slip through the door that led to the loft above the little shops littering the street. When East Cambridge underwent the gentrification process back in the nineties, most of the old factories had been turned into commercial buildings and residential lofts. He'd snagged a loft across the street from the restaurant the Sheridans frequented ten years ago, paying out the nose for the location.

His phone rang as he hit the stairs, and he cursed at the now-familiar number. "What do you want?"

"As convenient as it would be for me if you took a bullet to the chest—again, from what I hear—I want Romanov more than I want you."

Jude had spent enough time as a man on a vengeance mission to recognize that trait in another person. As much as Romanov wanted the O'Malleys dead and gone, it appeared Aiden wanted the same for him—with interest.

Still, all *Jude* wanted was to take out whoever Romanov had sent to frame him and get Sloan somewhere where they would be left alone. "I'm not interested in whatever war you're planning."

"Not war. Never that."

"You're wasting my time." He started up the stairs.

"I know Romanov wants to use you against Colm."

That brought him up short. "You seem to know a whole hell of a lot that you shouldn't." He might have tapped his brother's phone, but there's no way he could have tapped Jude's. It struck him that he'd underestimated Aiden, and that didn't sit well with him in the least. "I'm listening."

"Romanov won't take your double-cross well. There's little he hates more than someone breaking their word. He'll bring everything in his power to make an example of you."

That was what worried him more than anything else. He could keep Sloan safe. He wasn't worried about that. But Sloan was a woman who would crave roots—her time in Callaway Rock had more than proven that. It might take some time, but eventually she'd resent him for keeping them on the move and under the radar.

And that wasn't even taking the kid into the equation. A life on the run was no way to raise a child. "You have thirty seconds to give me your pitch before I hang up."

"I know that you do extensive research on both enemy and ally, and that you know things no one else can seem to pin down. I want what you have on Romanov—all of it."

It seemed a small enough thing to ask, but Jude wasn't the trusting sort. "I'll pass it over with the condition that you tell me exactly what you're planning—and keep me updated on the process."

"Yes to the former. No to the latter."

"Aiden, this isn't a negotiation." He needed warning if he was going to get Sloan out of wherever they were before Romanov brought his wrath down upon them. He paused at the top of the stairs. "Take out whatever Romanov has set up as a backup plan and we'll talk when I deliver the information to you."

"We'll talk about my sister, too. We've reached the restaurant." Aiden hung up, leaving Jude more irritated than he should be. His life had been so much simpler when he kept to the shadows and didn't tangle with powerful men. Aiden and Dmitri might think themselves so different, but they were just two sides of the same coin. The only difference that mattered to him was that one had tried to blackmail him and the other was willing to work with him.

He took a careful breath, and then another, letting all that fall away. There was a fight waiting for him on the other side of the door, and he couldn't afford to be distracted.

The door opened before he could move, revealing a man with tattoos crawling down his arms and up his neck, and whose face was marked with scars. His eyes went wide, but Jude didn't give him a chance to call out a warning. He chopped him in the throat, grabbing his body as he started to tumble and shoving him into the loft.

The man hit the ground, gurgling, and Jude shut the door behind him and locked it for good measure. Someone could kick it down, even with the reinforced wood, but he'd hear them coming and have warning.

He kicked the fallen man, the force of it flipping him onto his back, where he lay still. He wouldn't be getting up anytime soon. Jude stalked farther into the loft, avoiding the creaky boards. There wasn't furniture to deal with, because he'd never bothered to furnish the place, and so he had a clear line of sight to the second man kneeling before the window, a rifle in his hands, his attention on the building across the street.

"Stop." The man didn't look up, didn't move, his Russian accent confirming what Jude already knew.

He slipped his hand behind his back, palming the .45 he had tucked into his waistband. "If you pull that trigger, I'm going to shoot you in the back of the head."

"And you—"

Jude whipped his gun out and shot him in the back. He rushed across the distance and yanked the Russian away from the window just in case he got some funny ideas about trying to shoot Callista even with a bullet in him.

It turned out to be for nothing. His shot had aimed true. The man hit the ground, his eyes vacant with death. Jude walked back and put a bullet in the still-struggling second guy. He needed all his focus for what came next, and having some piece-of-shit Russian shoot him was not on the agenda.

He walked back to the sniper setup and knelt in the same place the man had, hissing out a breath when his bullet wound protested so much movement in such a short time. The rifle was an M4, which was fucking pathetic, but they didn't need the range of a true sniper rifle. Still, there were a dozen better choices for this job. He took out his phone and dialed Aiden, putting it on speaker as he used the scope to scan the buildings across from them.

"I'm busy."

"I've removed one sniper." Jude paused at the building

next door, taking in the dark-dressed man with a rifle similar to his own. "There's another one in the building to the south, second floor, three rooms from the street. He's overlooking the alley where the restaurant's back door leads."

Aiden's voice became muffled, but Jude still heard him order two of his men to deal with the threat.

He finished searching those windows and moved on. "Do you have my side of the street covered?"

"We've dealt with the threat we found two buildings down."

Three men. Romanov hadn't been taking any chances. He watched the man across the street get taken down by two O'Malley men. "I don't see anyone else."

More murmuring, though this time Jude couldn't pick up on the words. Finally, Aiden came back on the line. "We're moving them."

"I'll provide cover."

"See that that's *all* you do."

Jude hung up and watched as a group of people hurried out the back door into the alley that he'd just helped clear. He saw Callista, her blond head close to her husband's, his arm around her shoulders. Behind her...

He went still.

Colm Sheridan looked the same as he had the last time Jude observed him, his hair gray, though it hadn't thinned in the least, his face weathered and *old*. Even his shoulders were hunched as he walked in the middle of his men.

He had a clear shot. All he had to do was pull the trigger and he could avenge his family's memory. His *mother's* memory.

Jude's finger stroked the trigger, the feel of the metal a

comfort and a torment. It wouldn't take much, the slightest bit of pressure, and this would all end.

It wouldn't be the only thing that ended.

Sloan might forgive him for killing Colm. She understood his need for vengeance, and there was no arguing that man more than deserved death at his hands.

But the O'Malley men wouldn't see things his way. Callista Sheridan wouldn't, either. If he killed Colm now, there would be no alliance with Aiden. There would just be him facing down O'Malley, Sheridan, Romanov, and possibly even Halloran.

Sloan didn't deserve that.

Their child didn't deserve that.

Jude hissed out a breath as a dark SUV pulled up to the curb and Colm disappeared from view. He waited for the guilt of a missed opportunity to pull him under, but there was nothing except a growing need to hold Sloan. To reassure himself that she was whole.

First, though, he had one last task to accomplish before he could go to her.

CHAPTER THIRTY-ONE

It took Sloan thirty minutes to talk herself into action. Part of her just wanted to stay in this room until it was all over, keeping her baby safe, but her fear that something would happen to Jude rose with every lap she paced around the room. He was more than capable of taking out a few of Romanov's men, but that didn't mean her brothers wouldn't double-cross him. She'd heard Aiden. He might say that he'd keep his word, but he wouldn't lift a single finger to help Jude if he was injured again.

Her gaze landed on the lamp sitting on the side table. *Hefty enough to do the job.* She turned to face the man she barely knew, but who cared about Callie. "You have to let me go. I'm the only one who can stop this."

Micah looked up from the chair he'd been sitting in since he hauled her into this room. He shook his head. "I have my orders. You don't walk out of this room until I get the all clear."

That was what she'd been afraid of, though she'd expected it. Sloan ducked her head, her hair falling forward to shield her face. She skittered back and let a droop into her shoulders that she hadn't had in what felt like a lifetime. "I didn't mean for any of this to happen."

Through the curtain of her hair, she saw Micah's expression soften. "I know. We all get in over our head sometimes. It happens. Once your brothers take care of this asshole, you can get back to normal."

Her hand closed around the base of the lamp. "That's what you don't understand," she whispered.

"What?" Micah frowned and stood. "I didn't catch that."

"I said..." She dropped her voice even further, drawing him a step closer. Sloan brought the lamp up with all her strength and slammed it into the side of Micah's head. She cried out as she did it, hating that she had to hurt him, but the alternative was out of the question.

He hit his knees, looking dazed, and she hit him again. She barely paused to listen to his groan before she grabbed his gun, leaped over him, and slammed the bedroom door. He wouldn't stay down. She'd heard too many stories from Callie about how tough her main bodyguard was—how driven.

She had to get out of the Sheridan house before he roused enough to sound the alarm.

Sloan retraced her steps to the front door, her heart pounding with every second, expecting someone to appear and demand to know why she wasn't where she was supposed to be.

But the house was eerily empty, her footsteps echoing on the hardwood floor.

This is what it will be like always if Jude isn't able to stop Dmitri Romanov.

She couldn't let him face that threat alone.

She just prayed she was in time.

A dark town car sat at the curb outside the house, and she slowed to a stop and stared. It was entirely possible that it belonged to the Sheridans—or even the O'Malleys—but some instinct made her walk toward it. She was painfully conscious of the gun in her hand, the metal warming against her skin.

The back window rolled down, and her breath caught in her throat. She'd only ever heard him described, but there was no way this attractive man with dark hair and eyes was anyone other than Dmitri Romanov. He motioned her closer with a hand marked with tattoos. "Sloan O'Malley." His Russian accent made her name sound exotic.

She could run. She might even get half a block before he or his men caught her. If some well-meaning neighbor tried to interfere, she'd be signing their death warrant. That, more than anything, had her drifting closer. "Dmitri Romanov."

"Smart girl."

The temper that had awoken during her time with Jude roared to the forefront. She lifted the gun and pointed it at him. "What the hell is wrong with you?"

He didn't so much as blink. "You'll have to be more specific."

"You tried to frame Jude. You are pushing a war with my brothers. You were going to *kill* Callie and her baby."

That got a reaction. He narrowed his eyes. "Baby..."

He didn't know. That didn't make it any more justifiable. He still had had every intention of murdering her friend. She braced the gun, her finger on the trigger. "I don't care if you didn't know Callie was pregnant. You're still a monster."

"Put that gun down before you hurt yourself."

"I don't think I will." She wasn't a murderer. She'd never given much thought to ending someone else's life, even after Devlin died and she'd hated the Hallorans as much as she hated anything in this world.

But Dmitri Romanov had been the cause of so much misery for her family. No one would cry if he died. It might even be the act that allowed her and Jude to be free.

"Your man broke his word to me." He said it casually, as if remarking on the weather.

"If you're dead, there will be no one here to collect on that." The gun was becoming heavy in her hands. She couldn't hold it like this much longer. She had to decide. "I want to bargain."

One corner of his mouth quirked up. "Do wonders never cease?"

She ignored that. "Let Jude go—let us both go—and I won't shoot you."

"Generous."

"Take it or leave it." She shifted her grip on the gun, hating the way her palms had gone sweaty.

"I have a counter offer. You and MacNamara leave. I'll search for you, but I won't search hard. After a reasonable amount of time, I'll let you go—*if* you never come back to Boston or New York."

It sounded too good to be true, which meant it likely was. She frowned. "Why?"

He chuckled. "As I said before—smart girl. I have my reasons, which are no concern to you. Suffice to say that allowing you to escape unscathed suits my current purposes."

Meaning he had a plan and would leverage her safety to get what he wanted. She didn't like the sound of that…but

Dmitri had her backed into a corner despite the fact that she held the gun. She gritted her teeth. "If I see you again, I *will* shoot you—and that's not even going into what Jude will do to you."

He gave her a smile that didn't quite reach his eyes. "It's been a pleasure." He rolled up the window before she could decide whether she should shoot him anyway, and she'd be lying if she said she didn't feel a bit of relief as his car pulled away from the curb and drove down the street.

She belatedly realized she was still holding the gun in a neighborhood where that sort of thing would be reported and lowered it.

"Sloan."

She jumped, and then mentally berated herself for jumping. Micah stood in the doorway, a truly impressive bruise blossoming on the side of his face. She tensed, starting to raise the gun again, but he shook his head. "There's a phone call for you."

"What?" She took the phone from him, though she kept ahold of the gun in case it was a trap. "Hello?"

"Start walking."

She obeyed before she registered that it was Aiden she was talking to. Sloan shot a glance over her shoulder, but Micah was nowhere to be seen. "What's going on?"

"Do you choose Jude?"

That, at least, she had no confusion about. "Yes."

"He's the one you want—truly want? It's not some Stockholm syndrome like Teague claims?"

She picked up her pace, reaching the end of the block and crossing the street. "I love him, Aiden. I won't have anyone but him."

Aiden cursed long and hard. "If you change your mind,

you call me. I don't care what time it is, or what I'm doing—I will come for you and I will get you out safely."

Hope burst in her chest, and she found herself grinning like a fool. "You're letting me go."

"Yes. I can't speak for Teague, though, so you need to get your ass to Carrigan's. She'll protect you until Jude comes for you, and then you two need to get the fuck out of Boston. Don't come back, Sloan. I won't look for you, and I'll have Cillian erase any path you do leave, but that's all I can promise. You won't have a safety net to fall back on."

"I don't need one." She'd miss Boston. She already knew and had made her peace with that. She even understood why Aiden was only offering this much. In the grand scheme of things, a sister's happiness ranked lower than the safety of the family. She didn't want to be the thing that pushed the situation in Boston into a full-blown war any more than Aiden wanted her to be. "I love you."

"I love you too, little sister. Be safe."

"You too." She hung up and flagged down a cab. Sloan dropped the phone in the trash can on the corner and slid into the backseat. "Southie." She rattled off the address Carrigan had made her memorize after they landed in Boston, and patiently waited for the cabbie to stop trying to talk her out of it. "I'll pay double if you get me there in half the time."

"You got it, lady." But he shot into the street and headed for Southie.

She sat back and wished she had taken the time to call Jude before she threw the phone away. It was too risky, though. The longer she had the phone, the greater the chance one of Teague's men would track her down. She had to trust that Jude would come back to her safely.

Worry battled with the hope still trying to take hold. She forced herself to set both aside. It could wait. Everything could wait until Jude was back with her. He was safe.

He had to be.

* * *

Jude walked into the O'Malley residence without knocking. Aiden knew he was coming and he didn't have the time or patience for a pissing contest with the hired muscle. He stopped in the foyer, taking in the place. Dark wood dominated the room, bold accents creating a look of understated elegance. It wasn't in-your-face, but the whole place reeked of money.

A man stepped out of the hallway leading deeper into the house. "Aiden is expecting you."

Jude nodded and followed the guy into the shadows. He led them to an office that was decorated in much the same way as the rest of the house, though the walls were a dark green that seemed to be present in every high-powered office in the country. Aiden sat behind a large desk, and he didn't stand when Jude walked in. "Sit."

He waited for the muscle to leave and close the door behind him before he tossed the file he'd brought onto the desk. "There's everything I know about Dmitri Romanov."

Aiden didn't touch the file. "I could pay you a significant amount to remove him from the equation."

There was no way in hell he'd touch *that* with a ten-foot pole. His only priority was keeping Sloan safe. The rest of the world could go to hell for all he cared—that included both Aiden and Dmitri. "Do you think that would solve your problems?"

He sighed. "No. Someone else would just rise to power, and they'd be an unknown quantity. At least I can roughly gauge where Romanov is going at any given time. He's not exactly predictable, but he's known all the same."

That just went to further show that Aiden was smarter than Jude had given him credit for. "You have a plan."

"I have a plan." Aiden smiled, and it was the coldest fucking thing Jude had ever seen. "Do you know who John Finch is?"

"Yes." Jude had made it his business to know everyone connected to the Sheridans, and that included the feds who investigated them. John Finch had his fingers in every organized crime family in both Boston and New York.

"Romanov was instrumental in Finch's daughter being wrongly branded a dirty cop."

Jude sat back, a little in awe despite himself. *He's going to use the daughter to take both Finch and Romanov out at the knees*. It didn't matter *how* Aiden would accomplish it, only that he was devious enough to use this woman to accomplish his goals. "That's cold."

"It's necessary." Aiden finally picked up the file and set it in a drawer next to him. "You love my sister."

Jude blinked at the change of topic. "I do." It was something that had been simmering in the back of his mind for days now, though he'd hesitated to give it voice. It turned out to be easier than he could have imagined. "She's everything."

Aiden nodded. "She chose you."

Even though he knew that she would, he relaxed a little bit. "So what do you think happens now?" Jude knew what *he* thought was going to happen. Even if Aiden broke his word, Jude would fight his way out of this house and back to Sloan. He'd find her and he'd take them somewhere safe. That was the only thing that mattered.

"I'll tell you the same thing I told her—retrieve her from the Halloran house. Get out of Boston, and don't look back. I can cover your tracks to a limited degree as long as you don't do anything stupid to put yourself in the spotlight." Something almost like warmth came into Aiden's green eyes. "Go have a life, marry my sister, have a boatload of kids, put the family business behind you—behind both of you. You have a chance at happiness, and you'd be a fucking idiot to pass it up."

It sounded almost too good to be true, but whatever else the O'Malley men were, they loved their siblings something fierce. Aiden was smart enough to take Sloan's word as truth, and essentially offer his blessing as a result. He stood, wanting nothing more than to get back to Sloan. He wouldn't be letting her out of his sight anytime in the next couple years. "Happy hunting, O'Malley."

"It will be."

He turned around and walked out of the office without looking back. He would keep his word, and that was all Jude needed to know. He was going to go get his woman and leave vengeance to Aiden O'Malley.

* * *

Darkness fell while Sloan paced the room Carrigan had given her. Her sister had tried to stay and keep her company, but she wasn't capable of holding down a conversation, her nerves stringing tighter and tighter with each hour that passed. There was no word, but there wouldn't be regardless of the outcome. It wasn't as if Aiden or Teague would ring Carrigan to tell her their dirty little secrets.

And they certainly wouldn't call Sloan.

She rubbed her arms, her skin feeling like it was too tight. Jude should have been back by now. There was no positive outcome that would cause him not to be here. She turned and looked at the window.

And shrieked.

"Let me in, sunshine."

"Jude!"

"It's okay." She turned and caught the door as it flew open, her sister charging in with a gun drawn.

Carrigan stopped. "You're okay?"

"I'm fine."

Carrigan stopped and huffed out a laugh when she saw the window. "That man of yours certainly knows how to make an impression. Let the poor bastard in before one of James's men shoots him." She stopped in the doorway, her eyes softening. "I'm glad he's okay."

"Me too." Sloan waited for the door to shut before she rushed to the window. "What were you *thinking*?" She shoved it open and backed up so he could climb through. "They have a front door."

"I didn't want to announce my presence." He shot her a look. "I didn't expect you to scream."

"It's a normal reaction when a person is startled." She started to reach for him and hesitated. "Are you hurt?" He wasn't wearing the same shirt she'd last seen him in, but he was moving well.

"I'm good." Jude seemed to be waiting for something.

"Thank God." She threw herself into his arms, needing to touch him, needing his skin on hers as physical proof to back up his words. She yanked off his shirt and ran her hands down his chest. There were several impressive bruises blossoming, and his gunshot wound had a new bandage on it, but he wasn't hiding any massive injury. "You *are* okay."

"You're not going to ask about Colm?"

She froze, her gaze still on the center of his chest. "I trust you did whatever you thought was best." She didn't want any more deaths on his conscience, but... She loved Jude, and that meant making her peace with even the darkest parts of him. Callie was alive—Sloan would have heard if she wasn't—and that was the most important thing.

"He's alive." He covered her hands with his own. "I almost pulled the trigger. I won't lie and try to tell you otherwise—I was *this* close, but I didn't do it. *You* are the most important thing in my life. That old bastard isn't long for this world, and he'll burn in hell for what he did to my family." His grip tightened and he made a visible effort to relax. "I won't risk you—either of you—by hunting him down and putting him out of his misery. And your oldest brother has given his word that he'll cover our tracks."

She could hardly believe it. She knew what Aiden had said, but hearing Jude confirm it was something else altogether. "You're saying..."

"I'm saying I love you. You were already starting to make me question everything I knew before we found out you were pregnant. I'm your man, Sloan. Forever. I'm not going to turn into a teddy bear overnight, but—"

"I love you, too." She kissed him, so full of emotion, it was a wonder she didn't burst. "God, I love you so much. You are who you are, Jude. We both are." She cupped his face. "We have the whole world. We're free. Where do you want to go?"

He grinned, his expression the happiest she'd ever seen.

"I have a place in Maine. I know it's not Oregon, but it's on the ocean and in the middle of a little town that would give Callaway Rock a run for its money."

"Yes, yes, a thousand times yes." She kissed him again, lingering, a slow heat building beneath her skin.

His hands skated down her sides to her hips, pulling her more firmly against him. "I'm going to marry you, sunshine. Not now, not when we're fresh off all this bullshit and still reeling. But once we've settled down, when things are what will pass for normal." He reached between them and pressed his hand against her stomach. "We'll do it on the beach, just us and this little one. Think we'll have a ring bearer or a flower girl?"

She hadn't even thought that far. "Does it matter?"

"No. Nothing fucking matters but us, sunshine. You and me and the whole of the future spread out before us."

ACKNOWLEDGMENTS

Sometimes I figure it's a little weird that I thank God first and foremost in all my dirty books, but I wouldn't have this mind if not for Him, so I'm running with it. This was one of those books that seemed to write itself, where I was just as shocked as anyone by some of the stuff that came out of Jude's mouth. God gave me this sense of humor and love of all dirty-talking heroes, and I thank Him daily for it.

A *huge* thank-you to my fabulous editor, Leah Hultenschmidt, for letting me hit for the fences with this book. I am so grateful for your trust in me, and I'm not even the least bit sorry that you had to read the sexy scenes on an airplane next to strangers. Drinks are on me next time!

Endless appreciation and thank-yous go to the team at Forever. You've given me amazing support, from those outstanding covers to copyedits to promotion, and this series wouldn't have been half as successful without you.

The seed of this book was planted a couple of years ago on a writers' retreat in Cannon Beach, so thank you to everyone who came on that trip! I had a blast walking the same beach that I imagined for Callaway Rock, and navigating the truly terrifying trip back to Portland alive! We should do it again soon!

Thank you to my reader group, The Rabble. I know I've been teasing you with Jude and Sloan excerpts for what feels like forever, and your enthusiasm made the experience that much more amazing. Thank you! I hope Jude and Sloan's story was worth the wait!

The process of writing a book—especially a book that is as immersive as this one was during the drafting process—can be hard on the people living with the author. So last, but certainly not least, all my love and thanks to Tim for putting up with my zoning out, never complaining about having to come up with dinner on the fly, and kicking me out of the house on a semi-regular basis to go out and do the things that real, live people do. Kisses!

ABOUT THE AUTHOR

Katee Robert (she/they) is a *New York Times* and *USA Today* bestselling author of contemporary romance and romantic suspense. *Entertainment Weekly* calls their writing "unspeakably hot." Their books have sold over a million copies.

Find out more at:
KateeRobert.com
Instagram @Katee_Robert
TikTok @AuthorKateeRobert
X @Katee_Robert
Facebook.com/AuthorKateeRobert